HE BEGINS

Descent Into Darkness

*E-Book Only
**Coming Soon

DESCENT INTO DARKNESS

VOLUME 1

HE BEGINS

DORIS ROSS

TRINITY GATEWAYS LLC

DESCENT INTO DARKNESS, VOL. 1: HE BEGINS

This is a work of fiction. All characters and events portrayed are fictional, and any resemblance to real people or incidents is purely coincidental.

Cover Art by Blue
Cover Design by Doris Ross

A Trinity Gateways LLC Publication
www.TrinityGateways.net

ISBN: 194142600X
ISBN-13: 978-1941426005

DEDICATIONS

For my readers,
The family and friends who have rooted for me,
Coffee Roasters of Florida,
And my fellow lovers of the bean,
You all keep me writing.

Descent Into Darkness
Volume 1

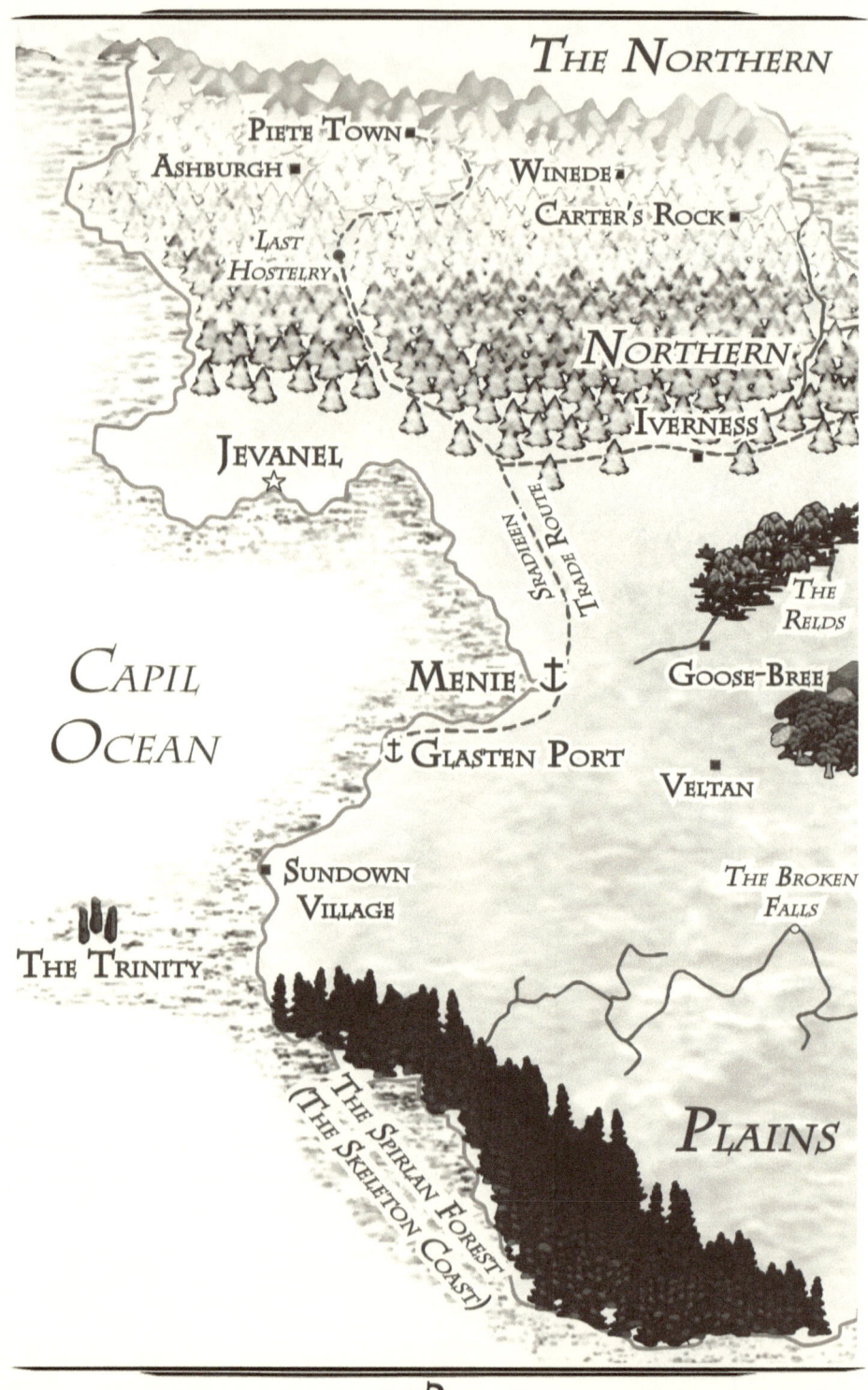

THE NORTHERN

PIETE TOWN ▪

ASHBURGH ▪

WINEDE ▪

CARTER'S ROCK ▪

LAST
HOSTELRY ▪

NORTHERN

IVERNESS

JEVANEL
☆

CAPIL

OCEAN

SRADIEEN

TRADE ROUTE

THE
RELDS

MENIE ⚓

GOOSE-BREE

‡ GLASTEN PORT

VELTAN

SUNDOWN
VILLAGE

THE BROKEN
FALLS

THE TRINITY

THE SPIRLAN FOREST
(THE SKELETON COAST)

PLAINS

ICE FIELDS

ULNET

YULLUM ROAD

TELMAR
BRIDGE

WILDERNESS

CHAL-EDON TRADE ROUTE

TRADE ROUTE

EDON PORT

MOORLANDS

RATHBURN

CHAL-EDON

CHALBROOKE

WOOD OF
DESTINY

MOORLANDS

DESTINY'S
WAY

OF GASTAEIA

Descent Into Darkness

Part 1

His Own

1

It began with a slight tremble. Not many noticed it at first. Those at sea only took notice of the lack of sea life if they made their living off it. Those atop the three towers of natural stone were either too busy to feel it, or thought it vertigo or nerves. Then it escalated.

Quickly.

The birds took flight, leaving behind nests, eggs, and flightless young. As the people stood ogling at the avian exodus, another caught their attention. Rats boiled up onto the wharves of the docking caverns like furred lava, milling about at the ends of the piers before spilling over into the water. Fleeing something unseen.

In a long forgotten basement, Ba'tvian Delthanurk, a student of the Trinity College of Magery, paused in his ritual preparations. Had that tremor been caused by an arcane mishap or was it something more serious? He extended his awareness, seeking out traces of magic use. The only ones he found were his own. The tower gave another brief shake. As the world steadied again, he knew he was running out of time.

For a quake to be felt out here, where none had been experienced before, it had to be monstrous. He needed to change plans. The purpose of his experiment in forbidden sorcery would not just be to collect more power; it had to preserve him and the Trinity. As the rock began to vibrate, he used chalk to alter the diagram he'd drawn on the floor. Snatching up the cages, he threw them into the center of it. Inside the little prisons, rats squealed, clawed, and bit.

The room moved violently. Ba'tvian braced himself as best he could, reaching for his notes on the ritual. He could all but smell the fear from the rats. The sour-sweet scent quickened his pulse. He licked his lips as he read.

He had to survive. If he died, he would never achieve greatness. If he succeeded, he may yet still be stripped of everything. It was the way of the world, to hold down and oppress those meant for more. He'd learned this long ago. Yet he might receive leniency for saving everyone. It was a thin hope, he knew. Still…He gave a hollow laugh. Even if they stripped him, he'd come back greater, more powerful, than before. He was certain that he would find a way.

With the words he needed burning in his mind, he flung out an arm. Magic surged through him. He heard the rats screech as the carvings on the floor flared with a sooty red light. He chanted the words even as the earth bucked. Rock strained, whined, cracked like a whip. Pieces of the ceiling fell as he determinedly finished the incantation. A section of stone from above broke to fall on the rats.

The world tilted, and he was tossed into darkness just as the last word was said.

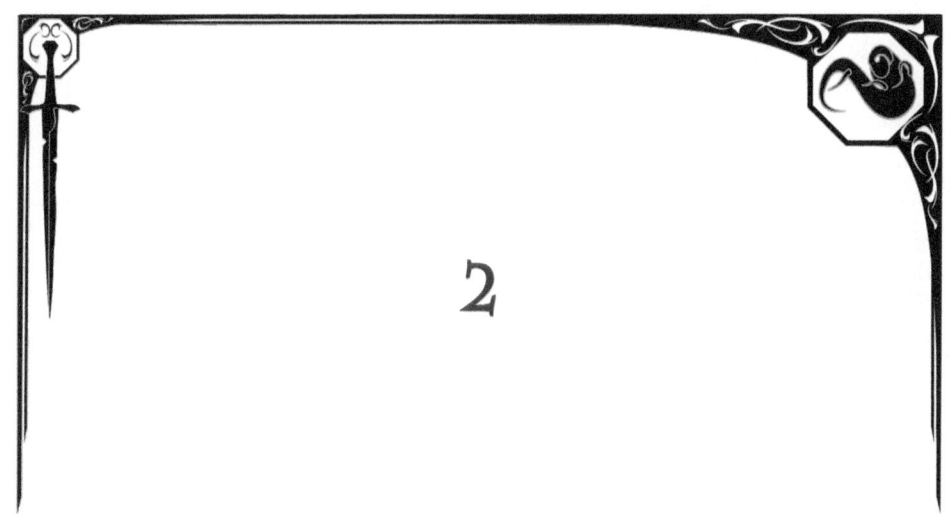

2

Ba'tvian awoke slowly. Grit dusted his face and his body felt stiff. How long he had lain sprawled on the floor, he didn't know. He couldn't even remember what had happened before opening his eyes.

All was quiet. Above him the stone ceiling had cracked, the fissures running out from the walls in a crazed spider web. Acrid, smoky air filled his nostrils. Something was burning nearby. The light illuminating the space was the wrong color to be from a fire. It was too bright.

A chip of ceiling fell to land on his shoulder. With it came his memory. An earthquake…the rats…the dim surge of power at the end…the violent dance of rock …

The world had stilled.

He listened to the rush of the wind. Turning his head, he could see the damage by the sunlight pouring through the massive rift in the stone wall. Part of the ceiling had collapsed in the far corner of the basement. By the new opening, a section of the floor had broken off into the sea far below. He saw that the rest of the basement floor was buckled, a fact that baffled him. The basement was at the top of huge tower of natural stone. He would have thought that the stone – was it granite? – would sooner topple than heave up and down as it had.

Well, he was no expert on the matter of earthen quakes or rock.

With a grunt, he levered himself up into a kneeling position.

Pebbles cascaded off him. Shaking out his brown hair to dislodge more of the debris, he looked around. He wouldn't be able to use this place again. The privacy this long-forgotten basement had provided was now compromised. All of the inscriptions, the symbols, and lines he'd carved into the stone facing were fractured or demolished. Useless they might be, they were evidence of what had transpired here, evidence that could be used against him. He should have thought of this eventuality before.

He would next time.

Someone would come looking soon, if only to inspect the damage. He had little time to cleanse the room.

Squashed rats, rubble, pieces of the whicker cages littered the center of the casting diagram. Reminded by them, he took another glance about the chamber then grinned. Heavy debris was everywhere – except the spot he had lain in. Elation filled him. He had survived. He had succeeded!

Still he could not be careless. Picking his way towards the carved pattern, he determined that he could easily throw most of the sacrificial evidence out the large hole into the water below. That, at least, would be simple. However, the blood staining the rock and the carvings could not be so easily remedied. Discovery was inevitable.

Ba'tvian curled his lip at the thought. A circus of accusations and trials would follow, he knew. He needed a plan, an escape. He knew the laws of the Trinity, in particular the laws concerning mage-craft. While he was certain that he wouldn't be executed because of his youth, he wasn't sure what the consequences would be. Exile? Incarceration? Maiming? The laws were not specific for blood mages below the age of eighteen. He wasn't about to wait around to find out.

Now that he had succeeded once, he wanted to see what else he could do.

At sixteen, Ba'tvian was a five-year student at the College of Magery of the Trinity. Called the Red Tower for the color of the rooftops, it was one of three schools here. Scholars studied in gold domed buildings, while artisans learned their craft under blue capped structures. They had held little interest to him. It had always been magery – magic – that had called to him. Magic, and secrets. The more closely guarded the secret, the more insatiable his need to know it.

With power added to the mix, he found it irresistible.

He was already suspect. His mentor at the college knew of his curiosity, knew that he'd been researching things in the libraries that were best left alone. Master Oknare had warned him away from the more fascinating practices, informing the librarians that he was not to go unmonitored when going through the texts. The man hadn't known that Ba'tvian had already concluded his research there. What he'd sought then could only be found in the protected caches at the heart of the college; he knew that he was not yet able to crack into them.

Still, he'd had enough to start experimenting.

Thinking of what lay ahead soured his mood. Scowling, he began to clean up. Perhaps, if he was lucky, he might be able to find his way into the docking caverns, then steal a boat. Food and water would be a problem, but he didn't think it insurmountable.

"Damn earthquake," he muttered as he gathered the rats to throw them away. "I should have planned for this, for when I had to leave..."

No matter what his options might have been, he knew that the time of learning was essentially over. The college was no longer a shelter. Returning home was not a choice he would even consider. The former was now an enemy, while the latter...

His parents and siblings despised him. The feeling was mutual.

All of his young life, they had tried to drag him down. They toiled in fields that weren't theirs, tended crops they wouldn't eat, looked no further than the work that was expected of them or each other. Instead of thinking of ways to improve their lot in life, they were grateful for it. They didn't own a thing, not even themselves, yet they were grateful. Ba'tvian found it pathetically sickening.

He had determined early on that he would be no one's slave. He had known that he was different, that he was gifted, that his destiny lay somewhere outside the life of his family's serfdom. They had ridiculed his belief, riddled his tiny soul with holes until whatever affection he'd felt for them had been drowned in defiance and pain.

He had thrown off that yoke when he'd been sponsored to the college. An accidental, harmless manifestation of power when he was eleven had caught the notice of their master. He had elected to have him trained so that he might serve as a full-mage when he reached adulthood. There would be no fields, no crops, no stabbing remarks of disapproval.

Yet he would still be obligated to – owned by – someone else.

Grimly, he tossed the rats out as he defied the thought.

Mage or not, Ba'tvian would be no one's serf, no one's servant. He'd studied hard. He'd achieved in five years the accomplishments of eight year students. His zeal had not gone unnoticed. Such prodigious talent had warranted a personal mentor so he had been charged to Master Oknare. He had been encouraged, guided – restricted.

He hated restrictions.

He hated cages. The image of himself being locked away in the cells to await punishment made his skin crawl. He wouldn't bear it. There had to be an alternative. Something. Anything. That meant leaving, somehow. He liked the idea of running about as much as he liked the idea of being caught. Of the two, however, it was the best choice.

Provided he could get out of the basement, then find a way off the Trinity and onto the mainland.

A serf didn't have money. A half-trained mage didn't much in the way of power. A trio of stone towers standing in the middle of the ocean didn't have many ways out. There had to be a way…there had to be…

First, he needed to get out of the ruined room.

Turning, he started through the debris. The stairs that led up to the concealed trap door he'd fashioned were still intact. He just hoped that the floor or ceiling of his room hadn't given way to obstruct the door in some way. Reaching the bottom step, he heard a sound and looked up.

He stared into the shocked face of his master.

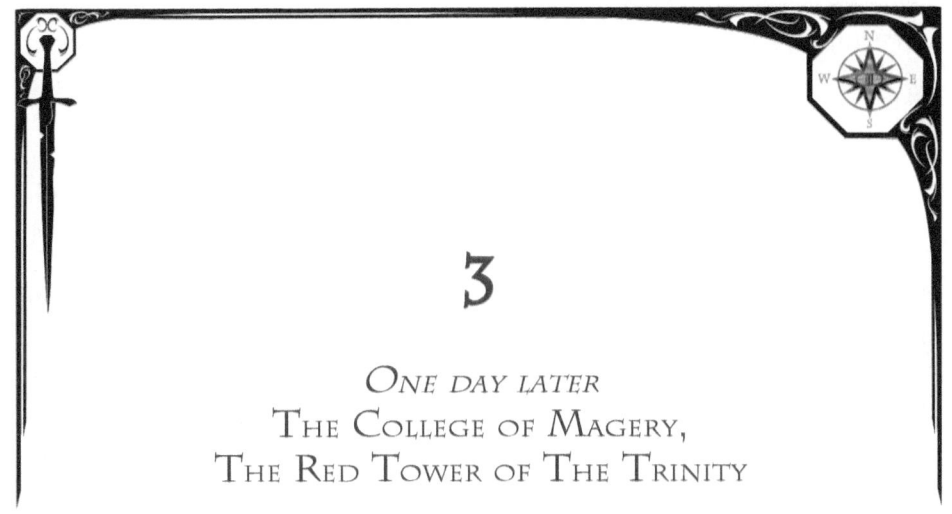

3

They called it the Cleric's Room. There was nothing religious about it, unless one counted the sanctimonious nature of the judging and sentencing that went on there. No one went in without invitation. Of those who did gain one, they were not usually seen again in the halls of the school, or the streets of the city that surrounded it.

It was rumored to be trimmed out with all kinds of arcane devices, each designed specifically winnow the truth from whosoever stepped inside. It was said that many of them were torturous, the procedures painful, the punishments for lying severe. Seeing it for himself, this room buried deep within the warren that was the college, Ba'tvian knew the hearsay to be nothing but manure.

"How could you? After all that we talked about, all the explaining I did, how could you, Ba'tvian?"

The betrayal in Oknare's voice made him want to sneer nastily.

Easily, old man. I won't be barred or chained by any one or thing, least of all you.

The words never left his lips. His former mentor seemed to hear them anyway. His expression changed from the look of the baffled father figure to the countenance of the disapproving adept mage he was. On either side of him stood the elderly, high-ranking mages who oversaw the school. Clad in the crimson and gold colors that indicated their affiliation, they stood as a silent wall of condemnation.

On each face was a frown of suspicion that deepened by the moment.

Ba'tvian suppressed a hateful snarl of defiance. The expressions mirrored the one so often worn by his father.

He detested his father.

He detested his surroundings. Upon being found in the basement, Oknare had dragged him back to the college to a cell, and now to the Cleric's Room. Inside it, he could sense the negativity, the fear, the defiance, the resentment, the burgeoning anger. Others had been here. He could almost smell the blood they'd spilt, the blood smeared on their hands that in turn was smeared on everything they touched. It intrigued him. That there were others of like mind had never occurred to him. Not students. It was something to think about, if there was an opportunity.

The room was barren save for a single wooden chair. The earthquake seemed not to have phased it in the least; there weren't even cracks in the plastered sheathing of the walls or floor. Ba'tvian sat sullenly in the chair, his limbs bound to it with rope. His apprehension had not been spectacular. He hadn't even run. He had simply stared in shock, giving his former master the chance take in the implications of the basement then to bind him with magery. His own reaction, or lack thereof, disgusted him. He should have fought. Run. Something other than stand there like a slack-faced serf, a lack-wit idiot.

"Have you nothing to say? No explanation to give?"

Ba'tvian remained silent. It seemed the best defense.

"You have this opportunity to attempt to exonerate yourself because Master Oknare requested it on your behalf," one of them stated sternly. Ba'tvian couldn't remember his name, but he would forever remember his face. His, and those of all who stood in the room. "You might gain leniency with a proper explanation."

They'd tied him up, treated him like a slave-turned-thief. He was already less than a mage in their eyes.

He didn't want their leniency.

As his silence stretched, the men exchanged grim looks and glances. It was Oknare who finally broke the quiet.

"Very well. You will stand trial for blood-magery, for violation of Trinity law," he said, his eyes never leaving Ba'tvian's. "You are expelled from the college. Your mage talents will be blocked in addition to whatever punishment the city courts decide."

Fury bubbled inside him, though he had already thought of this punishment. His power? They would strip him of his power – his most prized possession. The only thing in this world he truly owned. The only thing that made him more than the sludge he'd come from. They would take even that.

Seething, he glared at the men as they filed out, glared at Oknare who seemed to be waiting for some kind of response. Ba'tvian would be damned if he gave him the pleasure of an outburst. He bit his tongue to quiet himself, tasting blood as his teeth clenched. Pain joined rage in the red haze creeping over his vision.

Blood...he savored the taste of it, used it to focus. He had to think. A key – couldn't he make –

There was little time for plans. He tried anyway.

Two more college officials stepped inside, enforcers of mage law at the college. Their black-trimmed white robes were almost priest-like, and the similarity disgusted him. They were not priests, not superiors, though they would have others believe that. Through eyes narrowed to slits, he watched them confer briefly with Oknare. Together, the trio approached his seat to hold his head fast. Together, they took the only thing he loved.

Deep in his heart, the bitter flames of rage burned.

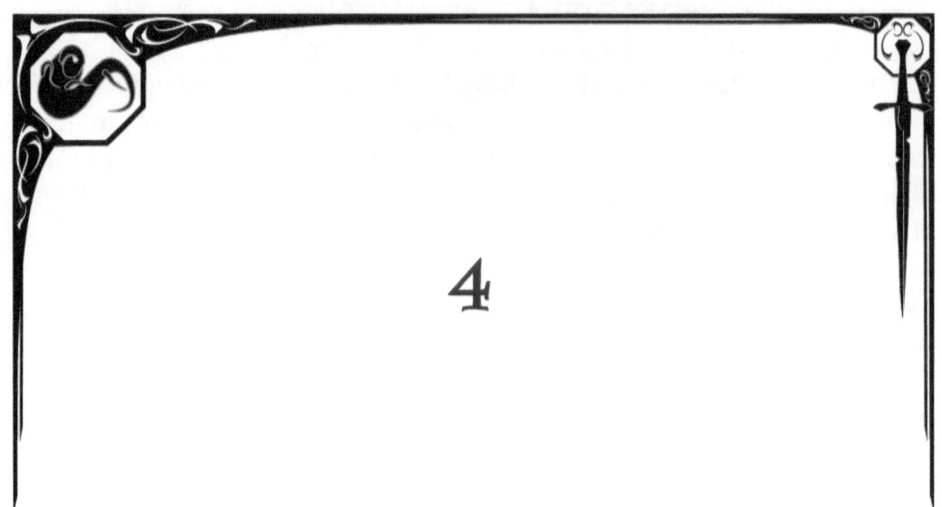

4

B a'tvian's unconscious body was unstrapped from the chair and removed to a holding cell. Master Oknare sighed wearily, turning to the far corner of the stark room. He gestured. There was a whisper of power. Another chair materialized with its occupant. Clad in robes of white-trimmed black, he sported the chain of law official from the city administration. With a sad shake of his head, the High Judge of the Red Tower spoke.

"I'm sorry, my friend. I know this isn't easy for you."

"It's not your doing."

"Nor yours. You did all you could, gave him every opportunity to change his course, give his defense, and he didn't take any of the chances afforded to him." The judge rose to place a hand on the mage's shoulder. "This isn't your fault."

"I know it." He gave another heavy sigh. "It doesn't make it any easier to lose a student like this. I liked him, Hamal. He had such potential."

They left room quietly, making their way through the myriad floors to reach Oknare's office. There, Hamal sat as Oknare opened a small cabinet to pour two mugs of the ale he kept there. He offered one to his friend.

"What is your verdict? I know it won't be the final one. Still, your words have a great of weight in the courts."

Hamal sipped the drink, taking a moment to consider.

"Expelling him from the school, stripping him of his power…the only thing the courts would add is exile from the Trinity. That's more of a formality. In effect, you've already done that. He's too young to warrant execution under our laws," he reminded. "The most likely sentence is immediate deportment to the mainland, on the first ship available. You've done the rest."

"At least it was only rats." Oknare wandered to the window behind his desk, stared out with the mug cradled in his hands. "He hadn't moved to a higher class of life. Doesn't excuse it, and I'm not trying to. At least he hadn't gone so low as to kill another sapient being."

"He could have used that, tried to defend himself with that. Perhaps make an argument for reformation and rehabilitation. There are precedents." Hamal leaned back into his seat thoughtfully. "Yet he didn't. He wouldn't. It troubles me, Oknare, that he didn't try to do so."

"He has a great deal of pride," the mage murmured. "He's very conscious of where he stands, how he's seen." He frowned, turned back. "I've known him to carry grudges. Yet I've also known him to give some kind of explanation, or attempt to, when he'd been found doing wrong in the past. I'd caught him in the library, skimming through texts that no student had any business with. He had tried to talk his way out of it. He'd had time, thought it through. He'd had the argument prepared."

"But not this time."

"No. Not this time. Now that I think on it, it puzzles me. Ba'tvian has always been one for preparation." He looked down at his ale, then drank. "The earthquake caught him off guard, I suppose. I know that it did the rest of us."

"I heard that the geomancers had traced the origin to the southwest, to Genoria."

"Just off the coast. A large piece of the continent has sheared off. It just collapsed into the sea." Oknare let a long moment of companionable silence pass by. When he spoke again, returning to the initial subject, his voice filled with regret. "If, as you say, the courts decide on immediate deportment, how soon would he be leaving?"

"Tomorrow, perhaps the day after, depending on how soon we

can get a ship captain to agree to the transport." Hamal set his mug on the desk and rose. "The school will have to confiscate his belongings. The law dictates that nothing is to be taken with him."

Oknare nodded, looking back out the window to the sea and overcast sky beyond. What a waste, he thought, as the High Judge took his leave. What a terrible, terrible waste.

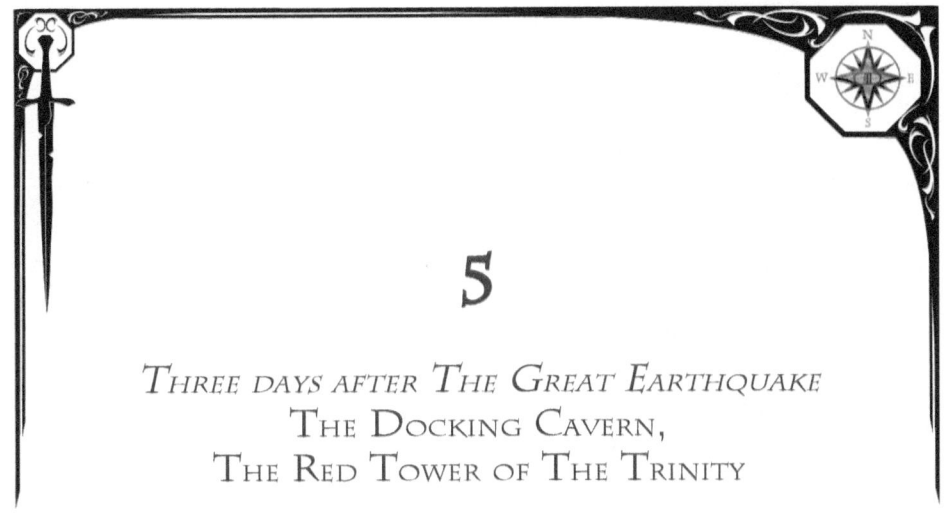

5

B a'tvian waited on the dock, flanked by the Trinity's armed escort, resolutely staring at the hugely gaping maw of the cavern's entrance. Below him, ocean water gently surged in and out, creating a muted rhythm for the dockworkers to follow as they went about their work. Overhead, seagulls swooped to and from their nesting sites or the open sea outside.

Looking at it, one wouldn't have thought that the world had been shaken violently enough to crack the cavern walls. Yet as calm as the waters were, as complacent as the birds seemed, there were other indications of it.

On any other day, the docks would be bustling with people off-loading mercantile goods. People and livestock would be boarding or disembarking. It would have been crowded. There would be such a tumultuous noise what with people shouting to one another over two rushing tides of life. One would be headed for the waiting ships, the other headed for the huge oxen-driven lifts that would carry them up to the top of the huge stone tower in stages.

Not today.

The earthquake didn't prevent them from coming. Of that, he was certain. *It's as if they are afraid of what I might do.*

As if he could do anything.

They had taken the clothes from his back, then dressed him in the drab gray garb of a convict. More, they had taken his magic, the one thing he'd had to call his own. Bitterness and despair welled up, filling that new emptiness inside him. How could he do anything to these people without the one thing he'd treasured above all else?

All he had left was the anger, the hate. They burned beneath his grief. Perhaps they were right to be afraid, yet the ones he wanted to fear him stood stoically beside him. He didn't acknowledge them. Still mourning his loss in silence, he promised himself that they would pay.

They had made him as the dirt under their feet.

None of them spoke, not even when the ship that would carry him into exile glided up gracefully to dock at the pier on which they stood. The mooring ropes were set, the gangplank lowered with a thud, and burly sailors took up positions on deck – defensive positions, the blood-mage noticed with a resentful mental sneer. The fear, the disgust was palpable.

A guard prodded him in the back. Ba'tvian walked up the gangplank. He didn't see the point in fighting his exile. As hurt as he was, as much as he hated, he wouldn't rebel. Nor would he let them see how they made him feel.

It would make vengeance all the sweeter, if he could obtain it.

If.

Armed members of the crew came forward to replace the escort sent by the college. Ba'tvian refused the urge to look back. Oknare was watching from the pier, impassive and grim. He was determined for that – for *him* – not to matter. Not on the surface.

Don't let them see, don't let them know. Don't give them the satisfaction.

He let his guards lead him below the deck, bit his tongue to hold back the vile words that sprang to his tongue when he was shoved down the steep, narrow steps. In his mind, he replayed the trial, the sham of it, the martyred, righteous looks of the mages who had testified against him. Their faces were already etched into his memory. He added the faces of the crew to the growing agenda.

They didn't understand. They never would. It didn't matter.

They had made him nothing.

That was all that mattered.

INTERLUDE 1

The ship was moving out as the rat watched on. There were many rats in the docking cavern, smart, lean, and common enough that few people took notice of them in the business of the day. There were always exceptions, usually when a young rat or a new one made the mistake of getting in the way of the humans that worked in their territory, but also when a rat was distracted by something. This one was. It was so intent on watching the exile that it failed to check its surroundings as it normally did.

Someone stepped on the rat's tail. Startled, the little creature squealed, whirling on the offending foot to sink its sharp incisors into the flesh above the boot leather. The dockworker, laden with canvas for sail repairs, let out a yelp of his own as he dropped the load onto the pier-side catwalk, flailing his leg in an effort to dislodge the rodent. Grappling with the leather, it held on, screeching as it the world dipped, shook, and spun in its vision. There was a muttered a curse, a strange series of hops, then a piling loomed large on one side – just as the man's boot hit it hard.

The rat let go with an agonized scream. It landed in the water. Stunned, body broken, hemorrhaging inside, the rodent could only watch as the dark sea water close over it. It sank down.

Pity.

As the rat's vision faded, so did the image in a mirror some distance away. The man who had been watching the former student go into exile contemplated the strange emptiness in the glass. Yes, quite a pity. He would have liked to have gotten a better measure of Oknare's reaction to this most recent turn of events. It could have been useful. Still, there were other ways, and definitely other little spies in his vast, largely unseen army. The loss of one tool was not a great impediment.

Labiyal Biyalban selected another now. This one, however, lived in a far different environment than the so-called Red Tower of the Trinity Schools. Nor was it a rodent. The subtle tug on the magic that linked him to his spy brought the mirror back to life on its stand. A scene flared up, mostly sky, as this particular set of eyes made its way to a perch suited to the task he required of it. It landed atop a miserable hovel, flipping small wings on its back and watching the dirt path nearby intently. A ways off in the sparrow's line of sight, several serfs toiled away in the field closest to their dwelling place.

More like slaves than serfs now. Ideal.

Circumstances had changed for these people over the last few years. While Ba'tvian had been sponsored to the college, they had undergone several small tragedies. The old lord had passed on, leaving his son now ruled the estates. The nearby port city of Menie, proving to be a harder, more stringent master to serve. The family of nine had lost the youngest two winters ago and the second oldest had suffered a blow to the head by one of the master's prized bulls. He was now permanently addled, rendering him next to useless.

One of the daughters had come up pregnant, he recalled, then had been turned out by their lord – the father of her child. She hadn't gotten far before Labiyal had scooped her up, though they wouldn't know of that. Wouldn't care to.

Hard times begot hard people, and hard people were the easiest pawns to deploy. He was more than willing to sacrifice a few pawns to gain a warrior, or even a priest.

The thought brought the shadow of a smile to his lips. He glanced at the *chesra* game he had set up on a small table to the left of his chair. He would have to indulge in a game later, perhaps when his father came to check on his progress. They both enjoyed it, though different reasons. It was really the only thing they had in common aside from blood. It was gratifyingly difficult to lose while trying to win.

Dismissing the prospective game from his mind, he returned his attention to the scrying mirror.

The Trinity Colleges were predictive in their handling of exiled students. They would have sent a messenger to all necessary parties – in this case, the family, the master, the sponsoring patron – so that they would be prepared for the disgraceful homecoming. There, trotting up the worn path depicted in the glass, was the messenger as expected, mounted on a mule.

He watched the rider's progress, as the sparrow did, saw him hail the workers in the field, observed the scene as an older, wretched looking man trudged up to speak with him. The bird was not close enough to hear the exchange. Still, sound was not needed to understand. The messenger had been given a letter, which he was even now reading out loud to the peasant. Labiyal knew every word by heart. As the lad's sponsor, he had been given a copy, as well.

By the time the messenger had finished, handed the grubby man his letter, then left for the manor in the far distance, he could see the bitter anger in the man's expression. More there was fear and resignation in the man's face. The new master was in the habit of meting out his punishments to all, not just the offender.

Ba'tvian was in for a traumatic time. It gave him a vague feeling of satisfaction.

The door opened at the far end of the darkened room. He released his spy, sitting back as the mirror went blank again. He gestured subtly. A mute servant appeared from the shadows to stand at his side.

"A chair and refreshment," he ordered absently, watching his visitor approach. "We are not to be disturbed."

The servant bowed then scuttled away.

The newcomer looked only marginally like the man seated opposite him. It was not surprising. A Daemon Lord could alter his appearance on a whim. His father preferred one that made him look sophisticated, regal, and powerful, if a little vain. A long golden mane spilled over his well-built frame, his face clean-shaven. His eyes were intensely purple. In all, he was quite unlike the dark red of his son's hair, the neatly-trimmed beard, the red-tinted amber of his irises. Labiyal's looks rarely changed without non-magical aid; he was only a half daemon.

"Spying again, spawnling?" his father queried with a thin smile. "On what or who this time?"

He ignored the insulting term, recognizing it as a test of proper discipline. Instead, he answered with a kind of casual indifference.

"Serfs, Lord Biyal." He never referred to the Daemon Lord in other way.

"What is the lot of serfs but to toil and suffer?" Biyal asked offhandedly. The servant appeared with the requested chair. Another brought a tray of delicate fare. The Daemon Lord sat, crooking a finger at the table set with the *chesra* game. Lifting gently, glided over the floor to settle between them. "What use is such an obvious fact to you?"

"Yes, they toil and suffer. Then they spread that suffering among those connected to them," he returned in the same tone. "They are the family of a particular mage I am interested in."

"Ah." Biyal's eyes flickered red as he gave his offspring a measuring stare. "A key for our King's lock, perhaps?"

Such was his mission, his purpose.

"I believe that he may serve, yes. He has the potential. He has already taken steps along the appropriate paths," he answered slowly, weighing each word as it was given. He did not wish to promise anything at this point. "At the moment, he is in disgrace. I wish to take more time with this one, to determine his suitability, to make him irredeemable. I do not want to repeat the mistakes of the past."

"No, you don't." His father regarded him shrewdly. "Time you have, Labiyal – for now. The King of Hell is not yet impatient. Still, he will want to know more."

"I will make a report to him as soon as I may, my Lord," Labiyal acknowledged with a nod that served as an informal bow. "I have no wish to anger our Sire."

"Nor I." Biyal leaned back, satisfied for the time being. "It is well for the moment, I think. Now, let us begin…"

A pawn slid forward on the board. Labiyal studied it and then made a move of his own. Yes, it was well.

The next move belonged to Ba'tvian Delthanurk.

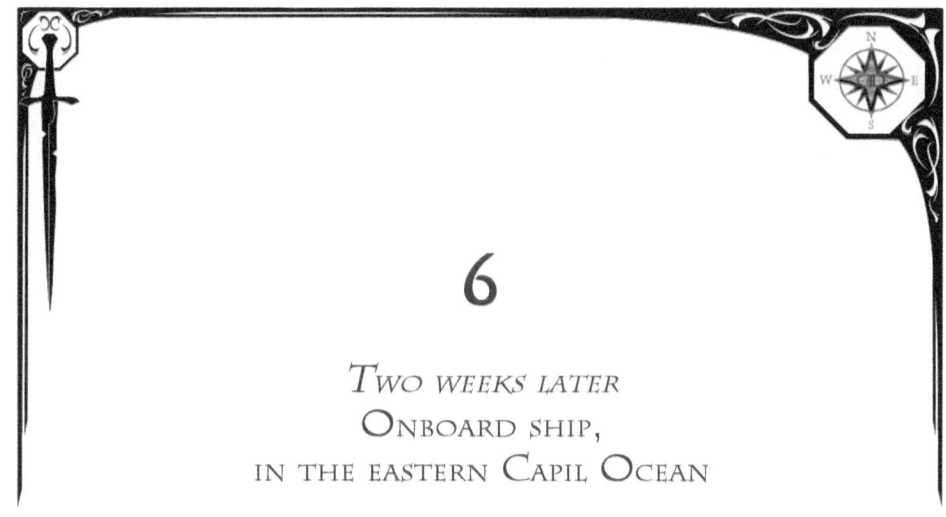

6

Two weeks later
Onboard ship,
in the eastern Capil Ocean

THE ship's name was *King's Folly*.

There were no kings in Orthanor, the continent they were headed to. There were records of them, accounts of their existence elsewhere on Einlienn, but there were none here; the lords who ruled the cities could not be called monarchs, nor did they claim to be. The captain, who owned the vessel, didn't deal with anyone that came close to that rank or title. No one seemed to care about the origins of the ship's name, or at least they didn't care discuss it within his hearing. Now it became a joke among a few of the crew members, one he heard entirely too much.

King's Folly. Ba'tvian's folly.

Even in the brig, he heard the derision, the scorning laughter. The guards posted outside the door didn't bother with tact or discretion. He had little choice in overhearing whatever they thought was amusing. Yet an interesting fact had surfaced, one that may well prove to be more than useful.

The crew didn't want to have anything to do with their prisoner – unless they were killing him. They hadn't bother to hide it, or the uneasiness that lay beneath their hostility and mockery. They feared him, a mage stripped of power. That fear had driven them to petition their captain, to hand him an ultimatum.

The prisoner went, or they would mutiny.

Since the guards now spoke with a kind of unholy glee, he

assumed that they were getting what they wanted. The glee rankled. He concentrated on that, not his own rising uncertainty; he refused to call it fear. Fear was weak, wasn't it? He was not weak. One day, they would know that. First, he had to survive whatever they planned.

They hadn't yet strung him up. He wasn't certain that this was altogether encouraging. A direct death wasn't what they'd been after, it seemed. Whatever it was, until it came to pass, they manhandled him, bruised him, dealt him pain and humiliation at every turn.

None of it would be forgotten.

Ba'tvian had kept a diary during the relatively short voyage, using only his mind for paper, pen, and ink. He harbored everything in his memory, consoling himself with promises. Those promises became more desperate, more hedged with anger, with every passing day.

He would get his powers back.

He would return.

He would grind them into the dirt beneath his heel.

Each of them would die in as many slow, creative ways as he could possibly imagine.

None of that would happen without power, so that search had to be his primary focus now. Not revenge, not pettiness. He couldn't let them distract him from that goal, no matter how appealing it might seem, or how much it was warranted.

There was a pounding on his door, startling him out of his reverie. It swung open to reveal the bosun standing there. This was it then. He braced himself.

"Well, then, get up, m'lord mage," the man said in a gruff, mocking tone. "Got yer way ashore all ready and waiting."

Ashore? Was he to be turned over port authorities after all?

When he didn't move instantly, two of the ship's guards came forward. He was roughly hauled him to his feet. One of them muttered about something about smelling pig swill or cesspools. Ba'tvian bit back a scathing retort. The stench was their fault, not his. They hadn't permitted him to bath in over two weeks, nor had they troubled themselves with cleaning out the chamber pot. His hands had been tied fast behind his back for the entire journey and none of the guards were willing help him with his trousers when needed. How did they think he was going smell?

They banged him into the door jam as they propelled him into the cramped corridor, marching topside. With every bullying shove, with every painful bruise, he gritted his teeth to keep himself quiet. By the time they stopped by the dingy being prepared for launch on deck, he was seething.

He was manhandled into the boat, hemmed in by guards, sitting sullenly as they were all lowered into the water. Staring over the shoulder of the bosun who had been the last to climb aboard, he studied the coast in an effort to place it on the maps he knew. It didn't look at all familiar. It was, for lack of a better description, a field of destruction. Broken, dead or dying trees looked is they'd been thrown up in the air to land on the shore any which way. Some of the trunks were massive. Where those spire trees?

The shore wasn't the only place that was a wreck. The water close to it was as well. Trees had either fallen into the ocean from the small cliffs, or, so it seemed, had been tossed there. The surf was muddy. One or two rocky edifices protruding from the water looked like seabed. The state of the ocean bottom couldn't be guaranteed, which explained why they'd launched the dinghy so far from shore.

Where was this? The Spirlan Coast? The forests there held many spire trees, yet this…this looked more like a wasteland than a forest.

Ba'tvian continued to watch the approaching shore as they navigated the hazards in the water silently. When the boat's bottom struck the rocky shore, two sailors leapt out to grab the bow. They didn't beach the dinghy completely as they otherwise might have done. Instead, everyone began to disembark directly into the water. The bosun and two of the guards climbed out, then he was nudged into rising. He wasn't half-risen from his seat when one of them shoved him hard. He fell over the side face first, swallowing seawater, choking, gasping, writhing manically as he struggled to get his head up. The bosun yanked him up by the back of his tunic. Sucking in air, trying not to vomit up the salt water, he got his legs under him. All around him, there were chuckles and snickering. The water was only waist high.

He'd barely gotten his footing when the bosun prodded him forward. Two sailors flanked him as he stumbled onto the shore. Once out of the surf, they forced him to his knees. One of the guards came around to bind his feet. Pebbles bit into his legs through the cloth of his pants as he looked up at the ship's officer. The man scowled at him.

"We wanted to slit yer throat and throw ye overboard." He yanked Ba'tvian's head back, set the edge of a small dagger against the exposed skin of his throat. "Captain's contract don't allow fer it. We be honorable in our way, so we won't be killing ye."

He released him so abruptly that Ba'tvian overbalanced, toppling onto his side.

"Ye get the maritime punishment. Ye don't deserve it," he growled contemptuously. "But yer not likely to live long enough for it to matter, so here it be."

He drove the dagger into the ground a body's length in front of Ba'tvian.

"It's all ye get, m'lord mage. May ye rot here 'til yer death." With that, he spat on him, then waded back to the dingy. The others followed suit.

With spittle dripping from his cheeks he watched them go. His eyes burned with tears.

And with hate.

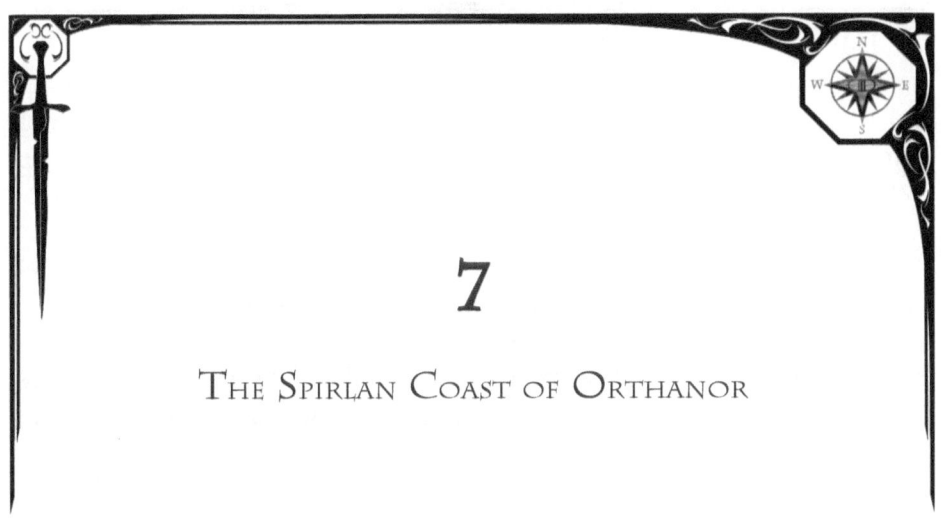

7

The Spirlan Coast of Orthanor

H E'D wept.
The shame of tears, though they were private, seared his pride. His gift, the one thing that had made him more than dirt, was gone, his hands bound, his belly hollow, his thirst savage. He'd strained first, felt the throbbing ache of joints positioned unnaturally, the burn of the rope cutting into his wrists. Anger had given way to frustration, then frustration had led to despair.

The course of emotion was done. His head hurt fiercely from the bout. At least his eyes were free of grit. The pain dulled as the despair leaked away. Renewed determination crept in. With it, came sullen anger and a new awareness.

There were things in this place. They kept to the shadows, watched from them, crept up close enough to touch him when the gradually shifting light allowed. They seemed to follow his every move.

Ba'tvian had first noticed them not an hour after he had spent those bitter tears. The sun had been westering in the sky, making the shadows had become more prominent. He could feel the eyes watching from the shade, hear the insect-like whispering in his ears. He didn't understand the words though he could hear them. He'd caught sight of one creeping, lizard-like, on the rocks as the sun descended. His only thought at that point was to get free. To try, again and again, until he had achieved it.

Hours later, he was still working at it.

He'd wriggled and rolled over to the dagger. As it had been buried to the hilt, he'd had to pry it up halfway with his toes. Sawing through the rope at his ankles had been the easiest part, he knew. When he repositioned himself to free his hands, he had only an inkling of how difficult the task would be.

He wasn't a notably flexible or athletic young man. His joints were screaming at him. He was certain that he had overstrained muscles in his limbs with all the maneuvering, possibly partially dislocated a shoulder. The temperature only added to the misery. The day had been murderously hot, and his body ached abominably in the cool of the night.

Not once did he take his attention off the things. He couldn't. He saw them. He heard them. He felt them.

He knelt in the sandy dirt, small rocks digging into his knees as he tried to make use of the sharp edge. The long night was almost over. He knew, just knew, that the things were waiting to strike yet couldn't think of why they hadn't before this. They'd had time, opportunity. A shadow flitted to his right, jerking his gaze in that direction. Fresh pain sliced through his palm.

Another surge of fear had him ignoring the pain. He jerked his bound hands up and down, straining to spread them wide as he did. All around him the shadows lengthened, deepened. The eyes of the things glinted dully. Slowly, their circle began to close.

Finally, the first ring of rope gave way. Panic and elation flooding through him, he worked his hands faster. He nicked his fingers, yet didn't care. More of the bindings began to loosen. From the feel of it, there was one, maybe two rings of rope left. They were coming undone quickly, but not quickly enough.

Blood had mixed with dirt on his hands as he'd struggled to get through the last of it. In the gloom of the night, the things watched. The things waited. When the first hint of predawn showed, the last strand snapped.

They swarmed.

Throwing himself flat, Ba'tvian made a grab for the dagger.

8

Aboard *The King's Folly*, *in the eastern Capil Ocean*

THE brig had been scrubbed clean with a meticulousness that was worthy of a king's palace. There was talk of having it cleansed by a priest when they made port. They were a superstitious lot, even the captain, though he didn't let it show as obviously as the rest. Until that little errand had been taken care of, they were on their best behavior just avoid the brig and whatever taint it may still hold.

They would all be happier once they reached Menie.

The day crew of the ship slumbered easily. The night crew enjoyed the quiet of the evening air, the cool breeze off the water, letting the creaking of the rigging soothe away any lingering uneasiness from having a blood mage onboard.

There were not many on deck. With the weather calm and sweet, there wasn't a need for more than a skeleton crew to mind the rigging. The coxswain stood at the helm, having lost the coin flips with the captain and bosun to determine who would pull the all-nighter to make up for some of the time they'd lost taking the bastard to the coast. He'd set them on course, locking the wheel in place so he could dozed a bit on his feet. The lull of the sea was just a bit too much to resist.

No one saw the shadows playing along the surface of the water behind them. No one saw them crawl up the wooden planking like an oily slick dripping in reverse. Those on deck heard the coxswain's violent oath clearly. Then even the crew below heard the shrillness of his screams. More cascaded into the night.

When they stopped, the *King's Folly* continued on her heading, as quiet as a tomb.

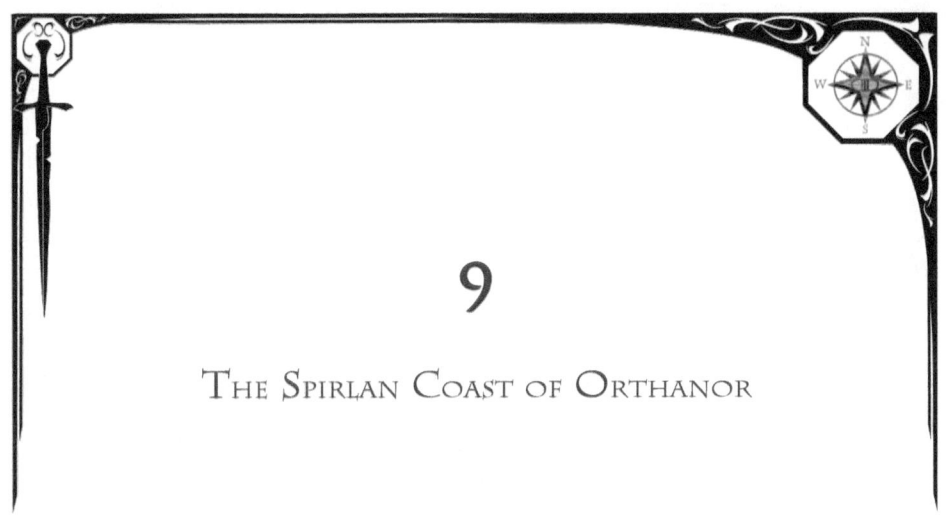

9

The Spirlan Coast of Orthanor

HE awoke in the dawning sun to find himself sprawled on his back, his limbs free., if incredibly sore The sun hovered over the eastern horizon, so he hadn't been out long. He rubbed his eyes, felt his hand began burn with pain as his cuts reopened. Dumbly, he stared at them. Blood seeped through the grime and grit, reviving his memory.

He shot upright, looking around wildly. The world spun. His stomach began to revolt. He had to let himself fall back to the rocky dirt. Closing his eyes, he took deep breathes in an attempt to calm the wave of nausea. Once it had passed, he slowly sat up.

His body was a mass of aches. He was weak on top of it all. Groaning a little at the discomfort, he peered around. There were a few shadows but nothing lurked in them. He cast his eyes to the ground around him, then saw the dagger. It was still buried in the black corpse of one of the creatures.

Even dead, the thing's outline blurred, shifted. It seemed filmy, almost transparent. He staggered to his feet, reaching out to touch it, to see if it was really there. It felt solid and very, very cold. He remembered dimly that they had been cold to the touch during the fight, too.

What had happened during the struggle was a blur after his hand had closed around the dagger's grip. Nothing was clear to him. The creatures had lunged all at once, he had lashed out blindly with the blade – had he screamed something? Yes…yes, he had. What he couldn't recall. His dagger had hit something, perhaps the one that lay dead now, and he'd shouted again.

I was furious. I thought I was going to die. He looked over his shoulder at the empty sea behind him. *I was going to die and never get my due. Never get my power, my vengeance. I'd be the dirt that they wanted me to be, that they made me to be.*

He couldn't be dirt. He couldn't be nothing.

He focused on the dagger again, grabbing hold of the hilt. He tugged it out of the thing's neck. It did not come out easily. It was as if the body was determined to keep it. The moment the blade was free of flesh, the corpse began to deteriorate rapidly. The stench it gave off as it did so was indescribable. Ba'tvian gagged, stumbling away from it. Still he couldn't stop watching as it rotted. A thousand questions rolled through his mind.

What was it? Where had it come from? Was it magical? Had the dagger killed it, or had there been something more?

If it was something more, could he use it?

His lips cracked as he found his first smile since the earthquake. Perhaps he could. It would be a start on what promised to be a long and painful road.

Especially for others.

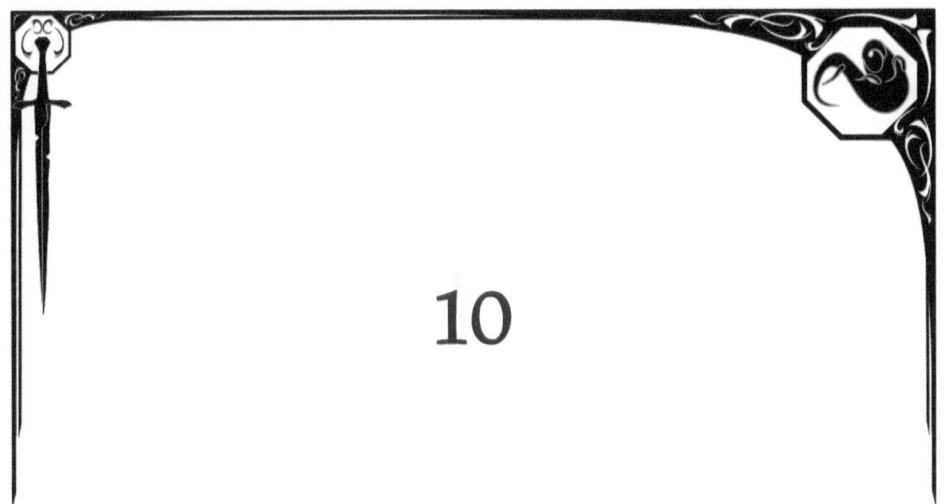

10

THEY watched him as he studied their deceased brother. From the shadows further out from the beach, they observed his reaction to his survival, the revelation that there was still power to be garnered. That he thought, that he planned, pleased them. They would be sure to watch his progress as he went along his path.

The death of one of their number was inconsequential. Shadows were as nothing to others of their kind, and often to each other. The death had proven what they had sensed, what they could scent.

This one. It was this one, this boy on the verge of manhood. Soon, there would be repayment. It had already begun.

The long wait was over.

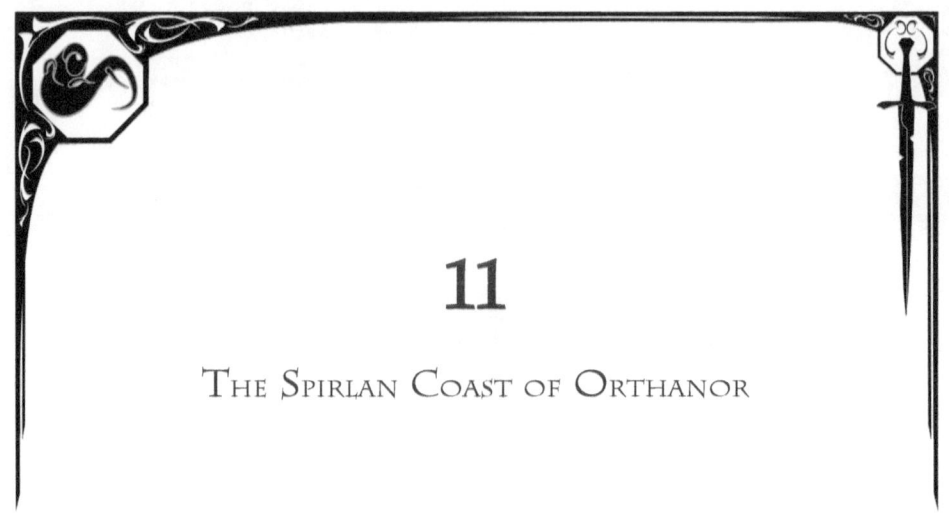

11

THE SPIRLAN COAST OF ORTHANOR

IT really was a wasteland. Dead trees, mud, dirt, all manner of rubble – that was all he saw. There didn't seem to be much that lived aside from a few plants that had somehow managed to cling on. Halfway through the morning, he'd discovered a blackberry bramble growing between fallen trunks. He'd stripped it clean of fruit. It did little to satiate his hunger and nothing to slake his thirst but it was something.

While he'd eaten, he'd seen them. Sliding over the wood, the ground, lurking in the shadows.

They made no move to attack, seeming content to watch him. It was unnerving, the way they stared, the way they ghosted around him. They didn't get too close, though. By midday what fear he'd felt was replaced by wary curiosity,

What were they? What did they want?

Ba'tvian pondered those questions while he searched for more blackberries and any remnants of civilization. He knew there had been cities in this forsaken place. They'd been perched on the boughs of the spire trees, filled with people. They'd grown and harvested crops in those trees, too. He had some hope that he if he found the ruins of a city, he could scavenge the foodstuffs they no longer needed.

The irony that he'd learned all of that from the very school who'd damned him here left a bitter taste in his mouth.

They will pay. That was a promise that he fully meant to keep. *They will pay dearly. They will remember what I did. They remember my name for all time.*

He spent hours stumbling through the jumbled landscape before he came up on a huge trunk, the roots torn up from the earth by the quake. Studying the base of the spire tree, he concluded that it had to be as high as the Red Tower. Surely, this tree had held a city.

He followed the length of it, noting a nasty, shattering break about thirty yards down. The rest of the tree tilted drunkenly on the sloping ground, its branches dipping into a shallow river below where he stood. He came down the slope quickly, half sliding in the dirt and mud, to kneel at the river's edge. The water wasn't clear, clouded a bit by the muck. Still, it was fresh water.

He was so thirsty.

He rinsed his hands in it, scrubbing them as clean as he could, then cupped them to catch the water to drink. It tasted a bit like earth. He didn't care. He drank his fill, having the sense of mind to do so slowly lest he be sick. Then he shed his clothing to bathe.

Ridding himself of the filth did much to restore his confidence. He wasn't a serf, a worker to toil in the fields, then come back to his hovel covered in his work – work done for someone else. He was a mage, a powerful and talented one. As soon as he found the most suitable sacrifices, he would break the seals Oknare had placed on his gifts. He would show them all. They would know then the true meaning of power.

His own.

He did what he could for his clothing, wishing that there was soap root nearby. He draped the fabric over a branch. Walking naked through the knee-high water, he inspected the rest of the tree. Around him, the shadows drifted forward.

Seeing them move, he stopped, frowning, watching. They slithered over the water's surface, the trunk, the limbs. They seemed to swarm over a particular spot just off a large branch up ahead. Cautiously, he approached them. The shadows slid into the space between that bough and the next. He followed, pausing as he found the place dark, the air foul. As his eyes adjusted to the lighting, he could see them waiting for him, sedately coasting to either side so that there was a path lined with them. It led to the half-buried body of a man.

He'd been dead for several days, probably since the quake. Ba'tvian studied the bloated body with a disdainful expression, then turned his attention to the debris around him. Chunks of wall, plaster and wood, some personal items scattered about, most of them broken. A dwelling, then. There were generally useful things in a dwelling.

A thin smile stretched his lips, causing the parched skin to split. He licked them, tasted his own blood, then decided that the shadows could be handy after all.

Ignoring the corpse, he began to rummage through the ruins, intent on what he could find.

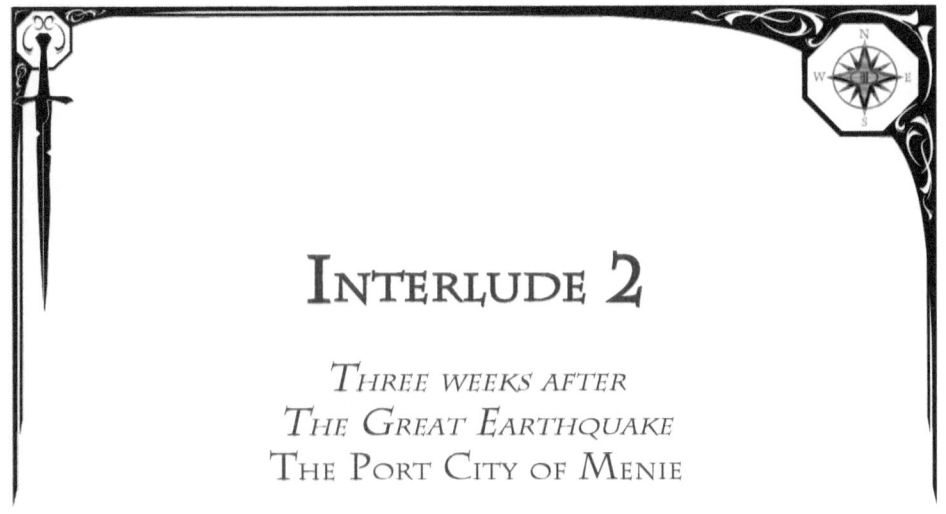

Interlude 2

Three weeks after
The Great Earthquake
The Port City of Menie

LABIYAL waited. It was something he was good at and had the patience for, unlike his father. Certainly, unlike most of his father's kind. He considered the trait a rare benefit of being a half-bred spawn.

He sat comfortably in the high-end room he'd rented, elegantly dressed as the eccentric man of wealth he portrayed when visiting places like the port. He was known as Sir Kendell in this guise, a man of diverse interests with deep wells of generosity. As Kendell, Labiyal had helped the late Lord Menie reform and rehabilitate the older, declining sections of the city. Together, they had implemented work projects that allowed the poor to not only earn their daily bread, but to climb up out of the pit of poverty.

Thinking of his programs, he made a mental note to check the work houses while he was in town. He didn't doubt that they needed culling. Promises of more work or better wages often had the twits willing to be led anywhere. Most of them ended up under the knives of one of his rites. Power demanded sacrifice; he needed that power to complete his task.

His existence depended on it.

He leaned back in his chair, idly contemplating the platter of fruit and cheese that had been laid out for him upon his arrival. Absently selecting a slice of good cheddar, he tapped the base of the small table mirror he'd set up. The gold was warm to the touch. It grew warmer as the mirror's surface fogged over, then cleared.

It was time to see if the tardy cargo vessel had arrived.

The docks came into view, with the bustling activity of fishermen, cargo haulers, merchants, and sailors. From the way the image spun out, close to the ground with a kind of quick scrambling movement, he could tell that the images were being relayed from one or several rats in the area. He made another note to acquire some of the seagulls that hung about the harbor. They were a bit more suited to what he wanted.

Twenty minutes of watching the mirror told him what he did not want to hear: the King's Folly still had not made port. Ba'tvian Delthanurk was nowhere to be found.

His gold eyes flared subtly with a crimson haze, then he drew the temper in, locked it coolly away. The boy must return home. There was too much that he had planned for him, too much that he had invested in him, for him to throw it all off course now.

With a flick of a hand, he dismissed the image in the mirror while he drew out a thin blade with the other. In an almost casual gesture, he nicked his thumb, saw the dark, dark red of his blood bead. He smeared it on the mirror frame, on the silvered glass, and murmured an incantation that had the black energies of forbidden magic stirring. At the end, he spoke Ba'tvian's name.

In the glass, he saw the boy stumbling along the coast, an escort of shadowy wraiths in tow.

12

B A'TVIAN had left the dead Spirlan Coast behind. For now, he followed the shore line north, led by the hazy recollection of a handful of fishing villages to the north. Beyond them lay Menie and the aristocratic estates his serf family worked to the bone. By the time he arrived there, he was certain that he would know what needed to be done next.

The shadows followed him. It had been a surprise, a gratifying one, to see them tagging behind him like a pack of favored of dogs. They were becoming the company that he hadn't known he'd craved, companions who listened to him without filling his own ears with noisome chatter. Over the last three days, he'd found that if he paid attention to them, they guided him to sources of food, water, and whatever supplies he deemed necessary.

Their cooperation made him wonder. The memory of their initial attack made him wary enough not to take them for granted, or to trust them completely. They seemed to approve of his reticence, though that may have been his imagination.

He wished he knew what they expected of him. They had expectations; he could feel the weight of them when they turned those gimlet white eyes towards him. He didn't ask or wonder aloud. Even if he thought they would answer him, he wouldn't ask. He could sense that figuring it out on his own was part of what they expected. Asking would be an admission that he couldn't do it on his own.

He damn well would.

Traveling over the rocky soil and grassy sprawl that comprised the coast gave him plenty of time to think. One thing he had concluded was that there was no such thing as true glory. Glory faded with death, faded with memory. It was as useful, as pratical as an ornamental dagger. There would be no glory for him.

Ba'tvian Delthanurk would settle for not being forgotten, by anyone.

Everlasting memory. That was a kind of immortality, one that could – and would; he'd see to it – carry with it the overtones of fascination, horror, admiration, power. The Great Quake, for instance, would be spoken of for generations to come with a kind of terrible awe for the damage it had dealt the world. He seemed to remember his keepers discussing how it had affected most of the southern hemisphere.

He would follow that example. He would brand himself into the memory of time.

It was a lofty ambition. As he scaled over yet another jagged outcropping on the shore, he thought about what he would need to do in order to achieve it. Power – his gifts – yes, he would have to regain those. That came first, before anything else. There was no point in doing any of it if he didn't have the one thing that made him better, that made him more the dirt.

Still, he would need others, wouldn't he? Soldiers, helpers, yet no partners. He didn't need or want partners. They wouldn't be equals. Still, a few had to be close, and they would have to be of like minds. A general had to have commanders after all.

Yet I've got to prove myself, don't I? Have to show them – the world – Oknare just what it is that I alone can do...

The thought slithered into his mind as he reached the summit of the rocky outcropping. Sprawled below him was a village. The buildings were in various states of repair, as were several boats beached for the work. Those closest to the water had taken the hardest beating from the waves tossed at them by the quake.

Belatedly, Ba'tvian crouched to merge the outline of his body with the rock around him. The shadows crept up alongside to peer at the hovels, the boats, the people hard at work. His heartbeat seemed to deepen, growing louder in his head. His blood began to hum. Watching the scene before him, he didn't think of food, of shelter, or of the possibility of aid.

He thought of prey.

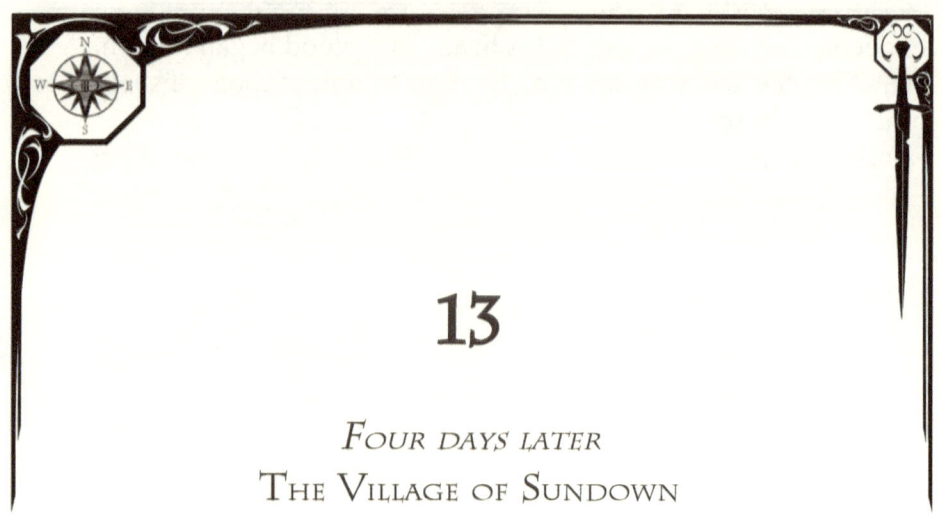

13

H E waited until dark. He was smart enough to know that he could do more to greater effect when most of the villagers were tucked into their beds. So he ignored the cramping of his belly, took stock of what he carried, and planned as the light waned.

He had several knives taken from the ruins in what had remained of the Spireling Forest. The clothing he'd salvaged was dark enough that it shouldn't attract attention if he kept to the shadows. It was all he needed for an attempt at a simplified blood rite, or so he hoped. He debated trying to scout around the edges of the village, to see who and what was where, but didn't think he could do so without being seen. He muttered about that, brooded over it, knowing that he could very well end up worse than just exiled if he was caught here.

The mainland wouldn't care about how old he was when it came to dealing with a blood mage.

So deeply mired in his thoughts was he that he didn't notice when most of the shadows slipped off. Two remained with him, silently observing his preparations. Only when night had finally fallen did Ba'tvian notice the absences. He frowned over them, eyeing the two who in turn eyed him. Eventually, he shrugged, then began to creep over the rock towards the village. He knew he couldn't rely on them.

He didn't go into the hamlet. Finding a comfortable hiding place inside the breached hull of small fishing boat on the shore, he waited until he saw the tiny lights in the hovels and cottages go out, one by one. As he waited, the shadows returned.

He spared them a momentary glance, biting back the urge to demand where they had been. Determined not to let it matter, he reined in the irritation. Leaving the boat, he led the way to the first dwelling.

His earlier observations of the people had led him to believe that a solitary fisherman lived in the humble shack. A single, older man, someone he could very well deal with on his own. He edged around the side of the dwelling and listened at the rickety door. Faint snores emitted from within. The sacrifice – it was best to think of him that way – was asleep. Slowly, he tried the latch, pausing with each squeak of the rusted metal to see if the oldster stirred. He didn't.

He allowed himself a sneer as the door inched open. Only in inconsequential places with nothing of value did one find doors without locks.

Checking to make sure that there was no one about to see him, he stepped inside, then closed the door behind him. The shadows ghosted through the cracks around the entrance, encircling the man as Ba'tvian unsheathed a knife and stalked towards him.

Interlude 3

The Port City of Menie

LABIYAL watched with some satisfaction. The boy was resourceful, even if he was ignorant.

As Ba'tvian had planned for his night attack, he had enjoyed a sumptuous dinner, an excellent bottle of wine, then some substantial planning of his own. The Shadowed Ones, he mused as blood spurted in the mirror, may change everything, if only slightly. He decided they were an encouraging sign.

The *Helkorex Noxim* mentioned them. His master had uttered every word in the tome, each syllable holding the power to create, to destroy. Some of the passages were rants, others observations, though the vast majority were statements of what was to be.

Yet the problem with prophecy is time and its very fluid nature.

The future was ever changing in accordance with choices, lives, deaths. None of that negated prophecy. It did change the method, timing, or impact of each occurrence. Labiyal tended to do without prophecy if at all possible. Still, as his orders – even his existence – were noted in Hell's tome, he couldn't ignore it altogether.

The Shadowed Ones were part of it. Hell had lamented their fall, spoken a tirade full of fury over their fate. They had been the first of Hell's Children. Very, very few had escaped The One's curse upon their kind. His own father, the Daemon Lord Biyal, was one.

"My Children shall hail My Key, My Favor, My Blessing, with My War to follow," he quoted to himself, watching the creatures that

had been of Hell's bloodline swarm over the remains of the old man. *"Safeguard him, for he is Mine, and should he please Me, he will be as Me."*

Yet if this lauded key failed, then his fate would be no more, yet no less, ignoble than Labiyal's own. Ba'tvian was on the correct path; he had no intention of letting him stumble off it. There was only one more step needed to seal him there.

Touching the dried, almost black smears on the mirror's frame, he uttered another incantation, calling blood to blood, and the boy to his childhood home.

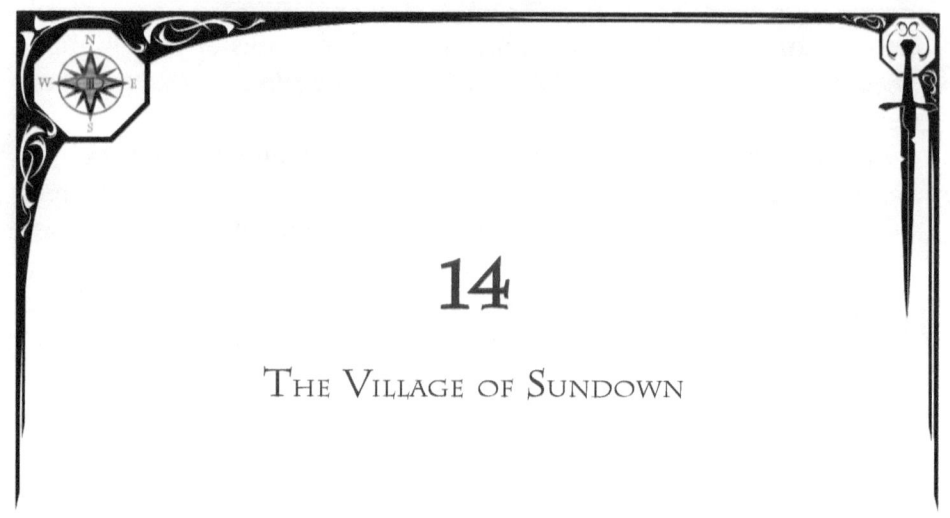

14

The Village of Sundown

HE could feel the power, feel the pain. The bindings on his gift strained, but held fast. It wasn't enough. Still, it was encouraging, even elating.

There was such joy in death.

With his gift bound, he could only direct the power as he might wield one of the great spire trees as a club. Still, the old man hadn't given him much. That was fine. For now, that was fine. He still had much to learn, still had a great deal of skill to master. The man hadn't lasted long at all, so he needed learn how to prolong it. There was power in the blood, the death, the spilling of life out of a body. More, there was power, in fear, in terror, in pain. It was a waste to harvest just the one and not the others.

Yet as wonderful as that had been, there was one thing that had proven to be even more so.

The shadows had spoken to him. Approved of him. Believed in him.

He could hear them now, their chittered whispers, words he now understood, sounding in his mind. He felt their greed, their lust, their sheer excitement over the death throes of the sacrifice, their anticipation of more to come.

And come it would.

With a fierce grin, he turned away from the mess on the bed to look down at himself. The sight of the gore covering his front had a harsh laugh clawing up his throat. He stifled it, promising himself a moment to revel in success later, when there was no chance of his jubilations waking his prey.

The Shadowed Ones, his own Shadowed Ones, swirled around his legs like eager puppies. Stepping outside into the night with them, he considered the nearest hovel and wondered in a sly whisper if it might be possible to keep them from running, to trap them in their homes until he got to them. He wanted – needed – the time to savor, to perfect.

You have only to call. You have only to command.

The words slithered into his brain, a predatory smile springing to his lips. Raising his bloodied arms, he gave the call. He gave the command.

He passed the rest of the night with pleasurable work.

15

The College of Mager,
The Red Tower of The Trinity

MASTER Oknare sat wearily at his desk, going over letters from patrons and parents who wished him to enroll their prospective students. With Ba'tvian Delthanurk no longer attending the school, he found himself with too much time on his hands. Too much time, he thought as he turned his gaze to stare blindly out his window at the sea, to wonder.

Where had he gone wrong? He kept circling back to that point. What had he done, or hadn't done, that had turned such a promising mage into the sullen, hateful potential for monstrosity he had been forced to exile? He had gone over everything in his mind, his notes, his reports, yet could see nothing that would give him answers.

Hamal had told him that the fault was not his. That opinion had been seconded by many of the senior staff at the college. How did they know? How could they know?

Dwelling on the questions wasn't getting the letters read or his decision made. He could only take one student. Perhaps, a few of the other masters could take more in the fall. At the moment, however, he was the only one in need of someone to teach.

It was a need. He needed another student, another pupil, to distract him from his failure – to prove that he could still guide a young mage properly. He wanted the reassurance. At his age, a man who was approaching his sixth decade, he needed reassurance. He gave a rueful chuckle at himself, rubbing at his eyes with one hand.

He looked over at a rap on his door. Before he could call out, it opened to admit his friend. The face Hamal wore was set and grim.

"It's rather late, Hamal." Oknare rose from his chair as the High Judge came forward. "What's wrong?"

"Would you recognize Ba'tvian's work?" he asked flatly. The mage felt all of the blood drain from his face.

"I – " He broke off, taking a deep breath to steel himself before meeting Hamal's eyes. "I believe I would, if he was somehow capable of it. What has happened?"

"The ship *King's Folly* was found drifting at sea, not too far from Port Menie. The crew's dead."

He could see the implications clearly in the judge's hard eyes. Dread balled heavily in his gut.

"Ba'tvian?"

"I do not know. All that I do know is that descriptions I've been given of the deaths are...unnatural, to say the least."

"What do you need me to do?" Oknare asked quietly.

"Gate us to Menie. We'll go from there."

Two hours later they stood on the deck of the *Folly* surveying the wreckage. The deck looked like the inside of a charnel house. Rusty crimson stained the wood and the reek of it was sickening. Even after several days in the open air, it still smelled. The bodies had been removed before their arrival, but one had only to look at the splotch pattern in the rust colored stains to see where they had lain.

Oknare, ignoring the nausea creeping over him, frowned as he studied the scene with experienced eyes.

"There's no sign of blood magery, nor are there sign of an attempt at it. Even attempts, unsuccessful or otherwise, leave some kind of indications if you know what to look for." He kept his manner brisk, the tone of his voice professional, though he knew that his pallor was gray. "Do we know what the bodies looked like?"

Hamal shook his head.

"They buried them at sea at the first given opportunity. The port authorities sent the mage-message after it was done. I was told that they had been exposed for several days. There's more of this below deck," he added, gesturing at the dried blood. "They said it was like the whole crew had gone mad. Some seemed to have been killed by other crewmen. Knife wounds were in evidence. Several had daggers buried in them. The rest..." He shook his head. "They couldn't say."

"And there is no sign of Ba'tvian."

"No. The lifeboats have all been accounted for and there is nothing in the captain's log to indicate an extra stop."

The mage tried to think of the ship's original itinerary. He had viewed it when they had selected the *Folly* to take Ba'tvian back to the mainland.

"They should have come straight here," he murmured. "How long would that have taken? When were they expected in port?"

Hamal went to speak with the dock master, who had refused to come aboard with them. While he waited, Oknare climbed up to the helm to see that there were similar stains there. Splatters on the ship's wheel, smears on the deck moving away from the wheel mount. He felt his blood run cold at the sight of bloodied hand prints on the grips. The victim had fought to keep from being drug backwards. It was a fight that he had lost.

What had dragged him away?

He turned as Hamal came up behind him.

"They were slated to arrive about a week ago. They sent a message via carrier pigeon stating they were running behind several days before they were due in port. They gave no reason for it, though they did give a time frame for their arrival. They should have arrived today – " He interrupted himself as he glanced at the still dark eastern horizon. "Well, yesterday."

"They made another stop," Oknare muttered. "He and his crew weren't happy to transport Ba'tvian. What are the odds that they dropped him off in the middle of nowhere, on some desolate coast? Or just dumped him in the ocean?"

"If this is his doing, whatever they did with him wasn't enough."

"It's not." The mage turned away from the wheel. "At least, not directly. I don't know what this is, Hamal. If he did it, then he's somehow broken the bindings we placed on his mage ability. The problem with that theory is that I should have felt the backlash from it. I would have known."

They made their way back to the pier, each silently speculating. Hamal spoke with the dock master again. Oknare listened with only half an ear, as his gaze tracked back to the *Folly*.

They would tow and scuttle ship. Superstition was as rampant on the high seas as fish, he supposed. No one would be willing to sail the *King's Folly* again. Now they would have to send word out. Had to, because he could be wrong. There were ways of breaking bindings without the mage who had set them knowing of it. On the mainland, there were people whose only job was the hunting of blood mages, their pets, the undead, and what daemons found their way into their world. Mancers, they were called. They would be alerted in the morning.

The Mancers would kill him. As heavily as the knowledge weighed on Oknare's shoulders, he couldn't help wondering if that wasn't for the best after all.

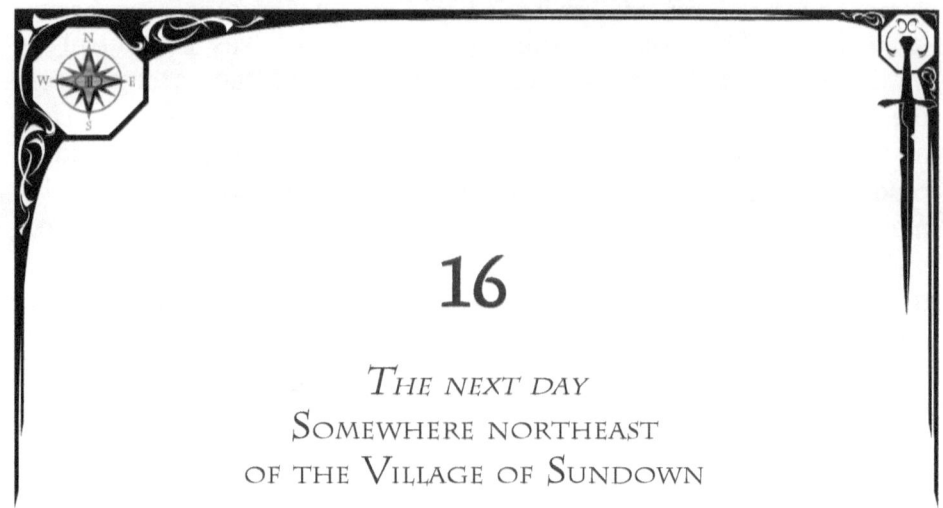

16

HE'D taken the time for a real bath, had slept most of the morning away in a real bed. Bathing meticulously after a night of gruesome, if enjoyable, work had been wondrous. Sleeping comfortably for the first time since the earthquake had been a gift from the gods. Neither had been particularly luxurious though they had felt like it.

There'd been a cow behind the house he'd slept in. Meat, he'd thought when he'd laid eyes on it. Fresh red meat, nothing scrounged or vegetative. He'd salivated heavily even as he'd butchered the bovine, carving it up into . He wouldn't be finding meat on the journey ahead; he'd every intention of taking as much as he could with him. He had cooked cutlets, raided the stores of salted fish, gathered every crumb of cheese and bread he could find. All of it went into a burlap sack he'd come across in the kitchen. By the time he'd finished, it had almost burst at the seams. He also procured a donkey from a dead man's pen, found it's saddle and bridle in the man's shed.

So the afternoon's journey had begun with Ba'tvian in high spirits.

His Shadows cavorted around him. The donkey he rode was stubborn and steady. It feared his Shadowed Ones yet was it was more or less obedient to his will. Wild-eyed, it carried him along the rocky coast.

Even having spent the morning in sleep or at work, he was making good time. He'd woken with a vague sense of needing to get home, which had puzzled him. As he'd fed himself, then procured his future meals, it had dawned on him as to why he should to go home, back to the filth, the drudgery that made up his family and their lives.

The one thing in the world he valued above all else.

There had been power during the night, released with the blood that he'd spilled, the pain he'd caused. It had been enough to test the bindings on his gifts though not enough to break them. Now, as the jenny he rode picked its way over a sandy ridge along the shore, he thought again of the reasoning he's come up with.

The greater the gain, the greater, more personal, the sacrifice needed. If he wanted to regain his powers, even to a small degree, he had to kill his so-called family in a blood rite – a full one, if he could manage it. The fact that he'd be using his own blood-kin, and whatever emotional ties there were, should magnify the power loosed. At least, he seemed to recall some text or other he'd read saying that. It had him digging deep into memories that he'd spent years trying to forget.

He recalled the layout of the fields, the hovel his father had built for his family, the proximity of other serfs and even the manor of the master. Some things he would have to ascertain anew. He was no longer sure of the number of people in the area, for instance, or what the rotation was for the fields around his childhood home. A fallow field would do well for a rite. He would have to find one that wasn't too close to the roads leading to the city.

The donkey suddenly skittered to one side, bucking. Clutching at the saddle one-handed, he clung to its back, yanking hard on the reins. It stumbled off the ridge, almost dislodging him, before galloping along the shore.

Water splashed up to soak his trousers as the mule ran into the surf. The shadows ran alongside it, then surged forward to form a kind of barrier in its direct path. Again, Ba'tvian jerked on the reins, this time taking up slack to pull straight back. The equine tossed its head, bucked again. It dug its hooves into the beach when it finally saw the Shadowed Ones ahead.

Braying manically, it backed up. Ba'tvian wrenched the reins to the left, spinning the miserable beast in circles until it stopped. It trembled where it stood as he scowled at it, then the ridge.

"What set the asinine thing off?" he muttered aloud, scanning the direction they'd come from. He didn't see anything. He hadn't really expected to.

A snake.

The sibilant voice slid into his mind smoothly. He turned to study the shadow that had slithered up to him, saw the white eyes glitter with intelligence. The jenny took one side-step into water, turning its head away, the whites of its eyes flashing.

It will not run now.

"Yes, I can see that." He considered the creature for a minute, adjusting his thinking. They'd been helpful, informative, the night before... "I don't suppose you would be able to tell me how much longer it will be until we arrive at Menie?"

Tomorrow. It blinked its leprous eyes. *If you travel into the night.*

He nodded slowly, mulled it over. The beast would suffer for it, but then why should he care if the wretched thing was ridden to foundering? It wouldn't be of any use to him once he reached the port city. A sly smile touched his lips. He would ride it to the ground, then take the time for a rite. The shadows would like the treat, and he could always use the practice.

"Good," he said. "Let's go."

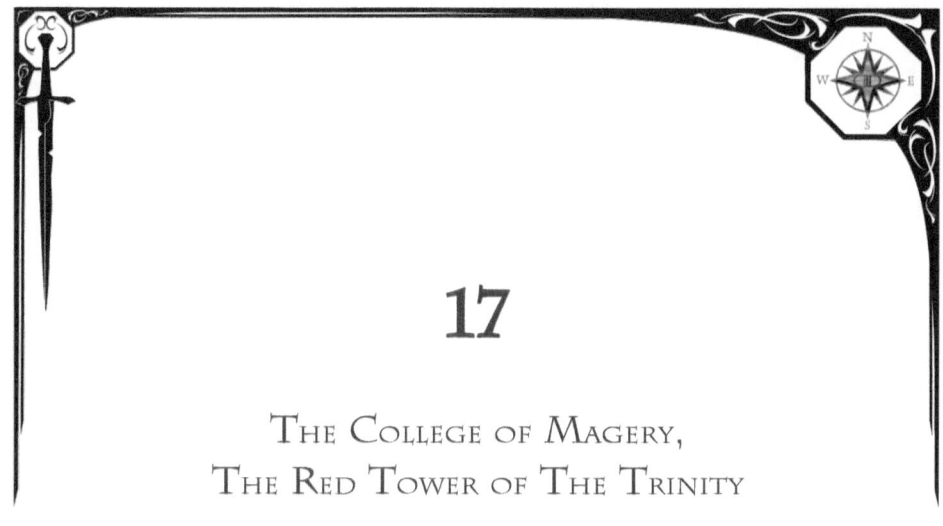

17

The College of Magery,
The Red Tower of The Trinity

"NERISSE se li Astorae."

Oknare was pleased as he studied the report on the girl's background. She was of the Elvanaer, an elven race that dwelled in the underground caverns of the Halsk Mountains in northern Orthanor. A mage and an empath, he noted, with what her people called the 'earth-sense.' She'd be sensitive to the state of the earth she stood on, attuned to its needs or moods, if he trusted their description of the ability. The land was her connection to life and death, which was why they'd already marked her for the priest sect.

The mage talent was the reason for Nerisse's attendance here. A very talented young woman, they had already taught her all they could. Having no mage higher than Master rank, they'd had little choice in sending her to an adept.

"I'll enjoy teaching her." He glanced up at Hamal as the High Judge contemplated the view through the window in his office. "You can't expect any news this quickly, my friend."

"I know it." He turned from the window with an impatient gesture. "The Trinity Council is considering revising the laws concerning blood magery, did I tell you?"

"No, you hadn't." Oknare set the prospect of a new student aside. He clasped his hands in front of him looselytrying not to think of why the laws were being revised. "They're amending the age limitation for executions?"

"That, and the procedure for deporting exiles. We've no jails here, no room for them, which is why we send our exiles to the mainland. There's talk now of sending them to Exile's Peril."

"Ah."

Oknare grimaced at the thought of the Peril. It was an island the size of a country, southwest of Orthanor. The landscape was inhospitable for most things, possessing a vast inland desert at its center. There were only two colonies on the Peril: an autonomous fishing village on the eastern side and a large penal colony on the western side.

The city-states of the mainland were in the habit of sending their criminals there. He couldn't remember what the arrangement was, exactly, though he knew that the colony had to import goods regularly. The place couldn't support itself on its own. It seemed sensible for goods to be sent in lieu of payment in taking other states' criminals.

"How would we get them there? Or is the previous practice of using whatever ship is available not going to change?" he asked.

"It'll change." Hamal went to the cupboard where he kept the jug of ale and mugs. He hefted the jug, held it out to him with a cocked eyebrow. Oknare nodded absently, waiting until the ale was poured.

"They haven't worked it out yet, have they?"

"No. It will probably be some time until they do." The judge sipped his drink as he stowed the jug away again, then brought Oknare his tankard. "We don't have a need for a ship standing by. It is my guess that they'll contract a prison vessel from the Peril to come by once a month. We can house an exile for that long."

"Yes, we could." He leaned back in his chair, cradling his drink in his hands. "What else is bothering you?"

Giving a half-laugh, Hamal dropped into the visitor's chair opposite his friend.

"That apparent, is it?" He shook his head. "The *King's Folly* bothers me, Oknare. I can't get it out of my head. It makes me think of where they'd been, what they'd done."

"We've no way of knowing for sure. We sent out messages to all the ports and mariners we know of to see if they'd been sighted during the allotted timeframe. Still, it is – what do the archers call it? – a long shot."

They drank in silence a moment.

"Not knowing what happened to Ba'tvian weighs on you," Hamal stated quietly.

"Some." He took a deep breath.. "I don't want to believe him capable of that level of atrocity. Part of me already does, and that makes me ill inside. He was mine, Hamal."

"It wasn't your fault."

"No, not my fault, still…he was my student. Yes, I know we've been down this road before." He did his best to shake the feeling. "It's done. He is no longer mine. This one is." He rested a hand on Nerisse's papers. "I'll do better by her."

"I know you will." The judge smiled, then glanced at the water-clock sitting on a shelf. "It's almost time for my next hearing in court. I'll just finish this particularly fine ale and be off."

"Take it with you, my friend." Oknare gave Hamal warm smile. "We both know you'll be back to return it."

18

B A'TVIAN wondered if his memories of the city were faulty. In his mind, the streets closest to the wharves were filthy, the allies liberally decorated with wasting humanity, the dock workers rough and mean. Farther inland, the city didn't get much better, at least, not at night. There may not have been quite as much in the way of wasted souls or malice, yet those elements slunk out of their holes once the sun went down. During the day, they weren't seen unless some fool stumbled into a dark corner.

Menie had changed. The streets weren't littered over with trash, the dregs of society weren't in evidence. The dock workers were still gruff, though they seemed more cautious with it now. More restrained. As Ba'tvian walked warily the byway that ran along the piers, he kept the hood up on his cloak. Around him, his Shadowed Ones flitted through the dark corners, blending in as best they could with the street and people. He couldn't say that they were truly hidden; he saw them just fine. Yet while he had no trouble picking each of them out, no one else took notice of them.

He filed that observation away to think about later, then stepped off the byway to head up the main road leading through the city. It would lead out all the way to the estates outside, he remembered. Following it, he wouldn't get lost. Still, he didn't let down his guard as he traversed the invisible border between the harbor and the merchants' sections.

I am in enemy territory.

He kept the thought firmly in mind as he scanned the area, seeing with satisfaction that his shadows had taken up vanguard positions. They knew it, too. The road may have been cleaner, the people appearing to be more kindly, the shops looking a bit more prosperous than his memory gave testament to, but this was the city they had sent him back to. This was the city that might have executed him.

He could see the main square up ahead. At its center stood a wooden platform. Speeches were made there when criminals weren't being hung there. As a young child, he had sometimes come with his mother on those rare occasions she had gone to the market for something. It had been years ago, in a time when life hadn't been so harsh or hard for the family, when the stipend they'd received from their lord would cover a treat or two every few months. They would come here, listen to the orators. He remembered being disappointed that no one had been hung or punished whenever they'd come.

He'd been foolish boy, Ba'tvian decided with a spiteful glare for the gallows. Now he hated things such as this. Death wasn't an entertainment – it was power. They wasted power here, let it slip through their fumbling fingers without realizing what it was. Their ignorance was criminal, their arrogance unforgivable. Structures like this, he vowed, would fall into disuse. He wouldn't have them in the world he would make his own.

What offends you, lord?

The whispered question hissed in his mind. He said nothing, merely gave a slight nod at the platform. He could see himself there, in his mind's eye. He could see what they would have done to him, with him, how his body would have jerked and danced in the air as the noose tightened. Once his struggles had stilled, they would have dragged him down, hung him from the old yardarm erected at the edge of the harbor to serve as dire warning for those who would break the law here. He could see it so clearly...

He was meant for greater things.

Take it down. The order snarled in his mind. He could feel the fury beating under it, prying and pushing in his mind. *Splinter it into dust.*

The shadows flowed away from him. He forced himself to leave, to watch them work. He kept his pace steady as he stalked through the square, vibrating with the image of his own execution. They would have made him food for the birds. Garbage. An example of inferiority. The bastards would pay. They would pay, and pay dearly...

He realized dimly that he was breathing heavily, that his rage was a muted roar in his ears. That – that wouldn't do. He had to be calm. He had to be in control. He wouldn't succeed in anything if he wasn't in control.

Behind him, he heard startled shouts. He turned automatically, like many others on the street, to stare at the crowded square. The gallows shook, shuddered. There was a resounding crack, like the sharp breaking of bone, then it collapsed.

It wasn't enough. He wanted it to burn. Needed to see it as ash. The desire rose in him, a rush of strength. Pain lanced through his head, racing down his spine. He stood, frozen, staring, as his mind lashed out in response. He felt something give inside him, just a little. Just enough.

It felt like a spike driving into his brain.

He couldn't make himself move. Couldn't even raise his hands to clutch his head. He wanted to. Oh, he wanted to. It hurt, it burned – *it wouldn't stop.*

Stop...

It had to stop. He would make it stop. He had to. No one else would do it for him. They didn't care if he suffered. No, he thought as his mind ruptured inside, no, they'd have enjoyed it. They'd laugh as he struggled for air, they'd snicker, or grin as he collapsed on the street. They'd kick at him, whip him, piss on him....

Rage and pain peaked. The breaking wood in the square exploded with flame.

He was so shocked that he forgot the hurt, the fury. He gaped at the scene. Sooty smoke boiled up from flames the color of blood. He closed his dry mouth, swallowing the faint elation that welled up inside him. It was gone. It was gone, it was burning. It had been him, not the shadows, that had done it.

Abruptly, he turned away, stumbling through the crowd, his mind whirling with aching fatigue. He needed to think – to assess, to plan. He needed to see if he could do it again.

Behind him, his Shadowed Ones drifted over the cobblestones, unseen and unheard. He felt their presence as he ducked down a side alley, seeking a quiet, dark corner. He could sense their thoughts.

He was indeed meant for greater things.

Interlude 4

The Port City of Menie

LABIYAL watched it all from his rooms on the corner of the square. The surge of raw, uncontrolled power had been a pleasant surprise. His blood still thrummed from the heat of it, and the sharp edge of awareness had yet to fade from his mind. Oh, they had been quick, the shadows, working to mask the signature of their leader as best they could. They hadn't been quite quick enough to block him from recognizing it.

Labiyal continued to stare at the window until the sullen red flames had reduced the wooden structure to embers. A slight, cold smile touched his lips. The boy was powerful, just as his former mentor had expected. He'd grown even more so in the past weeks, with rage, resentment, and blood enhancing the potency.

The bindings still held, however. Thoughtfully, he turned away from the square to glance at the mirror set up on the table. The glass was dark; it was likely to remain so. Ba'tvian was beginning to realize his potential, or would do so soon; he couldn't risk either him or his shadows detecting a scrying.

The Shadowed Ones...

He couldn't recall ever hearing of them going out of their way to protect whoever had command of them – not without orders. Again, he thought of the Helkorex Noxim, the prophetic sayings held therein, and wondered what the full extent of Ba'tvian's potential might be. There was so much the boy didn't know, he thought. So much that not even his own father, the Daemon Lord Biyal, or his master, the King of Hell, knew.

Labiyal did. That knowledge was another form of power.

"Blood will out," he murmured as he fingered the base of the mirror's frame absently.

If that was case, then this boy was the one, which meant his blood -connections had to be kept secret. There was more than just success at stake. Labiyal's very existence could be comprised.

He'd known seventeen years ago that this would be one of the greatest gambles of his life. Now everything rested on the shoulders of a boy barely old enough to call himself man. The boy would either die, with Labiyal's life hanging precariously in the wind, or become the mage his lineage demanded him to be.

He would wait, and he would see which he would take.

19

THE COLLEGE OF MAGERY
THE RED TOWER OF THE TRINITY

OKNARE had done it. He felt good about his decision. The girl had such promise, he thought, leaning on the railing of the terrace that provided a gorgeous view of the sea and the other two towers. It was wonderful to have something positive to look forward to. She was on her way there, due to arrive in about a month.

He wished briefly that he could share his good news with his friend. Hamal was in court and would be for most of the day. Well, he could wait. They'd get together for dinner that evening to discuss it. There was so much to do in preparation, as her family had requested that Nerisse be housed outside the college dorms. She needed space, they'd stated in the mage-sendings that had been going between them for the last several days. She was quiet, shy, sheltered.

He was inclined to give in to the request, but wanted to keep the girl close. He intended to keep a better eye on her, her interests, her activities. With that in mind, he made a mental note to speak with his own land lord. There was a vacancy in one of the suites. Though his building was generally reserved for teachers at the college, he was determined to explore the possibility of housing her there. She would be less likely to stray down the darker paths when surrounded by so many authority figures.

"Excuse me, Master Oknare."

He turned to see the white robed figure trimmed in black, recognized him as one of the leaders of the school. His expression was grave, his eyes tired.

"I'm afraid I must speak with you in regards to the Delthanurk matter."

"I see." He felt the pleasure of anticipation slip away, the weight of guilt sliding in to replace it. He glanced around, saw that they were the only ones on the garden terrace. "Here or elsewhere, College Master?"

"There's no one about so here will be fine. I will keep this brief." He stepped up to the rock-hewn railing beside Oknare to frown at the water below. "It was stated during the trial and in your reports on the matter that Ba'tvian Delthanurk was researching material in the library that is normally prohibited to students."

"Yes."

"Do you know what text, exactly?"

"I'm not entirely certain." He thought back to the time in question, tried to recall what the archivists had told him before he had confronted Ba'tvian on it. "I'd been told by the librarians that he had been using several of the black books, jotting down notes and the like. I confiscated the notes, then burned them. Most of them seemed to be about drawing power from various unorthodox sources, spilt blood being one."

"I just received an inquiry from the port authorities in Menie."

Oknare's head came up. His eyes narrowed, his stomach clenched.

"Ba'tvian."

"We've no way of knowing. However, given what happened to the *King's Folly* and the fact that he's missing, they have some valid concerns," he said, idly tapping a finger on the railing. "The hanging gallows in the main square has been destroyed. The wooden boards pulled apart as if by several men. Eye witness accounts state that several black forms slithered over the platform as it was broken. Then the wood suddenly combusted. The fire was described as being the color of old blood."

"His gifts are blocked." Still, Oknare could feel his face go pale.

"You and I both know that there are ways around that." The College Master sighed. "Though none of them are easy, or even likely. It is the black – well, shadows, I suppose – that I'm interested in. What are they?"

"I don't know." He struggled to set his dread aside. "The Mancers might, though."

"I've already sent off an inquiry. I am sure that the Menie authorities have done the same."

"Did you want me to see if I can narrow down the texts?"

"I do." He rubbed at his temple wearily. "I've been wracking my mind on this one, Oknare. We don't know what we're looking for, not really, and we thought that you might have a better idea."

"I might." He thought wistfully of his earlier good mood, then reluctantly of the change in his evening plans. "Well, then. Let me just clear my schedule so that I can to it."

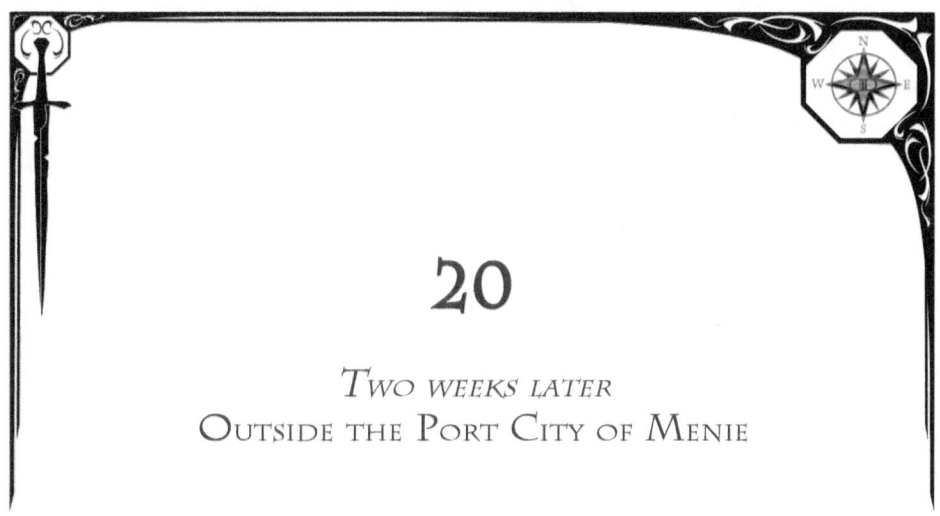

20

Two weeks later
Outside the Port City of Menie

H E'D waited.
The shadows were a tad impatient with him but he'd been adamant about waiting. It gave him a chance to plan. To think, to recover.

The headache and fatigue had persisted for two days after he'd burned the platform in the square. It was in his mind a small price to pay for the success. He would learn to work through it, master it. He couldn't afford the risk they posed if he'd acted in those two days. Dulled senses, slowed reactions – they spelled death for him. An inferior death, leaving him as little more than the dust on the well-worn roads outside the city.

If he had acted on the third day, he would have missed a few crucial details. He wouldn't have seen his family's new lord in town, the reactions of the port authorities, the lengths they were going through to find the culprit – him – or the arrival of one his enemies. The Mancer, he thought, was not the trifled with or underestimated.

Ba'tvian trudged along the road, mulling over the rumors and gossip he'd gleaned from the marketers. There were plenty of embellishments in what he'd overheard, yet there were also grains of truth.

The Mancer's name was Absol Omine. He was one of the better known Mancers in the region, never staying too long in one place. He was in his late thirties, his age being a testament to his dedication, skill, and rate of success; Mancers lived dangerous lives. Few saw their fourth decade.

Omine had come to Menie, though not because of the incident in the square. He had come to learn more of what had happened to the *King's Folly*, to gather more information for his hunt. A hunt, Ba'tvian had been nearly shocked to learn, with him as its focus.

The grass rustled on the side of the road. His head snapped up and around. He stopped in mid-stride, holding his breath as he waited. A mouse scurried out from the growth to run across the beaten cobbles. It dove into the tufts of long grass on the opposite side. He let himself breathe again, checked his surroundings warily, then continued on under the dark moon in the night sky.

The *King's Folly*. The fate of the crew, the superstitious scuttling of the ship, the fearful speculations – it all amused him. He might have wished to put every one of them under the knife with his hand on the hilt, still…one took one's pleasures where one found them. No one knew the cause of the deaths. Neither did he. However…

He slid a look at the shadows nearest him, considering. He didn't let himself entertain the half-formed notion for more than a second or two. His Shadowed Ones were entitled to a bit of fun, weren't they? If, that is, he was correct.

What had happened to the crew of the *Folly* was what had instigated the bounty. A bounty, he thought again, on his head. Part of him took perverse glee in the news. It meant that they believed him worthy of one, worthy of the trouble to send for specialists to deal with him. It was a sign of their inferiority, was it not, that they had to call in someone else? He liked to think so.

Yet it wouldn't do to let the dubious satisfaction of the bounty cloud his thinking. There was more at stake than reputation or worthiness. It was his freedom, his life, his power – everything that they would strip from him.

Omine would be an adversary to be wary of.

"You know the Mancer," he murmured. His shadows turned their gimlet eyes to him at the sound of his soft voice. "Does he know you?"

All Mancers know us.

"You can watch him, observe him." He flicked a glance at the field to his right, absently noting the hovels in the distance. "How likely is it that he will spot you?"

He is sharp of mind, keen of eye. He will see.

"I need to know where he is at all times." He wouldn't be caught now, not before he was prepared for a confrontation. That, he reasoned, was inevitable. Still, these were his allies. They'd proven too useful to risk callously.

Another can track him.

His eyes narrowed. He gave his full attention to the shadow who had spoken.

"Who?"

Another. The leprous white orbs blinked at him dully. *He is like you.*

Interesting, he thought. Another blood mage? A lesser one?

Yes.

What a fascinating thing to learn.

"How reliable is he?"

Enough. He will not betray. The Mancers are his enemy, as well.

"For what price?" Nothing came without one, just as no one or thing could be trusted in full. Ba'tvian weighed his options hurriedly, stepping off the road to wade through stalks of late summer corn. "For what currency?"

We can inquire.

"Do so. Now. If it is blood he wants, he'll get it."

The shadow peeled away as he moved out of the corn. There, in the far back with more corn behind it, was the isolated mud brick dwelling his family called home. The field closest to it held only sparse patches of grass, weeds, and wild clover. A fallow, or at least disused, field. He glanced back over his shoulder, estimated the distance from the road, considered the cover provided by the corn. It was best not to chance it.

Minutes later, he skirted the hovel, found a heavy beam of half-rotted wood leaning against the shed. The streaks of grime on it had him studying the place he'd once lived. A support? Part of the frame? Then he shook his head. It didn't matter. It served another purpose now, whatever its existence had been before this.

Gripping the wood, he hurried into the next cornfield and set to work.

INTERLUDE 5

THE PORT CITY OF MENIE

THE Mancer was indeed a problem.

The boy had gone to ground, further proof of his intelligence. As of yet, he had not made any moves to further his progress down the path that Labiyal had planned for him.

Someone would have to do something soon, though. Absol Omine was a man of determination and persistence. He would stay until either a more immediate hunt pulled him away or he caught his prey. As the man's prey was Ba'tvian Delthanurk, Labiyal had no intention of letting him remain in the area.

He must be led away...

A pawn must be sacrificed. He had plenty of pawns. Not many were of the suitable nature that would draw the attention of a Mancer. That would change with status, and status would come with success. More of it would come with unusual success, which was what he aimed for. The game was not the black and white of a *chesra* board; it was the shades of gray that were often disregarded by Daemon kind.

It was a Daemon he needed. A destructive one to be enraged. It was rare to find one of significant power on Einlienn. The few that managed to make their way there hid themselves too well. Perhaps his father had a rival in the area. It was possible, even probable. Biyal had not been secretive about his travels when checking on his spawnling's progress.

Labiyal took a moment to send a mage-message to his sire about the matter. If the older male was canny, as he usually was, he'd let hints of Labiyal's current project leak. It should be enough to tip the scales of reason, vindictiveness, or both in the desired direction.

It was the boy that mattered now.

At the far end of room, darkness flickered in the gloom. Labiyal sat absolutely still in his chair at the table, the mirror glinting with the muted light of the single candle lit by his hand. His blood stayed cool his mind stayed clear. He hadn't left this room since the Mancer's arrival, nor had anyone entered it.

Suspicion grew.

A Shadowed One slithered over the surface of the window sill. It slipped over the wood like oil on glass, its eyes glinting white, its semi-reptilian body like inky smoke. A detached part of his mind noted the broad, flat head, the lack of hind limbs in the form. Odd creatures. It was bewildering to think that they were related.

He had seen them before though never so close. He was not a Daemon Lord or Hell's Chosen Child. They would never follow him. Yet this one came to him now, drifting about the room before coiling in the center of the floor to staring at him. They studied each other for a long minute.

"Yes?" Labiyal kept his voice indifferent and level.

Our lord asks for a boon.

He raised an eyebrow. He had never heard of the Shadowed Ones speaking. Still, it was the implication in the statement that made him cautious. It would not do for the boy to be aware of too much so soon.

"Your lord knows of me?"

Yes.

"My name? My status?"

No. The careless, disinterested answer appeased him somewhat.

"What boon?"

Track the Mancer. What is the price?

"Ah." Interesting. He considered. There had to be a price, if only for the look of the thing. Leaning back in his seat, he let his muscles relax slightly. He could already see the potential in this arrangement. "He wishes a contract?"

The creature seemed to consider this before responding, *Yes.*

"One life per cycle of the moon, to be turned over before the moon is full. Alive. Allow me to draw this up properly."

Near constant contact with him. Oh, yes, he thought as he gathered paper, quill pen, and blood-ink from his kit, then sat at the table to write out the document. This definitely had potential.

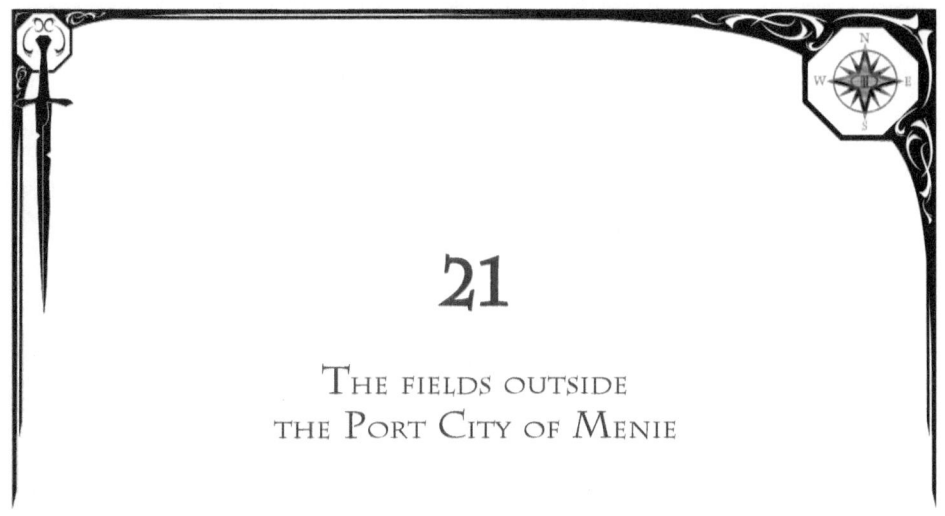

21

THE FIELDS OUTSIDE
THE PORT CITY OF MENIE

IT had been easier than he had anticipated. A life every twenty-eight days in return for information on the Mancer's activities. He could do that, handle it. As the protocol dictated in the contract demanded, he nicked his arm with the point of the blade he'd chosen to be his ritual knife, pressing his thumb first to the wound, then the parchment. The bloody print glowed crimson briefly. He rolled up the contract, tucking it within his jerkin for safekeeping. Turning, he studied his improvised work space.

The cornstalks were flattened in a rough circle, the ground covered with symbols he'd drawn in the blood of his family's goat. He'd found her, a breathing bag of bones and wiry muscle, asleep next to the house. The old nanny couldn't have been very useful. She'd been too old to produce milk, too old for her meat to be good for anything aside from stew.

Stew, he thought, wrinkling his nose. He hated goat meat, nor was he fond of the thin stew his mother prepared.

Well, neither was going to be a problem for him any longer. The goat didn't have to worry about it either.

Gesturing to his shadows, he led them back toward the house. They already knew what to do. They surged forward, a black wave that surrounded the hovel. They climbed up the walls. They slipped through the cracks. They squeezed in under the door. Ba'vian nudged the door, found it merely propped up. He opened it so that he had just enough space to pass through. He gazed around the single room, eyed the bodies crammed in among the ratty blankets on the floor.

He knew them. He'd grown up with them. Yet even now he couldn't quite remember their names. His brothers, his sisters, his parents – he didn't know them, not anymore. Just as they didn't know him. They never had.

He was so much more than they were.

The texts he'd read had stated that youth made for more vitality, more potential power. With his newly signed contract rubbing against the skin of his chest, he pointed to his youngest sister. The girl, perhaps ten or so summers old, was curled up in the far corner. Within moments, the shadows swarmed over her. The blanket that covered her was bundled more tightly around her as they began to drag her towards the entrance. She barely stirred through it.

They wouldn't kill her; she wasn't for them. Their treats were coming soon.

He signaled to the rest of escort. They slithered forward as he picked his way towards the wall where his parents slept. The Shadowed Ones crawled over everything, everyone. Tthose who had been startled into waking didn't move. They couldn't. He paused, watching the pair who'd raised him, then kicked the old man hard in the ribs. He woke with a cry, thrashing his limbs, glaring up with bleary eyes in the dark.

Ba'tvian grabbed his father's hair, yanked his head back. The man's mouth opened to shout. Quick as a snake, a lithe shadow darted up his torso to reach inside. It pulled hard on his tongue with claws like pincers. His eyes bulged. The old man began to gag, jerking his head. Ba'tvian tightened his grip, Ba'tvian drawing his knife to slice the tongue off. His grin was cruel as the blood pumped out, the muffled scream sounded.

"Hello, father," he said, making the title sound as if it were the most vile word in existence. "I've come home."

Lifting the old man up as if he weighed nothing, he half dragged him out into the cornfield to show just how much he'd learned.

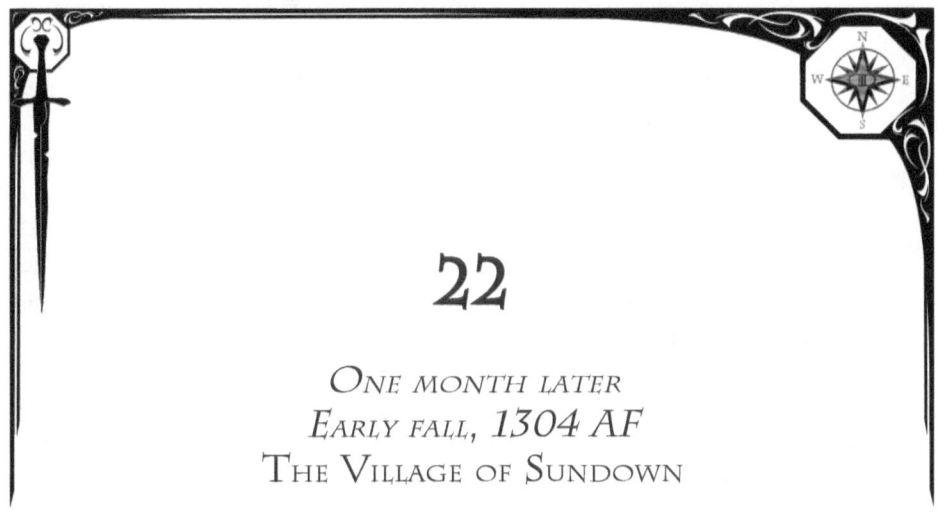

22

To the outside, the village seemed still. Empty. Standing among the shacks and tiny houses that made up the dwellings here, one got the impression of life interrupted. There were few tools left out or tasks left unfinished, unless one counted the beached boat with a hull in need of repair. There was water in the animal troughs, feed put out for the livestock. It was almost as if everyone had done their chores, then vanished.

The scent in the air told a different story.

Absol Omine had left his horse tethered on the beach. The animal tended to be skittish and he hadn't wanted to be distracted with having to deal with it inside the hamlet. It had been a good decision. The stench would have set the gelding off.

It smelled like a charnel house. After entering the first shack, after seeing what lay inside, he knew that it was worse than one. Intuition had told him that the rest of the villagers had met similar fates. Still he had to investigate each hovel. He wasn't certain that he had ever seen anything like the slaughter here. Not on this scale. A family, a small group of people – nothing over ten or eleven victims at a time.

The state of the bodies could tell him little as to how they died; there was simply too much damage done to the flesh. Decomposition was also far advanced at this point. The way they'd been laid out, though, conveyed enough. He'd seen a similar, fresher scene of carnage on the estates lying outside Menie several weeks before.

By the time he'd investigated the seventh dwelling, he needed a break from the carnage. More, he needed fresh air to breathe.

As he came out into the open, he felt the surge of static power that signaled the opening of a portal in the area. A dim sense of relief washed over him. He needed the company now. Adults were bad enough. Children...there was always something about seeing the death of a child that got to him. Add to that the eerie quiet of the place, the faint buzzing of the flies, and he had a very surreal scene. Gruesomely surreal.

He walked back to the beach, catching a whiff of the clean breeze sweeping off the ocean. It felt like heaven. When this was done, he determined, there'd be a bath in surf.

He saw two men standing next to his horse as he crested a low lying dune on his back to the beach – back to clean air. He'd been expecting them. He raised a hand in greeting; they reciprocated the gesture.

This would be the first time Absol had met them in person, though they had corresponded many times of the last two months. Master Oknare of the Trinity was one of the premier Adepts on staff at the College of Magery. The High Judge Hamal was purported to be even-handed, level-heade. Both were had a vested interest in the recent incidents that might involve a former student of the Trinity, which was why he'd sent for them.

"Master Oknare, Judge Hamal," he said as he drew near. "Thank you for coming. I'd offer you my hand, but you'd regret it, frankly. This is not pleasant." He waved a hand in the direction he'd come from. "Nor is it recent. You saw what had been left of the Deltanurk family?"

"Yes." Oknare looked pale now. Lines of weariness and sorrow were carved deep into his visage. "We arrived after you'd left already. That was Ba'tvian's work."

Absol had heard that conclusion from the Menie authorities.

"I had managed to track him north of the city, then lost him as he turned inland. I might have caught him as he'd done it," he speculated in a quiet voice. Oh, to be able to go back, to do it over. "A Daemon had surfaced to the west. Since I had no leads on Ba'tvian, I'd left to deal with it. Within hours after that, he killed his family. I'd just finished my hunt when I got the news."

"One evil or another. You couldn't be in both places at once," the judge reasoned. "What led you here?"

"I'd lost the track. I thought that he might have circled around. A blood mage that goes after his family like that usually has a vendetta in mind." He breathed deeply of the wind coming on-shore. He could still smell death in his nostrils, could almost taste it in the back of his throat. "Or a goal. A big goal, one that's almost always personal. Power, revenge, what have you. So I did plenty of asking. When I'd heard that you'd pinpointed him as the culprit, I got one of the bounty sketches the authorities had drawn up. Passed it around the market place, the square, the docks. Found two workers that thought they'd seen him come into the area from the south."

"That's mostly rock, isn't it?" Oknare frowned as he tried to remember to harbor. "There's a kind of rocky hill on that side of the inlet."

"Which is why these two remembered him." The rogue mage had been seen clearly against the sky atop that hill. It had been a lucky break for him. "So I started south. I had to detour away from it for a few weeks. I have a child in my care that I've left with friends so had to check back with them." Thinking of the little boy he'd found in the aftermath of Great Earthquake, he tried not to wince. He felt bad enough that he couldn't take him along as it was. "Once I got back to the area it didn't take me long to find this."

"You think it might be Ba'tvian." Hamal gazed at the buildings in the behind the Mancer with a kind of tired resignation. "Your mage-sending said that you wanted confirmation."

"I do. If this is his work, he's more of a threat than anyone may have realized."

"I didn't train him for this. I didn't train him to be this way." Oknare's voice was low, dismal. Absol could see the guilt eating away at him, had to stop himself from placing an encouraging hand on the man's shoulder. He could see the compassion on the judge's face. If compassion hadn't helped the adept with this burden by now, it likely never would.

"Blood mages are not taught, Oknare. Not in the way you mean." He waited until the mage's eyes met his. "Whether they are born with the inclination, or are driven to it in order to obtain a goal, they find these ways on their own. They make the choice to go that path, despite everything they are taught, how they were raised, or where they came from. That choice is wholly theirs. So is the fault."

He nodded, taking a deep breath.

"Do we need to see everything?"

Absol thought of the decaying horrors he'd witnessed. He shook his head. He gestured them to follow, leading the way to the nearest shack.

"I hope you've strong stomachs, gentlemen. This isn't for the faint of heart." The Mancer pushed the door open, then stepped aside so they could go in. He heard Oknare choke on the stench that rolled out. Hamal seemed to be made of sterner stuff.

They were inside for perhaps five minutes. The time seemed to be exponentially longer. When they came out, both were pale. Oknare looked green. Absol didn't press for a verdict. Instead, he took them back to the beach. Stripping off his gloves, he untied the canteen attached to his saddle and offered it. The mage sipped gingerly. Closing his eyes, did what looked to be breathing exercises. When his pallor improved, he opened eyes again.

"It was him." He took another swig of the water. "There's the same sense of other about the place, as if he was being aided by or attempting to summon something unnatural. It's not quite as strong as with the Delthanurk killings."

"Shadow daemons," the Mancer supplied. "The cursed children of Hell. They tend to follow Daemons of higher ranks. I've never heard of them following a human unless ordered to by a Daemon Lord."

"You think he's fallen in league with a Daemon?" Hamal glanced at Oknare who considered the possibility, then slowly shook his head.

"Ba'tvian wouldn't put himself in that situation without some kind of gain. He obeyed me – or seemed to –because he could learn from me."

"Whichever may be the case here, the fact that the shadow daemons are working with him can't be dismissed. I'll spread the word to the other Mancers about this. He's probably moved out of my area by now." He took the canteen back from the Adept for a drink. "Do you want to be informed of any news concerning this?"

"Yes." Hamal exchanged a look with his friend. "Both of us, and the Red Tower College Masters if it's not too much trouble."

"It shouldn't be."

"Is there anything else we can do?" Oknare queried.

"How much time do you have?"

"A few hours." He gave a wan smile. "I'm expecting my new student to arrive later today."

"You can help by collecting driftwood." Absol nodded back to the village. "I'd rather this was burned to the ground than just left here."

"If only everything was so easily dealt with." Hamal shook his head, then the three men got to the task at hand.

23

THE DOCKING CAVERN,
THE RED TOWER OF THE TRINITY

OKNARE waited on the pier, trying to forget the unpleasantness of the earlier portion of the day. He'd washed away the grime, had meditated to purge the memory as best he could. The scent of it still lingered in his nostrils but was slowly being remedied by the salty air.

It didn't do to meet his new student with it blighting his mind.

Hamal's presence helped. They spoke lightly of everyday things as they waited, even agreed to play a game of *chesra* later that evening. Then the ship they'd been waiting for glided up to the dock, the wooden ramp sliding out into place.

He couldn't help smiling at the shy figure that appeared at the top. She was charming, he mused, dressed in a simple gown that reflected her eventual calling as priestess. She hesitated there, scanning the people on the pier. He could tell when she'd spotted him by the way she seemed to relax. She came down the ramp as he paced forward to meet her at its foot.

"Hello, Nerisse." He took her hand gently in his, gave it an encouraging squeeze. "Welcome to the Trinity. This is my good friend, the High Judge Hamal. Shall we step aside and wait for your baggage?"

He guided her to the side of the pier, thinking how wonderful and clean the future – this student – was looking to be.

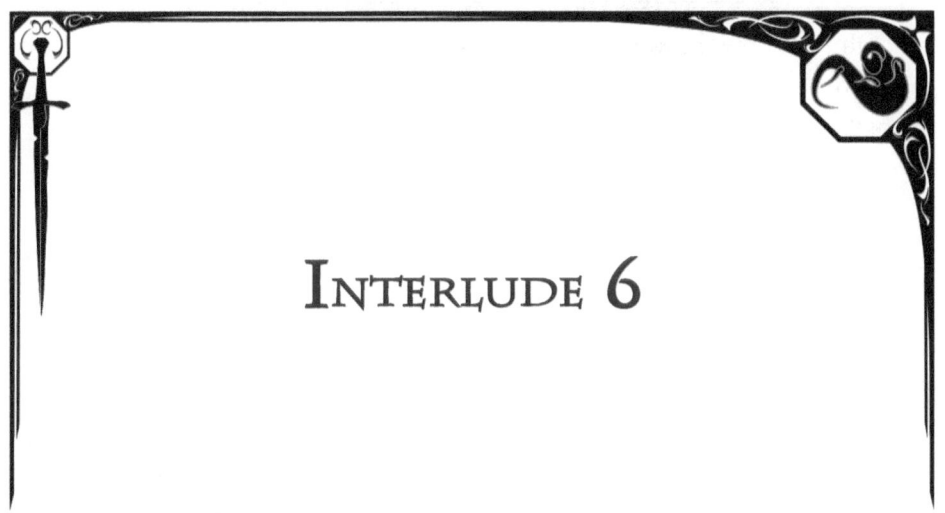

Interlude 6

LABIYAL stood amidst the crowds off the piers, waiting. He could see Master Oknare and the High Judge Hamal from his niche between stalls selling refreshments for anyone who desired them. He had bought a mug full of ale, more to appease the vendors than out of a desire for drink. It had been worth the small expense. This spot was isolated enough that he wouldn't be jostled, with a good view of the docks.

Ba'tvian had disappeared. He had vanished a month before, reappearing only to make the delivery of that the second contracted sacrifice. For the moment, Labiyal was content to let him be. The boy used his intelligence. Because he thought, because he planned, he would survive.

Yet while Labiyal was content to let the boy do as he would for the moment, he was by no means finished with this little project. There was too much potential to exploit.

He watched as the next player in this little drama sailed in on her ship. The elven chit would serve him well. He sipped the tepid ale absently as the vessel docked. It wasn't an entirely awful brew, he decided. He'd tolerated worse libations.

The off-loading ramp was lowered to the pier, the girl coming down towards the waiting Oknare. She was of the Elvanarae, with the slate blue skin and white hair of her race. Pretty, he mused, dressed in a modest wrap-style gown of white. She was young. She was malleable.

Oh, yes, he thought with the slightest of smiles. She would do nicely.

DESCENT INTO DARKNESS

PART 2

HER LORD

24

B A'TVIAN Delthanurk dragged the last of his bound captives into the back room of the basement he'd taken over for tonight's work. A torch mounted on the wall illuminated his harvest. The prisoner wasn't much of a sacrifice, as most of them weren't. They were street people, vagrants, malnourished, too old or too young, and half of them had some illness or other. Killing them could be seen as a small mercy.

He wasn't interested in mercy. Tonight was the full-moon. There was payment to be made.

A flicker of darkness at the light's edge caught his attention. He turned away from the twelve people he'd collected to watch one of his Shadows slither across the floor to his side.

He comes. The soft words slid into his mind. Its dull white eyes gleamed as it swung its lizard-like head to point in the direction of the basement doors that let out into the alley above. *We watch.*

"Good." He waited, ignoring the muffled groans and whines of his 'currency' in the heap behind him. That's what they were, he thought. The currency with which he paid for information, as per the agreement he'd made months ago.

A moment later, he heard the rusty hinges of the doors creak. He strode forward to meet his guest, a pale man with golden eyes and hair the color of fresh blood. He was well-dressed in non-descript garments that were nevertheless finely made. A mage of means, with enough connections to be able to operate without much interference, he provided Ba'tvian with information in exchange for victims. Neither had given their names when they'd struck their agreement. Ba'tvian called him Red; Red called him Shadow Master.

The younger mage considered the title both an acknowledgement of his alliance with the creatures that now circled the room as well as a mockery of Ba'tvian's ambition.

They exchanged nods of greeting, then went to the back where the captives were being held. Red raised an eyebrow as he surveyed them.

"I don't believe I require more than one as payment," he said mildly.

"Choose one then." Ba'tvian stood, impassive, as Red studied each prisoner. In the end, he chose a scruffy child who looked to be the healthiest of the lot. With little effort, the child was hauled up and set apart from the rest.

"The Mancer Absol Omine is headed to Glasten, Shadow Master." Red paused to see what his companion's reaction was. When one wasn't forthcoming, he continued. "He travels alone, on horseback. He is perhaps two days behind you, but could arrive earlier than that if he's determined enough. At present, he is the only Mancer near enough to be of any concern."

"What other news have you?"

Red gave a negligent shrug.

"The Port City of Menie has doubled the bounty on your head. The present lord there is very put out with you."

Ba'tvian nodded. One day, he might pay the lord a visit.

"There is a rumor that Absol is caring for – or at least paying for the care of – a child he found in the ruins of the Spirlan Forest. I have not yet confirmed if this is true. If it is, the child is likely at Destiny's Way, a place the Mancer seems to visit often. It is not a place I can obtain much information from." Red tilted his head. "Confirming the rumor will take extra time and effort."

Meaning, the younger man thought, a larger payment. He mulled it over, then shook his head.

"It can wait. I may ask for it at a later date, however."

Red nodded, then gave a short report on the current political atmosphere. There wasn't much of one. The cities were self-governing, the trade agreements solid, all active laws and policies more or less accepted from place to place. Orthanor was such a politically stable continent that the only unrest to surface was a dispute over a herd of cattle that had wandered between territories.

"Ah, yes. There was also a man over in Chalbrooke that had killed his family. At first, it was believed that you might have been responsible. They called in a local Mancer who determined that the murders were not committed by any blood mage, let alone you." Red smiled. "Your infamy has spread to the eastern coast. There isn't much else, Shadow Master. Unless you had something specific in mind?"

"No."

"Then I will trust you will take care of yourself."

Ba'tvian watched as Red picked up his prize. The older mage carried the urchin out of the basement without another word. Ba'tvian didn't move until he heard the basement doors slam shut. Then he kicked at the nearest captive, catching him in the ribs. As the old man wheezed into his gag, he took several deep breaths, seeking calm.

Infamy wasn't what he wanted. It only made moving about more difficult. Now with Absol nipping at his heels, he had little time to do what he'd come to Glasten to do. He would succeed. He had to. Turning to his Shadows, he gestured them closer.

"Watch the wharves. We need a ship. You know what to look for."

As they slithered away, he went to his pack for his knives. It was time to get to work.

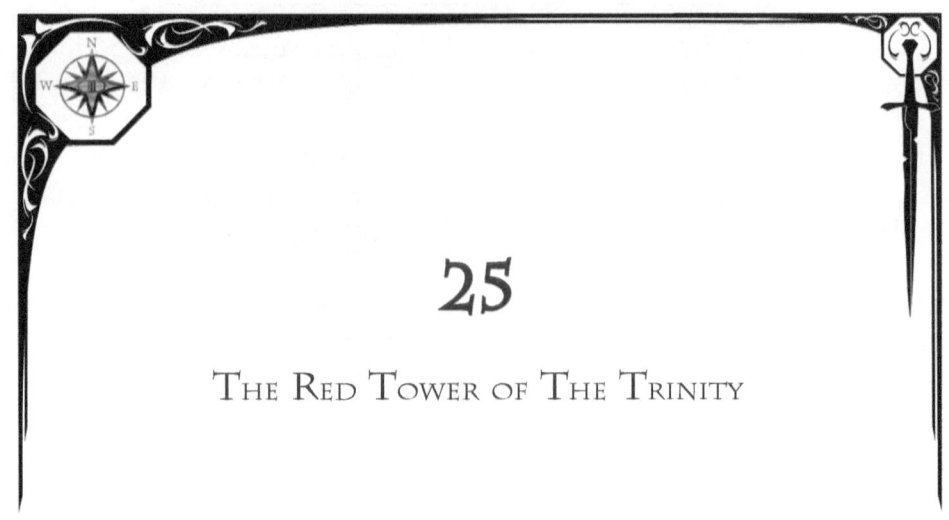

25

The Red Tower of The Trinity

NERISSE se li Astorae ran down the steps to the corridor, then out the heavy doors that opened to the street in front of the College of Magery. Her white hair flashed in the sun, showing starkly against her slate blue skin as she moved. The skirt of her bleached woolen frock whipped about her legs, her booted feet slapped on the chilled pavement. She dodged passersby on the street, murmuring apologies as she cut around them, through them. She couldn't afford to slow her pace; she was already late.

Dashing through the city that perched atop the natural column of stone that was the Red Tower, she wondered just who would be there. She still wasn't comfortable with the crowded conditions here. There were so many people all piled on top of each other…she was still trying to get used to it. Back home, she hadn't had to deal with this overwhelming populace; so few were there that she had been familiar with their faces, their names, their families. Here, that was impossible. Even among the student body, the number was too great to recognize them all. In truth, the sheer amount of people there was intimidating. Still, curiosity sometimes pushed her past the threshold of her natural bashfulness. She had made a few friends.

Today marked the end of her first six months at the Trinity, and the anniversary of the day of her birth. A few of her classmates were meeting her at the Dragon's Head Tavern for a small celebration. She wasn't the only one to have reason to commemorate the day, as one of them had just passed the first trials that were a prelude to becoming a Master Mage.

She was intrigued by his recent experience. Her own trials had been different from those held at the Trinity. Part of that difference was cultural, part of it was the nature of her magic. Her magery was specialized, with a primary focus on the magic of the mind and a secondary focus on that of earth. Kyle's magery was more generalized, not leaning toward any one type of magic. Perhaps he would be open to discussing the particulars...

Turning the corner sharply, she saw the carved wooden dragon's head that was the trademark of the tavern. The sight sent her stomach jumping with nerves. She forced herself to stop, taking a few bracing breathes. Self-conscious now, she smoothed her hair. Her nerves weren't soothed. Ah, well...she couldn't keep everyone waiting on her much longer.

Opening the door, she stepped inside.

INTERLUDE 7

HE had many names and faces. Today, he was Master Thursden of Gunvar. A tastefully dressed, well-moneyed man of low-birth with a reputation for philanthropy, he played the role to the fullest. He was eccentric by some standards, irresponsible by others, yet none could say was not generous. That generosity was the key to his presence here. One of the things this persona was reputed for was keeping track of the mages he'd invested in, funding the simple parties that were thrown after a successful hallmark in a mage's rites of passage.

Unlike Sir Kendell of Menie Port, Master Thursden didn't mind the antics of boisterous students in a mediocre pub.

So from his discreet seat in the far corner of the tavern, he watched with an amused air of detached interest as a group of students toasted one of their own. They were loud – they always were at these things. They were free with congratulations, sharing stories of other trials. Large quantities of ale, cheese, and bread were consumed as the conversation flew about the room. By the end of the night, there would be a mess for the barmaids to clean up.

He let his gaze drift toward the elven chit in white. Nerisse se li Astorae. Oknare's newest apprentice. She sat among them with a slightly anxious smile, trying to blend in with her peers. She failed utterly.

She was an oddity. An Elvanarae, one of the oldest races in the world, and slated for the priesthood, he had found it surprising that her people had allowed her to leave their northern caverns. Then he'd seen her, seen the mage-potential. He had understood. The Elvanarae did not often produce adept-level mages. It was extremely rare that they possessed more than one at any given time. Nerisse was the first in several centuries to have that kind of power. So they had sent her here to learn what she needed to before she became a priestess.

She blushed now, her blue cheeks flushing dark as the attention turned to her. As they began to sing a ditty off-key, he realized that it was her birthday. A slight smile touched his lips. Excellent.

He would wait, and see what happened next.

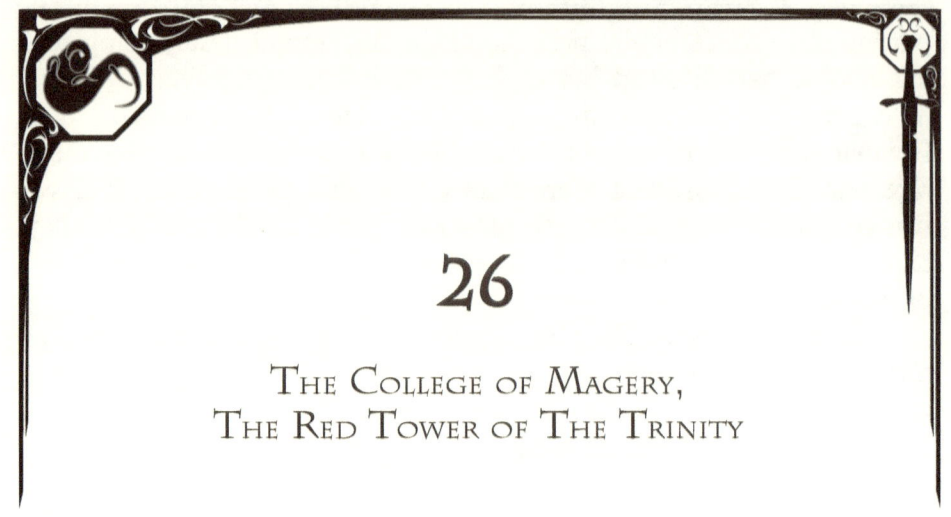

26

THE COLLEGE OF MAGERY, THE RED TOWER OF THE TRINITY

OKNARE tended a small potted plant on his desk with loving care. It had been a gift from his student not long after she had first arrived, an herb that could be brewed to make a relaxing tea. He snipped some of the leaves now, placing them in two mugs. He had a visitor coming. He also had a sinking feeling that he would not like the direction of the discussion to be had. Taking up the waiting kettle, he poured hot water over the leaves just as a knock sounded on the door. Kettle still in hand, he answered the door and waved the newcomer inside.

"Welcome to the Red Tower, Mancer Omine," he greeted, gesturing him to a chair before he rounded the desk to take his seat. "You indicated in your mage-sending that you had questions for me."

"I do, and it's just Absol, Master Oknare." The doffed his hood, running a gauntleted hand through his unkempt brown hair. "Do you want to go through the social niceties first or get to the meat of it?"

"You're a blunt one." Oknare smiled slightly. "I've tea steeping for us. Other than that, well, we might as well get on."

"What do you know of the Shadowed Ones?"

"Not a great deal. Ba'tvian Delthanurk is suspected of dealing with them. The few texts that mention them at all refer to them as the Cursed Ones and label them as Daemons as well as death-eaters." He grimaced as he said the last. Death-eaters consumed or absorb the spirit of the newly dead, overtaking them before they had properly moved on. He hadn't cared for the descriptions. It was common knowledge, however, that the Mancers dealt with such on a regularly basis.

"That's the gist of them, though not the whole. They're on the lowest ranking of Daemon society. They tend to be disregarded by higher Daemons. Not, however, by Daemon Lords. At least, not some of them. If they're smart, they'll pay attention to what they do, who they follow," Absol explained. "Generally, they'll align themselves with the strongest or the most promising Daemon Lord on the rise. Or they'll strike out on their own, giving allegiance to none. We, the Mancers, mostly encounter the latter."

"But...if they're following Ba'tvian..." Oknare's brow furrowed. "What would that mean, Absol? He's mortal, a human."

"That's what we're trying to figure out. He's not just suspected of leading a band of them anymore; it's been confirmed by another Mancer."

Oknare took a measured breath. He found that, surprisingly, he didn't feel shocked or guilty over the news. Resignation and disappointment laid heavy on him, yet the guilt that had plagued him months before was gone.

"Would your comrade speak with me, perchance? I'd like ask him specifics about the encounter."

"He died shortly after confirming the identity of his attackers." The quiet statement left Oknare staring at him.

"He – I'm sorry, Absol." Now the guilt came, a thin wash of it over his heart. "I didn't realize."

"It happens." The Mancer sighed, shaking his head. "There's no need to apologize for it. Ba'tvian Delthanurk is who is responsible. We just don't know what else he might be besides a blood mage on the run. Daemons don't follow humans unless enslaved. They turn on their masters in the blink of an eye. These...the Shadows were protective of him."

"This troubles me, my friend." Idly, he took up one of the mugs and a spoon to stir the leaves in the hot liquid. "Would you say that he has found a way around the blocks we've placed on his gifts?"

"I couldn't say for sure. Blood magery's tricky in that regard. It doesn't always require a mage gift. Still, all accounts that I've heard indicate that he hasn't been able to break the blocks. Strain them, maybe. Loosen them just enough for some wild and uncontrolled power to slip out briefly. Do you remember the gallows incident in Menie?"

Oknare nodded, tasting his tea to test its strength. He decided to let it brew a bit longer.

"It burst into blood-red flames. That's where the Shadows were first sighted."

"If he was able to do that consistently, he would have. He hasn't. There's been very little evidence of that kind of power. What there is of it doesn't show a great deal of control." Absol lifted his mug from the desk to sniff the steam. "Chamomile?"

"Yes." Oknare was a bit pleased that the Mancer had recognized the scent. "I find it soothing."

"I've a good friend who drinks nothing else." He sipped, then returned to the subject. "Ba'tvian uses the Shadows more than anything else, outside of blood-rites."

"What is he trying to accomplish?"

"Aside from regaining his gifts? I don't know."

The Shadows followed him...Oknare couldn't keep that thought far from his mind.

"He may well want revenge," he said softly. "For that, he will eventually come here."

"I think vengeance is a given. In my experience, it is one of the most prevalent reasons for someone to become a blood mage. You had best take precautions here."

He sipped, then stared broodingly into the tea.

"Still, it's what comes after that I'm truly worried about."

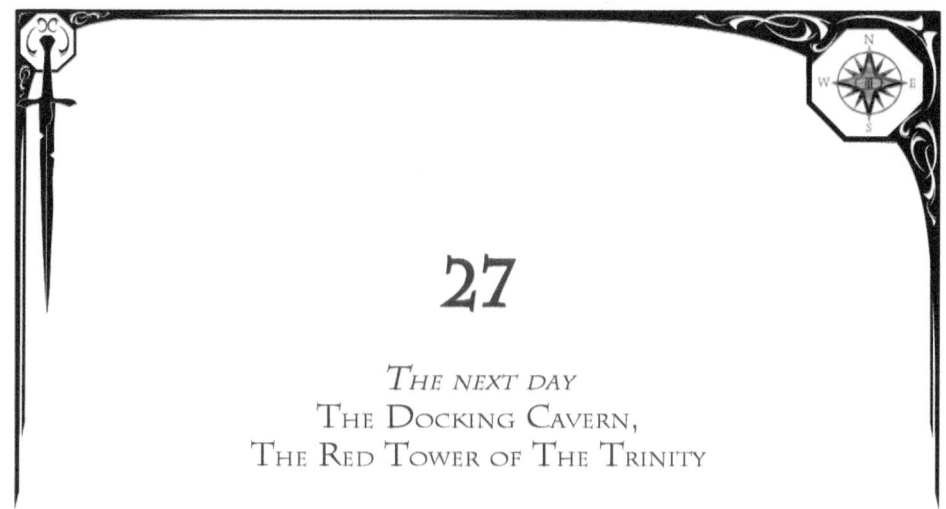

27

HERS were a people belonging to the earth, yet the sea fascinated her. As Nerisse sat on the stone outcropping just beyond the cavern that served as the Tower's harbor she watched waves lap at the rock, with gulls kiting above. A few of her fellow students try their hand at fishing. Securely perched on a boulder, she tugged at her woolen cloak, scanning the water for ships. It was a favorite past-time. If there were no ships and the birds lost her interest, the sea alone was worth the effort of traversing the narrow ledge that led out this way.

She found it soothing, though not nearly as great a comfort as the caves of home.

There weren't many gulls today, and only one small fishing vessel in the distance. The sky was clouding up; a storm coming in, she supposed. The wind began to pick up. She saw the small waves turn choppy. As the students began to pack up their fishing gear, she decided that going back was probably a good idea. She moved with slow care along the slick rock to the ledge to the shelter of the harbor.

"Bad storm a-brewing," muttered a dockhand as she neared the catwalk that butted up against the ledge. He looked up at her, nodded in greeting. "Anymore of yon out there?"

"No, sir," she replied softly. She looked over her shoulder to see the rest following her back. "We were all that was out there."

"That's good, then. You have a good day, miss. Be sure to keep dry."

She gave a shy smile, then moved along the docks, finding herself reluctant to go back to the top and her dorm room. She was tired of studying. She had to admit, too, that she felt a yearning for home. The people of the Red Tower weren't bad, boring, or really all that uncomfortable for her to be around. She had friends, though not any close ones, a caring mentor, respect, and admiration from her peers. She didn't lack for a social life; the party she'd attended at the tavern a few days ago had been enjoyable. Still, it didn't replace home in her heart.

Home had been like being in the womb of the earth, warm, welcoming, nurturing. It was unfortunate that her education in magery had to be finished in such a remote place, surrounded by so much water. Being out in the ocean like this cut her off from home, from the earth her people lived – it made her feel bereft.

It wasn't isolation, she thought as she paused to stare out the harbor's mouth where the sea was beginning to churn. It was... loneliness. The earth had always welcomed her before, like an old friend. This stone spire was a veritable stranger to her senses.

Still, it won't last for long. I have this assurance. I will return home to take my place among the priesthood to serve my people.

Turning away from the water, she stepped off the wooden planking of the boardwalk onto solid stone.

The world spun, dipped, darkened. She felt the rumble of earth, heard sharp cracking, crumbling of stone. Blood filled her nostrils; she gagged on it. Rats – there were so many rats – they scurried over the rock in a mad frenzy, freed from broken cages on a filthy, desecrated floor. She could hear them in the dark, see them in her mind. Then the vision all fell away, leaving her standing in the harbor cavern with her ears ringing.

Images overlaid the present like phantoms, gliding silently through the living. A ship docked at the pier behind her. She didn't have to turn around to know it was there. Just as she didn't have to look ahead to see the procession as it approached.

A young man clad simply in a drab colored tunic and pants, cloaked, his face obscured by a hood, was led by an armed escort. A prisoner, was her first thought. She could see the ropes binding his wrists, the hobble linking his feet. Behind him, she saw her mentor, Master Oknare, as well as another man she had seen but whose name she didn't know. Oknare was outwardly impassive. She could feel echoes of his pain, shame, disappointment. It flowed over her until the prisoner looked up. Their eyes met.

Furious resentment slammed into her. Humiliation and vengeance swirled around her. She felt fear, true terror, as she gazed at this man. He was young, handsome. His eyes, though, were hot, hard. They seemed to glow.

He's not looking at me. He can't see me. This is past, only the past. He's staring at the ship –

The procession advanced on her. She couldn't seem to move. She couldn't think of it. All she saw were his eyes, the dark glint of them, like drops of blood in the darkness. The guards passed through her easily, then the prisoner.

She fainted.

Interlude 8

Elsewhere...

WASN'T that interesting?

Labiyal watched from the safety of his tavern quarters. The little elven priestess, with her close link to the world, fell in an ungraceful heap on the stone. He leaned back as the dockhands in the mirror hurried over to see what was wrong.

What had she seen, he wondered. There were several possibilities. He knew what path she had stood upon, knew what impressions the earth may have stored. Yet she wasn't linked to the tower, was she?

"Earth priestesses must have ties to the land, one born of birth, one born of blood, or one born of destiny." Considering, he tapped mirror's frame. The scene vanished abruptly. "Well, then. It would seem that some of the King's prophecies are proving true."

It would be wise to re-familiarize himself with the Helkorex Noxim – the Written Word of the King of Hell. It meant returning to his current base of operations, though. Taking the tome into what was technically enemy territory was foolish. So it was time leave. Not, however, before he laid a final layer of foundation for what was to come.

After all, not even prophecy was guaranteed.

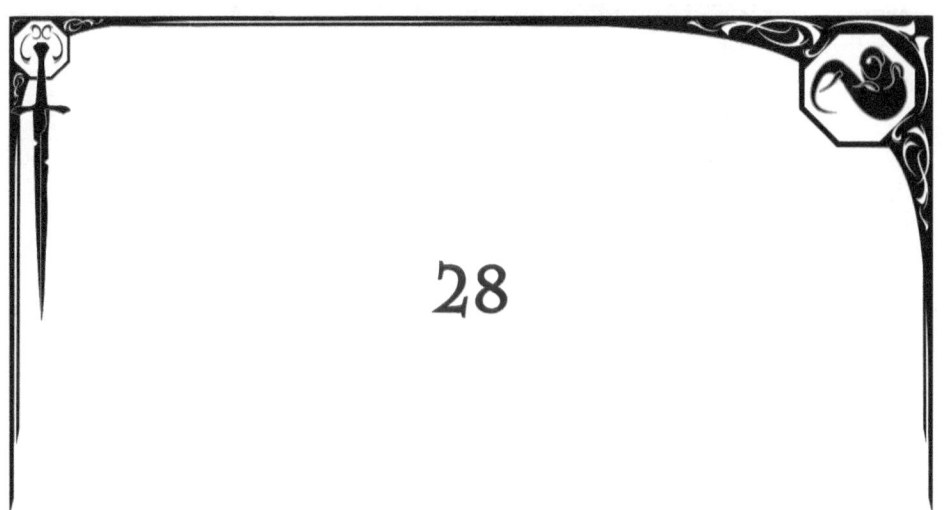

28

OKNARE rushed into the Healing House adjacent to the school, bursting through the doors quickly. An elderly matron gave him a disgruntled look as she planted herself firmly in his way as he tried to bolt through the lobby area. He skidded to a halt, ignoring the attention he was getting the few others waiting for treatment.

"Hold fast, now, Master Oknare. I take it you're here for the female student just admitted in my house?"

"Nerisse, yes. What happened?" He rubbed at his temple. "Is she ill? Injured?"

"It's not serious; just a bruise on her head from when she hit the ground. While she's not ill, she hasn't woken up as yet. She's in fine health, and should rouse soon." She pursed her lips momentarily. "Dockworkers brought her up from the harbor. Said she fainted dead away. I've asked one of the Emp Healers to come take a look," she explained, referring the healers that specialized in problems of the mind. "He'll be along shortly. I don't suppose you might know of any mage abilities that might have contributed to her current state?"

"Ah, well." Oknare ran a hand through his hand, found it damp. Had it been drizzling outside as he'd run? He couldn't remember, he'd been so focused on getting here. "She's slated to be an earth priestess when she gets back to her people. She has a strong sensitivity to the earth, can sometimes experience visions or such like. Traditionally, they don't train in that area until they join the priesthood, but it's possible that she may have picked up on something."

"I'll pass that along. Now you wait here." She nodded to the benches where the kin and friends of patients sat. "I'll let you know when the Emp Healer arrives."

29

Glasten Port,
the western coast of Orthanor

A bloodied, empty body was flung to one side to be engulfed in a crowd of Shadows. Fury pumped through Ba'tvian, hot and rich. He reveled in the dark taste of it on his tongue. It reminded him of fresh blood. So thinking, he grabbed the last of the bound street urchins he'd captured, bent the boy over the makeshift altar. He began to carve.

It served to relieve only part of his frustration.

He was tired of being hunted. He was tired of failing to break the blocks on his mage gifts. And he hated – absolutely hated – having to hide.

Yet he was learning more now than he ever had at the Trinity. That was some consolation. Not enough, he thought as he drew a precise diagram on the boy's chest, not nearly enough. Still, it was a start. Now it was time for the rest.

He'd killed a Mancer not long ago, a young man with little magic who'd been a few years older than he was. The memory brought a cold smile to his lips. It had been something of a rite of passage for him; his Shadows had been very pleased with the success. Mancers were the bane of his existence, the bane of every blood mage's existence. Still, he couldn't fully address that threat, could he, with his own powers limited to the time it took for blood to flow and a life to die.

He had been lucky with that Mancer, as it was. If the man had been more experienced, if he'd had just a bit more power, if Ba'tvian hadn't been so furious over his arcane impotence, he might not have succeeded.

In instances like that, rage helped, bursting up from within to bend his bindings just enough to free a bit of his power. Yet it wasn't consistent or reliable. What was reliable were rituals like this one, where the death magic could be harvested, then stored. He'd created vessels for that, some physical, some living.

His gaze flicked to his Shadows. The loyal, guiding allies, the ones that knew his true value. The only ones who knew, the only ones who acknowledged it. Soon they wouldn't be the only ones.

He had a plan. Before it was done, everyone would recognize the greatest power.

His own.

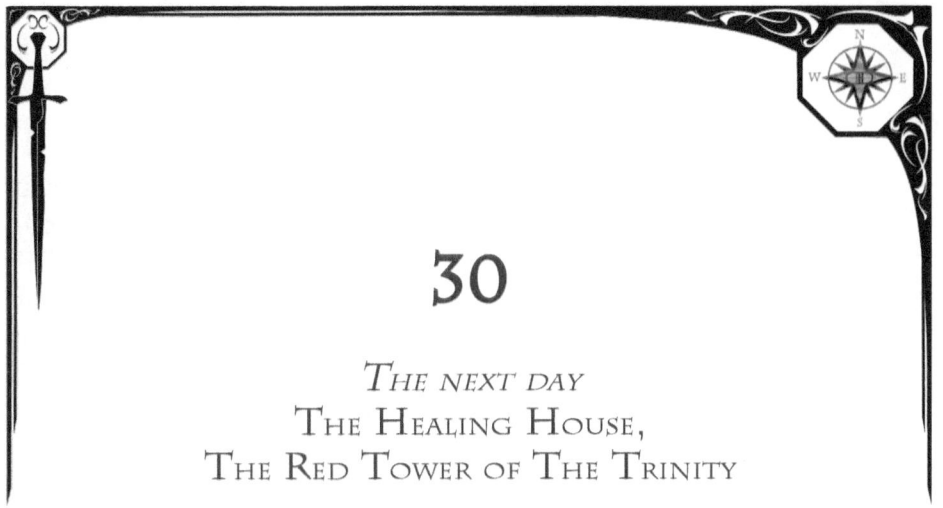

30

THERE were whispers in her dreams. She barely heard them, couldn't quite make out the words. The tone, though, the tone was different, wasn't it? The earth had always spoken to her but that voice didn't sound like this one. It was soft, silky, almost fluid, she supposed. It was reassuring, she found herself straining to listen more closely to what it was saying. The words blurred in her ears, became addled in her mind. Finally, she gave up on deciphering them. The moment she let go of the voice, the whispers ceased.

She woke to find herself on a strange cot, a healer and her mentor hovering at her side.

"Nerisse." Master Oknare gave her a welcoming smile, patting her hand.

"Master?" She blinked her eyes, turned her head. The movement brought the headache to her attention. *Ugh, where did that come from?*

"Allow me," the healer murmured, seeing her wince. She laid a hand on her brow, the pain easing. "I'm Adrianne, an empathic healer. Better?"

"Much. Thank you." She gave them both a confused stare. "Where am I?"

"The Healing House. You were brought up from the harbor after you fainted." Oknare's expression took on a concerned edge. "Do you remember what happened?"

"I – think so." It was coming back to her now. "I was coming back up. A storm was coming in. I left the docks, just stepped off the walk and I saw them. The rock showed them to me."

"Saw what?" Adrianne asked.

"Images. People. A memory. May I sit up?" They eased back from her to allow her to raise herself slowly into a sitting position. "There were guards, a prisoner, and – " She turned to the mage. " – you. You were there, with someone else. I think he was a friend of yours. You watched the guards lead the prisoner to a ship on the docks."

The healer regarded Nerisse thoughtfully as Oknare's expression shuttered.

"What was the name of the ship?"

She saw it in her mind, even though she had never seen it in the memory that the stone had shown to her.

"The King's Folly."

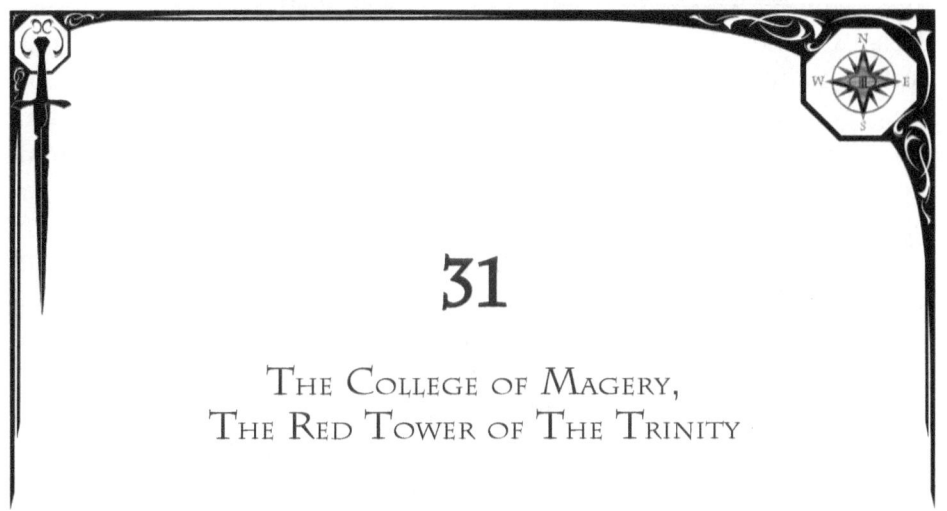

31

The College of Magery,
The Red Tower of The Trinity

THE words reverberated in Oknare's ears long after his student had been released from the healer's and seen to her quarters. After the incident, he sat in his study, thinking of the questions he had evaded. She had asked many.

Should he tell her? He sighed as he considered the gossiping nature of those living on the Tower as well as her own inquisitiveness. As shy as she was, Nerisse was very good at prying out the answers she needed. She would turn to books, to peers, to the very stone they stood upon. None of that appealed to him. Especially if she managed to find the location of Ba'tvian's experiments. Fainting was only a shade of could happened.

"Best to keep a handle on it," he muttered. He would give her some answers – suitably edited answers – in the morning. Until then, there were other things to consider, other things to question.

With great care for the words he chose, he composed a mage-born message, then sent it winging off to Nerisse's family. He needed to know what the priests would say about her vision, what their interpretation of her apparent link to the Red Tower may be. There were no visions without links. That was the way of the earth-sensitives, was it not? A bond between a particular bit of land and them? Until he heard what they had to say on the matter, he couldn't be sure how significant a role that bond played in visions.

As an afterthought, a sent a similar message on the recent event to

Absol Omine. The Mancer was probably still at sea, having set out for the mainland the day before. He'd spent his time at the College of Magery studying the records on Ba'tvian Delthanurk, going over the texts that they believed he'd accessed during time as a student. He'd interviewed many people who had interacted with Ba'tvian on regular basis. How helpful his efforts had been, Oknare had no idea.

The High Judge, along with the college's officiating staff, had coordinated a similar investigation in the wake of Ba'tvian's initial apprehension. No one here dealt with blood mages or daemon summoners as often as the Mancers did. More the former than the latter, he had to admit, and they hadn't known about, or even suspected, that Ba'tvian may have been daemon summoning until the gallows had been destroyed in the port of Menie.

Daemons…the Shadows…

Thinking of them made Oknare glance uneasily towards the shadows within the room. There was nothing there, of course. There never was.

Willfully dismissing the issue from his mind, he set a kettle on the hook above the hearth for tea. Regardless of what else went on in the world, he still had work to do. A resident Master class mage was applying for the trial that would make him an Adept; he needed to review to reports on the man before giving a recommendation. So he returned to his desk, dug up the necessary files from the stack of papers on the corner, and began to peruse them.

As he read, he never noticed the slip darkness that slithered along the baseboards of the room to exit underneath the door..

32

GLASTEN PORT,
THE WESTERN COAST OF ORTHANOR

*T*HERE.

Ba'tvian observed a small cargo vessel as it was loaded on the docks. He had seen it come in, watched its crew, familiarized himself with the captain and his habits. It could work, especially since the word 'small' was only relative. The ship was large enough to accommodate several oxen. The draft animals were used to power the pulley systems some ancient engineer had designed for the series of elevators linking the Docking Caverns to the tops of the Trinity's Towers. Teams of them were swapped out periodically. This vessel would carry one such team to the Gold Tower.

First, he had to get there.

Supplies were being loaded now. The livestock would board just prior to cast off, which would be the following morning. That meant that he had to sequester himself in the hold tonight.

The moon was absent tonight, hiding behind the cover storm clouds. The storm would prove useful. It had blown in from farther out to sea, the worst of its fury already spent. Still, the rain meant fewer people would be out. Even those on watch would be inclined to stand under some kind of shelter from the wet, despite being clad in oilskins.

He waited until the rain started before signaling his Shadows.

They drifted over the cobblestones, wood, and plaster, some gathering around him protectively, others gliding towards the ship.

His scouts, his escort, he thought. Ba'tvian might still puzzle at why they had chosen him at odd moments, yet that explanation didn't matter. Their loyalty did.

Two keep watch on deck.

The thought slid into his mind like a droplet into water. He wasn't certain which of the Shadowed Ones had spoken to him and it wasn't important enough for him to care.

Two stand under the eaves across from the gangplank.

There are no others.

All was in order then. He pulled his cloak more tightly around him, then turned to the trembling urchin standing just down the street. He hadn't sacrificed this one, nor had he intended to. At his approach, the boy jumped, his eyes skittering around him as the two Shadows that had been assigned as his keepers circled once, then away.

"Your fee." Ba'tvian dropped a few coins on the ground, waited until the boy hesitantly picked them up. "If you succeed, you keep it. If you fail, you die. Understood?"

He jerked his head in a nod. He couldn't be more than eight years old, the blood mage mused, watching him go. Young, vital, and cocky when they'd met. He smiled coldly. It had been a small pleasure to teach him fear.

Trusting the keepers to trail after the boy, he took up his own position to keep an ear out. There was a curse from the watchmen under the eaves.

"Watch it, boy."

"Sorry, mister," was the apologetic response. "Tripped over me own feet."

"Better not have taken anything." There was a pause, then another vile curse as small feet slapped on wet cobbles, landed in puddles. "You! Boy! Thief!" Threats and heavier footfalls followed the young pickpocket through the rain.

The other watches his shipmate from his post.

Moving as unobtrusively as possible, Ba'tvian willed his Shadows to cloak him as he made his way onto the gangplank.

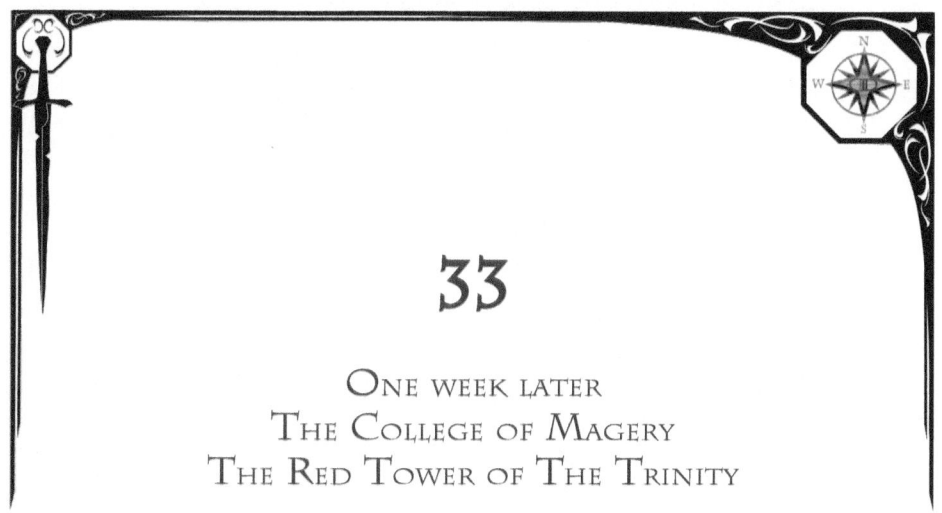

33

L IGHT from the morning sun streamed through the window across from Nerisse as she nodded amiably while her master finished the brief story of his last student. He gave no details of his crimes, only stating that they involved blood magery. Given Master Oknare's tight expression, she knew better than to interrupt, waiting until he was done.

"Do you have any concerns or questions about this?"

"Only one." Clasping her hands in her lap, she looked up at him from across his desk. "Priests and shaman sometimes use the spilling of blood in rituals that involve magery. I'm not familiar with the other practices. Could you please explain the difference?"

He lifted his brows in surprise, then lowered them with a half-smile.

"I do tend to forget how isolated your people can be. Though there are no universal laws concerning the use of blood in magic, many communities, city-states, and nations have variations of rules that are more or less the same. They all prohibit the use of animal or human blood in mage-practices that are for self-gain. Any practices that result in power derived from the blood or death of an unwilling victim are considered anathema."

He reached for the pot of tea that sat on his crowded desk. He poured the steaming liquid into her mug, then his own.

"Religions that utilize blood obtain it first from willing

participants. Those are almost always priests or shaman themselves. In most cases, the blood is given as an offering, with nothing taken by the ritual practitioners Death is seldom asked for, yet when it is, it is always for the community as a whole, not for an individual, or for power of any kind. Animals are used by some sects as offerings. In those instances, the whole of the sacrifice is usually burned.

"Ba'tvian Delthanurk was not religious." He cradled his mug in his hands and sipped. "What he did was for his own gain. The laws of the Trinity take a very strong stand on such matters; they have to. They have an entire school of mages in their house, so-to-speak, after all. Does that suffice?"

"It does." She took a token sip of the tea he had poured her. She had never been fond of chamomile; it seemed that it was all her master drank.

"Then let us set it aside. Today I want you to study the laws of magery, how they differ in the major nations or races of this world. The Library Archivists are expecting you. They should have the necessary texts set aside for you."

"Am I to be tested on them?" She hoped not. There was enough to prepare for with her next Mastery test looming not even six months away.

"Though some of it may come into your Mastery trial, I will not be quizzing you. I would, however, like an oral report on your findings. Then we'll discuss them." His lips curved a little at that. She knew he enjoyed debates on magery. She gave him a relieved nod.

After her dismissal, she walked through halls of the college, absently noting how few students there were in the corridors. Most of them would be classes. She let her thoughts go back to what Oknare had told her earlier. She couldn't help but note the gaps.

What, precisely, had Ba'tvian done? Had he killed someone? An animal? She didn't dispute the innate wrongness of killing a living creature for corrupt purposes. Corrupted power was cruel, cold. It invited curses on the one did the deed, or so her people had long believed. Oknare may have thought that Ba'tvian had gone that route; she wasn't so sure. The stone held a different kind of knowledge.

Ba'tvian Delthanurk had prevented the Tower from tumbling into the sea.

34

G LASTEN used to be a bustling city, full of color, trade, and tall -tales. It boasted no harbor yet the docks spanned the length of the beach. Man-made-jetties had been built from rubble to protect moored ships from the worst antics of the sea. A thriving fishery, the main source of revenue for the city, had called this place home until they had over-fished the waters. When it finally closed down, prosperity took a long downward slide.

Other ports had opened along the coast, though; Menie with its harbor to the north, for one. Merchants and shipmasters who could afford the higher harbor fees left Glasten, leaving behind their poorer fellows. Now the city was derelict, on the verge of being a pit. The people who lived here now had no other place to go. Those who used the wharves were shady at best, criminal at worst. Others occasionally weighed anchor here when they had little choice otherwise.

It was not the sort of place that in which Ba'tvian Delthanurk usually spent time.

He preferred places with a higher margin of prosperity, where murder was uncommon. Places, Absol Omine mused, where ritual killings were a shock to the soul. The Mancer had managed to pick up the fugitive's trail in Goose-Bree, a village further inland. Ba'tvian had slain a farmer there, then butchered some of the livestock for meat. From there, he had wound through the countryside, dipped south towards the settlement of Destiny's Way, and then decisively struck out for the western coast. The Mancer had been almost three weeks behind him in the beginning; he'd made up two of those weeks up to this point.

His progress had been due to a stroke of luck. Glasten, as run-down as it may have been, had a guard patrol to police the more blatant criminal activity. The captain had sent out word that there was a bounty available here for the disposal of an unnatural creature. Ba'tvian's trail had led in that general direction so Absol wasted no time in responding.

Now he followed a rough-n-tumble guardsman through the maze of alleyways that existed beyond the drab streets. They were filled with filth, garbage, vermin, some of the bolder of the low-standing criminal element, the homeless. Night time concealed much of it in darkness. It did nothing for the smell. There was very little in the world, Absol thought, which reeked quite like fish guts, waste, and stale urine.

"Ah, poor sod."

The muttered remark had the Mancer glancing up sharply. In the light of the guard's firebrand, he could see the form of an old man. He lay half in this alley, half in another, his dirty body stripped bare. There were no wounds or signs of struggle. Judging by the morbidity, he'd been dead for less than a day.

"Natural death."

"Eyah. Not a mark, see? So it's natural. Bugger's been dead a bit but that's not what we'd called ye fer." Handing the brand to Absol, he reached down to drag the body back through the alley, closer to the main street. "Dead wagon'll pick him up in a few hours."

The two resumed trudging through the narrow lanes carefully. Further in, the trash and stench wasn't so bad. Or perhaps it was just not as fresh. At this point, he couldn't tell. His nose had shut down in protest some time before.

They began to see signs of a community before long. Rags, old boards, all manner of junk became tents. The street people of Glasten made use of anything they found, turning it into sleeping pads, coverings, or portable homes. The denizens here huddled in their dwellings, others staring. A few more may have been dead.

There was an air of despair here. It was enhanced by the

emptiness in one pair of eyes or the balefulness in another. Children, adults, oldsters – age or mental state made no difference. Each type was represented.

Moving beyond the community, Absol felt himself relax marginally. He hated the sadness of these places. It was why he would never live in a city or town. When his time for retirement came, if he managed to live that long, he would have a small cottage and garden in Destiny's Way. His days would be spent in cheerful debate with his old friend, the abbot at the local shrine. Sighing inwardly, he pushed his dream aside to pay attention to the harshness of reality.

It was the silence that caught his attention. They were in an alley that was no less filthy, no less empty, than the rest. Elsewhere, things had moved, scuttling in the dark. That was not so here.

"No rats." That was a sure sign, wasn't it? They were sensitive to this kind of death, this kind of fear...

"Beg pardon, sir?" The guard slowed, glancing at him. "What'd ye say?"

"There are no rats through here, yet there's enough refuse scattered about to attract them." He looked around thoughtfully. "It's just interesting."

"Ah..." His companion – Absol couldn't recall the man's name – looked momentarily baffled. "I didn't notice. Is it important, ye think?"

"No." He gave a slight smile. "How close are we?"

"Oh, just 'round the corner there." Pointing, his escort resumed leading the way at a more cautious pace. He gestured at a building up ahead. "This place hasn't been used in all the time that I've been guard in Glasten. Fire gutted it a ways back. The cellar's intact, though."

They turned the corner, then stopped at a set of basement doors. They had been cleared of debris. Several long, rusty metal rods had been put through the door handles. No one had been posted to make sure that the creature stayed trapped, he noted with some consternation. What if it had gotten loose? What if that had been the intention, to add confusion, to cover up the summoner's trail? Did these people not think?

"Ah, now, the thing had been eating down there. We didn't want it loose or anything so, ah, the bodies…"

"Were left for it." He had already been told by the captain, so waved the explanation aside. "That's fine. Odds are that if you hadn't, it would have gone looking for someone to chew on. Is there anything else you feel I should know?"

He scratched his head under his hat, shuffled his feet.

"Well, the captain's looking for the boy that told us about the place. Thieving little bugger, yet honest enough, considering. Oh, haven't seen for meself but I heard the critter down there's as big as a man. Al, he said it had bulging eyes as big as the moon and everything. Can't say if that helps, though."

"It might." There was a strain of daemon-goblin that fit that description. If this was indeed Ba'tvian's work, it was an oddity. As far as the Mancers had been able to determine, he had never summoned a creature before this. Absol hadn't thought that he'd been able to.

"Er, sir?" The guard drew his attention, fidgeting. "How'd ye want to go 'bout this? Yer the professional and all…um, did ye need me to…do anything?"

Both exasperated and amused by his obvious reluctance, he shook his head.

"You just stay here, stand at the door."

"Ah, good." Relief oozed out of the guard. He stood straighter. "Right. Well, best get it done."

"Of course." He waited for the metal rods to be removed, opened one of the doors himself. In the gloom below were steep stairs. "Oh, and be ready."

"Fer what?"

"If I miss the first strike, it will be up to you to catch it when it flees." He didn't look back at the nervous sound the man made. Satisfied with the jab's response, Absol descended into the cellar.

35

GLASTEN PORT,
THE WESTERN COAST OF ORTHANOR

HE could hear it breathing in the dark. It sounded heavy, rasping, wet. It grunted to the unsteady rhythm of something meaty being torn apart. The creature wasn't moving around much; the noises only came from one direction. Feeding on a body – a rotten one, if the stench down here was any indication. Which way was it facing?

Absol felt along the wall ahead of him, creeping along as stealthily as he could. He stopped when his groping fingers encountered the corner. Edging closer to it, he peered around it into the gloom of the space beyond. There was no light anywhere. Listening to the thing as it ate, he considered his options.

He didn't have much in the way of mage capability. Most Mancers didn't, ironically enough. Those that did rarely developed them beyond the apprentice level. Too much of their time was spent training for, then fighting against, the Daemon influences in their world. He was no different, yet he did know enough to conjure a mage-light. It would give him the advantage of knowing what lay on the floor, precisely where the creature was. It would also enable him to identify the type of creature he was about to engage. The drawback was that the creature would have the same advantages.

This is its turf. It's likely to know it far better than I...

He conjured the mage-light with a habitual gesture, bringing it into being in the close to the center of the space ahead of him. The cellar room took on a golden cast from the light. His eyes adjusted quickly to the change even as the sounds of feeding stopped.

Absol remained out of sight, perfectly still. The creature growled, snuffling around as it investigated. He studied the portion of the room he could see, noting the piles of stripped bones the odd corpse yet to be eaten. They looked to have died only days before. The growling deepened, becoming harsher, closer. It had scented him.

He dove for the open, whirling around, unsheathing his sword and long knife. Seeing the creature for the first time, he knew what it was. Built like a man with scaly skin, a fanged, frog-like face, bulging eyes, and swollen pot-belly, it was a greater gremlin. The lesser gremlins were dwarfed variations of their larger cousins. They were more cowardly. This one would move fast, but tire easily. In close quarters, he'd have to be careful.

Hissing, it charged. He sidestepped, the sword slashing outward as he turned with the strike. The blade bit into the arm, the tip trailed along the back. It roared. Grabbing up bones, it flung them at him. He dodged, feinted, circled as it lunged. It grabbed his sword blade, trying to drag him forward. Absol pulled hard to the side. He brought the knife up. The steel sliced in deep, across the back of the neck.

Then both of them tripped over the scattered bones, jerking apart. The sword fell to the ground. The Mancer turned the fall into a roll, coming up in a crouch. The gremlin scrambled up facing away, clawing at the earthen floor, the skeletal debris. Its footing slipped, skidded, throwing it off-balance. Absol launched another attack.

The long knife flew like a spear through the air, piercing the creature's hamstring. The leg collapsed under its weight. A smaller dagger was thrown, driving into the shoulder joint on the same side. The gremlin rolled onto its back, forcing both blades deeper as he snatched up his larger weapon. It flailed its claw-tipped limbs at his approach. He made as if to attack several more times, letting the thing exhaust itself as it tried to defend itself.

Black ichor was making the littered ground slick.

Judging its waning reaction time, he feinted, dodged, then kicked. His foot had it cringing away, exposing its back once again. Seeing the opening, he stabbed his sword clean through the back of the neck.

Its death was typical of Daemon kind when struck down by

consecrated weapons, or by one of their own. The body decayed rapidly. Within minutes, all that was left of it was a darkly putrid sludge.

He turned away from it to take a closer study of the site. Most of the bodies had been eaten already; one had been partially consumed. Two more lay tossed on the ground nearby. The heads were missing. Greater gremlins considered the human brain a delicacy, so it wasn't unusual. They would have been devoured first. He searched, counting sternum bones to come up with a total of nineteen victims. A sizeable rite, especially for one so recently on the blood path.

There was little doubt that Ba'tvian Delthanurk was a determined, almost fanatic, devotee of blood magery. He had practiced frequently, though never on this scale. The Mancers as a whole had taken an interest in the hunt by this point, having found traces of his rites throughout the central region of Orthanor. He'd stayed south of the strange Wood of Destiny and north of the Plains of Gestia, never traveling to the eastern coast of the continent.

It had been Ba'tvian's work here. The feel of the rite, the taste of the lingering power he'd left behind, told him that it was. But why? Why had he been so careful about cleaning up after himself from the time he'd killed his family only to leave a site sloppily taken care of now? A gremlin would only take care of the bodies. It would do nothing to mask the unseen presence of power signatures that could be tied to the practitioner who'd conducted the ritual.

That left another question in need of an answer. Ba'tvian's mage ability had been blocked. How had he summoned a greater gremlin without it? Or had he? The possibilities of an unknown partner or Ba'tvian having found a way around the block ran through Absol's mind. He was going to have figure out which one it was.

Resigned to being in Glasten for a bit longer, he finished his search of the cellar. It was time, he thought as he ascended the steep stairs leading to the alley above, to check back with the guard captain and see if they'd found the boy. Hopefully, the child would be able to give him some answers.

36

THE DRAGON'S HEAD TAVERN,
THE RED TOWER OF THE TRINITY

"I'D always thought him handsome, if a bit broody. Shame that he turned out to be such an evil person."

"Handsome? He looked a bit homely to me. And it doesn't surprise me in the least that went bad that way. Just look at what he'd come from: a serf family. They probably didn't know to teach him any better…"

"I wouldn't judge a man by where he'd come from. Everyone looks up to the High Judge and he's low-born."

"That's true. You have to wonder, though, as to where he learned it all, don't you? Maybe he found it in some of those books at the college library or maybe he even found a tutor somewhere…"

"It would explain why he was so secretive…"

Nerisse listened to her peers chatter and gossip. The storm of words echoed in her ears, bussed in her brain. Had Ba'tvian really been evil? Could anyone so evil have done so much to save the Trinity from destruction? She'd come to the Dragon's Head Tavern to find out. Students of every rank spent their time there. She had thought that some of them would have known him. Few of them, if any, did.

Students of both sexes described him as aloof, a bit self-centered, a diligent student who seemed to think himself more superior than anyone else as he gained more recognition in his studies. One his classmates had admitted that though he'd been only been at the Red

Tower for four years he'd been on the verge of attaining his Mastery. Most didn't achieve that until their seventh or eighth year. Those who had been there longer, or were from a higher social class, had tended to look down on him. The hints of jealousy, coupled with his anti-social nature, likely accounted for their claims of his superior attitude.

They don't like that he was better than they...

He had to have known about it. Living with these people, working with them, how could he not? Yet he had done what he could to save the Red Tower from toppling into the sea.

"So what's your interest in him, Nerisse?"

The question jarred her out of her reverie. She looked up at the young man who'd asked it. The brooch pinned to his heavy tunic indicated that he was a Master Mage.

"Oh, it was just…something that Master Oknare had mentioned." She gave him a hesitant smile. "He didn't give a thorough explanation and I was a bit curious."

"I can see that your reputation for inquisitiveness is well-earned." His lips curved warmly. "I've always thought it curious myself that Master Oknare is still called 'master' when he's of Adept status. Adepts usually warrant the 'lord' mode of address."

"He's modest."

The conversation turned to college teachers. She let her mind drift off the subject, back to Ba'tvian as the others talked, laughed, enjoying the evening. She just couldn't let the matter go. It nagged at her mind, prodding at her to learn more, to judge for herself.

Their opinions were obviously biased. Where could she go to find an objective description of him and the events that had led to his exile? Exile… An exile required a trial, didn't it? An official trial, an official sentencing – the reports would be filed in the public records. That was her answer.

Satisfied, she let herself relax. Wrong they might be about Ba'tvian but that didn't make enjoying their company onerous. She'd pass the evening with them, then find the time later to search the records.

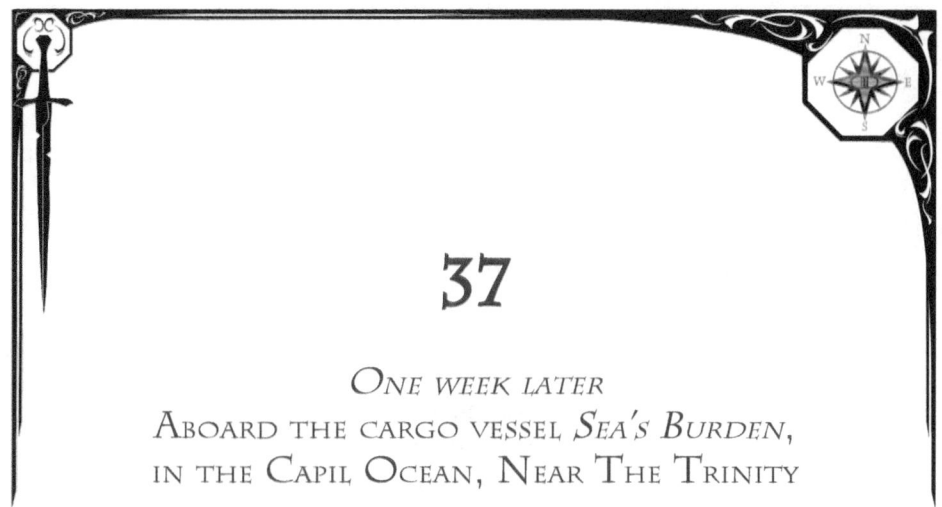

37

ONE WEEK LATER
ABOARD THE CARGO VESSEL *SEA'S BURDEN*,
IN THE CAPIL OCEAN, NEAR THE TRINITY

H E hated cargo holds. They were overcrowded, dark, dank. This one smelled.

The stink of the bilge lingered in his throat, tainting the stale bread he'd packed for the journey. When he nibbled on the bread, he could taste the foulness. The water skin was no less affected. Sipping sparingly from it, he grimaced at the flavor.

The voyage had not been comfortable, though it had gone relatively smoothly so far. There had been no storms, the sea had been restless only a day or two, the crew seldom came down to do anything more than a cursory check to make sure that nothing had shifted around. The Shadows gave him warning whenever someone came near, enough so that he could hide from them.

He absently licked his parched lips. How much longer would they be at sea? He'd stretched his supplies as far as he could. Already, the skin – the last of three he'd smuggled on board – holding his water was nearing empty. Soon, he would have to chance another night-time raid on the ship's water supply barrels in the galley. He had managed that tricky bit of business only once before.

A ship's crew never truly slept.

Three columns of stone have been sighted.

Distracted, Ba'tvian glanced to the right of his hunched position. The white eyes of one of his 'scouts' glittered back at him.

"How close are we?" His voice was raspy. He wasn't certain if it was the lack of sufficient water or general disuse that caused it. There hadn't been much need to talk on the voyage.

A few hours, perhaps. Another Shadow glided over the wooden planks of the floor, coming from the steep stairs ahead of him. The first slithered over to the side, merging with the darkness of the hold as it made room for its comrade.

"Have you found out which of the towers the ship will dock at?"

The one with the yellow roofs, the second replied, referring to the Golden Tower of the Trinity. It blinked its eyes lazily. *It is not the one we want.*

"No." It would have been too easy, wouldn't it, if the Red Tower had been their destination? He pondered this new issue silently for a moment. "Tell me of our approach. Will we pass the Red Tower at any point?"

Yes.

The other Shadows were stirring now. They drifted towards him, around him. They watched, waited. He ignored them as he continued to think and re-think possibilities. The one that held the most promise, also held the greatest health risk. There wasn't much choice, though, if he was to succeed – and he needed to. More than his life hung in the balance.

"What is the time of day?"

Mid-day.

Daylight would make this tricky, yet not impossible. It would also be a matter of timing. He couldn't afford discovery, or leaving behind any evidence that he or his Shadows were in the area. The incident of the *King's Folly* was too well known. That story, a ship found drifting near shore, its crew slaughtered by forces unseen, was not likely to fade anytime soon.

How long would it take him to reach the aft deck? Was there rigging to hang off of? If there was...

The ship has two anchors, one at each end, on opposite sides.

Perfect.

"Find me some rope." Two Shadows skittered away as he gave new orders to the rest.

38

The docks of Menie Port,
on the western coast of Orthanor

"GOOD to see you again, Mancer. What brings you to our fair port this time?"

Absol Omine stepped through the doorway of the Harbor Master's office. It was a simple structure, a veritable shack that was positioned in the middle of Menie's array of docks. The man who manned the desk most likely didn't work at it very often during the day. His leathery skin spoke of sun, hard labor, and sea salt. One eye was covered with a black patch; a scar running from forehead to cheek indicated how that eye had been lost.

"I have need of a ship. Which of your vessels in port are headed towards the Trinity?"

"Hmm." The Harbor Master scratched at his rugged gray beard as he pulled out a logbook. Flipping it open, he scanned the listings. "The *Fisher's Delight*. They head out tomorrow morning. Captain's Terik Wayford." The man's good eye flicked up to stare uneasily at him. "This isn't…spooky business, is it?"

"Not in the way you mean, no." He might not have bothered to elaborate – wouldn't have thought to if the Master hadn't seen what had been wrought aboard the *King's Folly*. Finding himself restless, Absol began to pace the cramped space of the office. "I tracked my quarry to Glasten. He'd left dead in his wake, and something from Hell to clean it up. The port guard already knew of it when I got there. A young thief had tipped them to it."

"Your…quarry…he didn't come here, did he?" The gruff voice was harsh with anxiety. He knew what Mancers hunted: blood mages, daemons, the undead. They were things that few wanted part of in their lives.

"Again, no. The thief had disappeared, the quarry long gone when I arrived. We searched for the boy. I hadn't spoken with him before dealing with the rest, only the guards had. He was dead when we finally found him."

Torn apart, he thought. The Shadows had taken him in a frenzy. Whether they had been ordered to do so regardless or only as punishment for telling, he might never know.

"I questioned everyone I could. One of the guards mentioned that the boy had been roughed up by sailors on the docks the day before he reported the…spooky business," he continued, borrowing the other man's term. "The sailors were gone with their ship that morning. I suspect that the one I seek was onboard as well."

"Headed to the Trinity…" The man pulled at his beard absently. "It's him. The one they exiled, the one that was sent out on the *Folly*. It's him."

"Ba'tvian Delthanurk." He stopped pacing to face the Harbor Master. "Yes, it's him."

Absol watched as the man brooded down at his log.

"I knew the captain of that ship. Good man. Good sailor." He made a notation next to the entry for *Fisher's Delight*. "Captain Wayford's likely at dock twelve, where his ship is. I know him, as well. Another good sailor. I'd hate to lose him."

"You won't. Thank you." He gave a salute, then turned to head out. He thought he heard the old man wish him good luck as he left but didn't turn back.

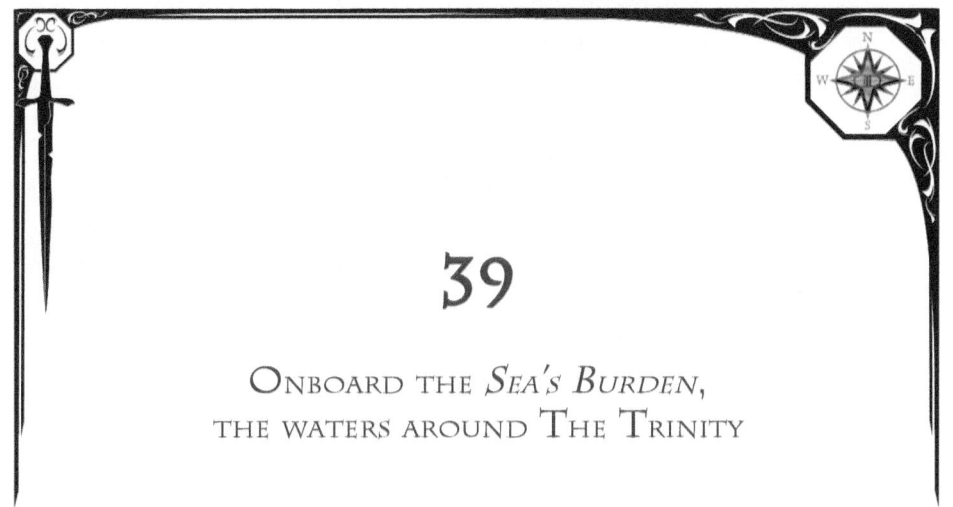

39

WITH the Shadows as scouts, Ba'tvian worked his way up from the hold. They glided ahead, warning him of the crew, as he climbed steps so steep that they were truly more like ladders. Thankfully, the ship possessed only four levels, including the main deck. With everyone busy with preparations to make port, there wasn't anyone to encounter on the third level. The second was not as clear and free as the first.

There are two down the corridor from the step-ladder.

He froze just below the opening leading up into the passageway. Possibilities flitted through his mind. Most of them had to be rejected – secrecy was paramount. He waited, muscles cramping from holding his position on the steps. The two down the hall did not move. Anger and impatience rose within him. He didn't have time for this.

Lead them away. He focused the order at the Shadows, underscoring with his thoughts the need for discretion. He didn't see them leave. Straining to hear, he listened to the faint murmur of voices at the far end of the hall. They stopped abruptly. Taking the risk of being sighted, he moved up just enough so that he could see down the hall. The two sailors were looking at something down a side passage with the next step ladder leading up top behind them. One said something – he couldn't quite catch the words – then they left. Their body language spoke of caution but not alarm or fear.

He waited another moment before pulling himself up. Hugging the wall, he crept over to the stairs. Two Shadows slithered over the floorboards of the deck to wait idly for him by the bottom step. He didn't wasted time in taking the hint.

He came out on the main deck off to the side of bridge. Barrels were lashed into place against the platform, providing him with cover. He crouched behind them, careful of any sound made the crew as they did whatever it was that sailors did onboard a ship. He heard shouted orders concerning the main sail and remembered that some of the crew would be on the masts. Would they see him as he left the ship? He didn't know.

There is no one aft.

He adjusted the rope he had slung over his shoulder, rolled onto the balls of his feet, and ran hunched over in the direction that his Shadows had indicated. Once at the rail, he carefully peered over to locate the anchor.

Now was not the time to worry about being seen. With the Shadows standing as lookouts, he took up the rope he'd brought with him. One end had been looped like a noose. He lowered it, swinging it to catch hold of one of the anchor arms. It took several tries. Heart pounding, teeth gritted, he concentrated on his task, jolting whenever he heard someone shout at the crew from the bridge above him.

It caught. He lowered more of the rope length over the side of the ship. Finally, he took up the rest, hugged the rail, then slid over the side.

He hit the icy water with a solid splash that caught no one's notice. His grip on the rope kept him from going under as the ship cut through the water on its way past the Red and Blue Towers. Ba'tvian braced his feet against the hull, holding on until the ship was almost perpendicular to his destination. He shoved off the hull, let go of the rope.

The Shadows swarmed the waters around him as he swam towards the stone column holding the College of Magery.

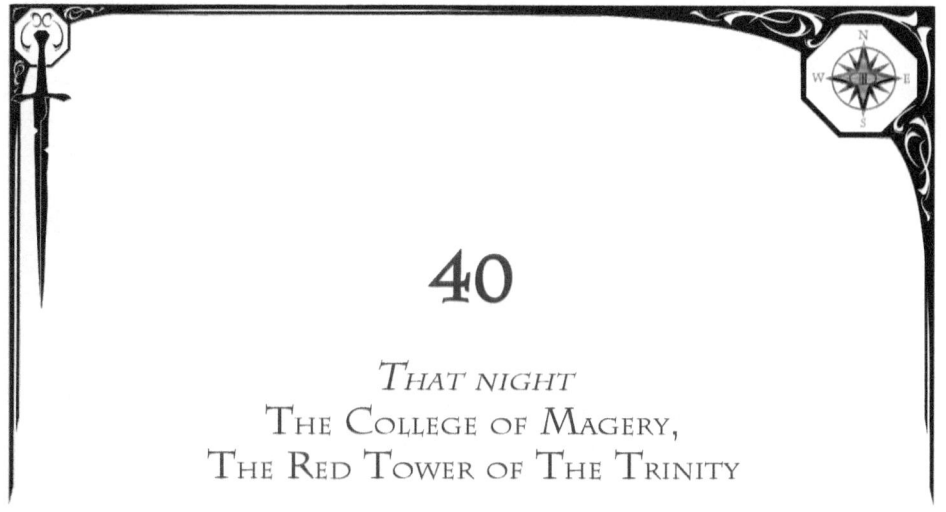

40

THE memory of stone haunted her dreams. Nerisse struggled out of them, the sounds of shrieking rats and stone echoing in her ears as she thrashed in her bed. She could feel the grinding of the rock, the damnation of the Trinity authorities, the hiss of something in the dark. She saw the ship, the dock, then *him* being drug through the frigid waters.

She woke, heart thudding. Sitting up, she extricated herself from the tangled blankets around her to perch on the edge of the bed, her head in her hands. She knew that the earth of the Trinity was calling out to her. She could sense it though its message wasn't clear.

It's so...garbled. It didn't use to be...

The longer she stayed here, the more confusing it was. It was as if the stone was trying to make her understand something about Ba'tvian, yet she couldn't see it, translate it. Becoming frustrated over her inability to interpret the tumultuous dream, she decided to take a walk. Clear her mind. She wanted to be at peace again before she made another bid for sleep.

She dressed warmly and ventured out of the dormitory. It was past curfew for students so she was careful to be quiet. Once outside, she shivered in the wind as she set off briskly with no particular destination in mind. The moon rose high in the sky, a bright light to guide her as she ambled along the streets. She tried to think only of the serene picture the city made at night. She lost track of time, letting her feet carry her wherever.

As she passed by the Courthouse Square, her mind wandered back to her venture into the city records. She hadn't been successful there. The archivist in charge had kept a beady on her the whole time she'd been there, delving into student records on the pretext of researching a project. It had been a weak lie, she knew. She hadn't thought to come up with one beforehand. Still, the archivist had let her dig through the papers and scrolls for examples of the laws in action. There was a great deal to go through. Unless she asked about the court files directly, it was unlikely she'd find them anytime soon. She'd try again in a few days.

She stopped when she came to the lifts that brought people up from the docks far below at the tower base. Housed in barn-like structures to protect them from elements, they operated at all hours of the day and night, hauling supplies, cargo, and people to or from the docking cavern. She thought wistfully of riding down, of watching the ocean under the moon. It was late, though. She had lessons tomorrow.

The earth tugged at her mind with violent urgency. She saw him among the rocks, shivering with cold. Shadows flitted all around him, as the ocean lapped at the stone, at him.

She blinked, reaching out a hand to side of the nearest lift-house to steady herself. He was – here? He'd come out of exile to return... why? How? Did he mean to come back for redemption? To clear his name? But – they didn't understand. They didn't want to know that he'd saved them all by doing what he'd done.

They'll kill him. The laws have changed regarding blood mages. The age of execution... She closed her eyes as she saw him shivering in the wet cold in her mind.

Hurrying into the lift-house, she boarded the next one headed down

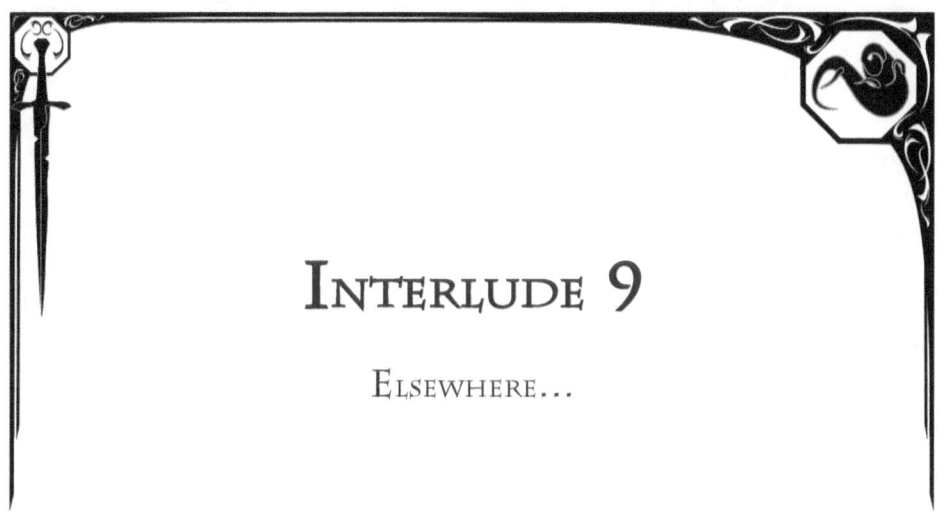

INTERLUDE 9

ELSEWHERE...

"FINALLY."

Labiyal Biyalban allowed himself a small smile. In the mirror across from him was a bird's eye view of what was transpiring at the Red Tower. He watched as Nerisse picked her way over the rocks to the jetty outside. Huddled there, guarded by his allies, was Ba'tvian. The boy had done well in getting back to the Trinity. Yet without intervention, he might have died of hypothermia. That he hadn't done so already spoke of great resilience.

Now he had a new ally, one that Labiyal had chosen for him. He'd monitored the progress of the work he'd set in motion within her mind, playing upon her interests, curiosity, and the one thing that her people considered holy: her tie to the earth. It was gratifying to see a plan unfold as expected.

Nerisse shed one of her coats to cover Ba'tvian with it, then spoke to him for a few moments before helping him to his feet. Together, they entered the docking cavern. Ba'tvian kept his head down, making an effort to walk on his own with minimal support needed from his new companion. All around the two, the Shadows swarmed. Did they recognize her for what she was to be? It was impossible to tell. The Shadowed Ones were a mystery to all but perhaps Hell himself.

She doesn't know what they are, what they mean.

She would soon enough. By then, it would be too late to turn back.

His eyes tracked from the mirror to another. The silvered glass showed a ship at sea, the Mancer Absol Omine pacing its deck. He would also be too late. That had been simple enough to arrange. Intercepting a mage-sending was easily enough done, if one knew who lay at both ends of it.

A second message had been sent more recently, after Omine had taken sail on the sea. Labiyal had allowed it to pass through without interference. Gating would not be feasible at this point, so it didn't matter. The damage he had intended had been done.

With a gesture, he sent the mirrors back into slumber. He didn't want them playing their scenes in the background while he made his report to his sire, and his king.

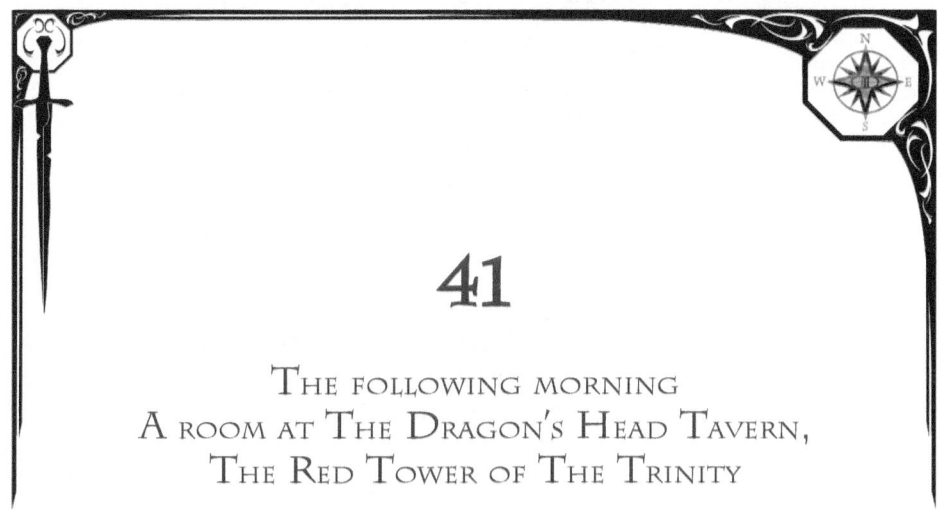

41

The following morning
A room at The Dragon's Head Tavern,
The Red Tower of The Trinity

BA'TVIAN roused in the bed. The first thing that registered in his brain was the warmth. The hours of numbing cold had passed.

Opening his eyes, he studied the room. Finding no one else there save for his shadowy comrades, he sat up stiffly. A whiff of aroma caught his attention, drawing his gaze to the small table by the bed. A bowl of soup had left for him, along with a note. His stomach growled, cramping painfully. Ignoring it for the moment, he picked up the piece of paper, and curled his lip. It was a set of instructions from someone named Nerisse. Nerisse. He frowned over the name. The girl. The girl that had come to him in the night...

"They'll kill you if you're found. They don't understand what you did or why. Come with me. I know of a place to keep you safe."

The note told him to stay put, not to venture out even for food. She would be by after her lessons at the college to see to his needs. He set it down, then picked up the bowl and spoon. Despite his hunger, he took a careful sniff at the food, then held it out to the Shadows. He had learned months ago that they could detect things he couldn't – like poison. One ventured forth to inspect the bowl.

It is clean. Eat.

"What of the girl?" he asked, as he took his first spoonful of soup.

She is Elvanaer, an elf of the underground. We have kept watch. She is a student here. Her master is the one you seek.

The spoon clattered on the floor as anger flared. The Shadows glided close, one of them dipping low to nudge meaningfully at the fallen utensil. He leaned over to snatch it up but did not resume eating.

She has told no one that you are here, one assured.

She believes that they are wrong in what they know of you. This came from the largest of his Shadows. It seemed almost amused. *She thinks of you as a savior of the Trinity.*

A savior? Now that was interesting. He allowed his anger to die down as he considered the ramifications of this little bit of information. He ate absently while he did so. Yes, he could work with that.

"Scout out the area. I want to know where Oknare and High Judge Hamal are at all times." His mind supplied them with images of both men as he named them. "Track her throughout the day. Find out as much as you can about her – lessons, schedule, family, expectations, desires. Everything. Find the library, the texts that I need – you know what to look for."

Yes, lord. Dull white eyes blinked lazily at him. *What will you do with the girl?*

"She is a tool. I will use her as one."

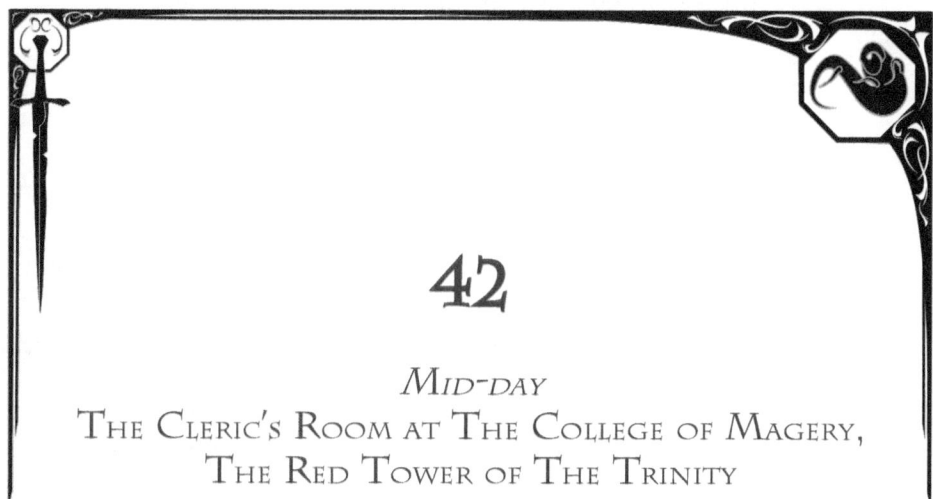

42

"HE'S coming back?"

"According to the Mancer Absol Omine, yes." Oknare paced the room restlessly, the robes of his office flapping around him as he moved. He'd received the news just after finishing a lecture for candidates for the trials of Adept-hood. He had immediately contacted the High Judge for a meet. Hamal had come, cutting one of his court sessions short. Now he looked on with concern in one of the most private rooms on the tower.

"You can't take this on, Oknare. He is not your fault."

The adept waved the words away.

"That's not the issue, my friend. The issue is his pride. I've thought of this time and again, pummeled it in my mind, and the one thing I keep coming back to is Ba'tvian's pride." He stopped to turn to his companion. "Do you know he came from a serf family?"

"No."

"I'd almost forgotten it myself. He doesn't act like a serf, or a farmer. Yet he once told me that he wanted to be a mage so that he would no longer be the dirt that everyone else walked over." He began to pace again. "We took that from him. Shut the magic away – with just cause. Now he's returning, with those things the Mancers call Shadowed Ones. Do you know why?"

"Revenge." The judge said it with a sigh, sitting in the single chair that the room held at its center. "What will you do about

Nerisse?"

Oknare paused in midstride, grimaced.

"Put her on the next boat back to her people. I don't want her touched by this. Aside from that, she may become a target for him."

"The sooner you see her off, the better. When does Omine arrive?"

"In a few days. He sent the message while at sea, or I'd have offered to gate him here." He rubbed at his temple. "A ship is forever changing position upon the sea; it makes gating to one nearly impossible."

A pounding on the door had both men turning. The door swung open to reveal one of the school officials in his trademark red and gold attire.

"Oknare, High Judge, we've determined where the ship, the *Sea's Burden*, is now. It is currently docked at the Golden Tower. They are searching the entirety of the column for Ba'tvian Delthanurk as we speak."

"The Golden Tower? What could he possibly want there?" Hamal stood as he spoke. "There is no one and nothing there that would help him regain his mage abilities."

"No." Oknare shook his head. "He's not there. Have the Red Tower searched. It's here he'll come, and it's likely me he'll want."

Absol had been right, he thought. Now they would have to deal with it. He wished, dearly wished, that he had been given the Mancer's warning message earlier. Why had it taken so long to get it?

As they exited the Cleric's Room, he turned to the official.

"Have someone find Nerisse. She will need to be protected."

43

The Dragon's Head Tavern, The Red Tower of The Trinity

NERISSE burst into the tavern, ignored those who hailed her, and darted up the steps. There was no time to waste with social niceties. He was in danger.

When she arrived in the room she'd booked for him, he stood at the window, staring out at the city. Around him was his shadowy escort. She didn't know quite what they were, but she could sense a kind of...welcoming from them. They turned her way know, blinking their glittery eyes at her.

"Ba'tvian, they know you're here, in the Trinity." The words tumbled out hurriedly. "They received a message from a Mancer at the school. They've found the ship that brought you at the Golden Tower so that's where they're looking now. It's only a short matter of time before they start searching here."

"It was...expected." His gaze swung from the window to pin her in place. He had such dark eyes, she thought. Dark, powerful eyes. "Where do you stand in this...Nerisse, isn't it?"

"Y-yes. I – " Where did she stand? She was Oknare's student, a Master Mage training for Adept-hood. He'd been wrong about Ba'tvian, though. Ba'tvian had saved the Trinity – the earth had made that clear. Remembering that, she answered without thinking. "I stand with you. You shouldn't be reviled for doing what you had to do to save everyone."

"Where did you learn of that?" he asked quietly. "That I saved everyone."

"The stone. It remembers. It showed me. It's that connection with the earth that has me slated for the priesthood upon my return home."

"A priestess." The Shadows began to glide in a slow, complicated pattern at their feet. She let her eyes drop from his to watch them. "Is that what you crave? To be a priestess? Separate from the world at large, a servant to your faith and your people?"

She'd never thought about it. It had always been expected of her.

"There's no reward in it," he continued quietly. "You serve, you cleanse, and you are taken for granted. You have no choice in your life. Most religious figures are not allowed love or marriage. They are restricted in their life, even the way they think. Much like this place."

"They took your magic from you," she said. "They didn't understand."

"You do. Can you comprehend – appreciate – what I have to do now? What I need?"

"Need?" She tore her gaze from the Shadows, their mesmerizing movements, to look back at him. "What do you need?"

"What is *mine*." His soft voice turned hard. "I need my magic back. They've made me as the dust beneath their feet, would make me even less that that if they could. With my power, I could better protect myself. I could make a haven that would welcome all with my plight."

"A haven…" Something shifted inside her. She couldn't say what it was, or what it meant. All she knew was that this young man, so sorely misunderstood, would change the world if he could. He didn't deserve the ruthless reputation they had given him. "It won't be easy."

"No, it won't. Nothing worth doing is."

His eyes. She was caught once again in his eyes. What was it about him that made her want to help, to protect? She fought to maintain her thoughts even as the feeling seeped in to gradually overwhelm.

"What price will you pay to make this sanctuary, to take back the means to create it?" There would be a price. Nothing like he proposed was without some kind of payment.

"Anything. It means that much to me."

She nodded, dropped her gaze to the Shadows once more as she tried to think. They were moving faster in their pattern now. So graceful, she thought.

"To free magic that has been locked away, you need one of three things. The first is to raise enough power to break it yourself. It carries the most risk, as the backlash often kills the one whose magic is sealed. The second is to convince the one who did the sealing to undo it."

He snorted derisively. She shook her head. No, that option wasn't truly viable, either. That left the third. Could she live with it? If he didn't take this last course, what lay ahead for him?

Failure. Death. Both wrongfully wrought by those who didn't care to understand.

"The last is to kill the one who locked the magic away." She raised her eyes to meet him, saw them glimmer darkly. She had to ask, though she already knew the answer.

"Who did it?"

"Oknare."

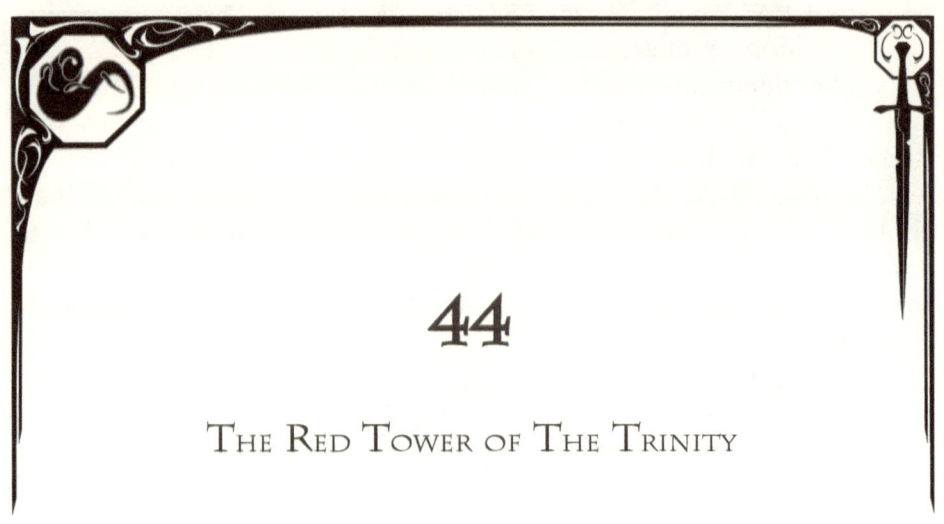

44

The Red Tower of The Trinity

B A'TVIAN followed Nerisse through the winding roads of the city. All around him were things that he remembered: shops, eateries, homes, fountains, statues. It triggered a sense of nostalgia, one that warred with purpose, banked rage, and hate. The streets were crowded. The Shadows had informed him that there were more people about than usual, that their mood was agitated. The search for him was on, just as she had said.

The elf was a puzzle to him. He had no exposure or experience to her people or culture prior to this, could not fathom why she had gravitated towards him. His escort, however, had seemed to expect her. They had not questioned her presence at his side, as he did. Instead, they were…anticipant. They wouldn't explain it. They never did, so he didn't bother asking or demanding.

He did feel though a weight with her beside him. There was something that he needed to do regarding her, something he was only just beginning to make out the shape of. For now, however, he shelved the feeling. Another task needed his attention.

Such as the city guard that trailed behind them.

Nerisse had taken no notice of them. He gave silent orders to his largely invisible contingent then moved up to grab her arm.

"We're being followed." He watched as her eyes darted behind him and back. "Ignore them for now. Find us a more isolated route."

With barely a nod, she turned down a side alley. Elsewhere in the press of people, someone screamed. She jerked in surprise, half-turning back before he placed a firm hand between her shoulders to propel her forward.

"Don't look. Just keep moving."

They left the crowd milling in confusion. The city guard that had been tracking them was slowed. By the time they made it the alley mouth, Ba'tvian and Nerisse were long gone.

45

The Hall of the City Council,
The Red Tower of The Trinity

REPORTS poured in via runners or mage-sendings. The Gold Tower had been thoroughly combed over to no avail. The fugitive was not there. The search of the Red Tower was still ongoing. Trouble had broken out on Carter's Street, one of the main thoroughfares of the city for people during the day and goods during the night. Someone had attacked a woman, slicing her thigh. The wound was superficial, yet the attack only served to confirm Ba'tvian's presence on the tower. The woman hadn't seen her assailant, stating that she'd glimpsed a flicker of something dark right before whoever it had been had cut through her dress into her leg.

While the city guard sorted out the mess, Oknare grimly conferred with Hamal and the Council.

"The College of Magery has been temporarily closed, the students evacuated away from the building."

"Do we have the guards in place yet? The mages, as well?" Hamal demanded.

The Captain of the Guard nodded.

"They're ready. Wish we had that Mancer fellow, though." He grimaced, flicking a glance at Oknare. "I know your school has Adepts and Masters in plenty. Still, this one's reputed to have shadow demons with him. Mancers deal with daemons, not us, not you."

"I understand perfectly, Captain. If Mancer Omine had sent his warning prior to when he did, we could have brought him here. Ah, well." He shook his head, pinching the bridge of his nose. "That's done. Has anyone managed to locate Nerisse, my student?"

"No. She was spotted briefly on Carter's Street before she was lost in the throng." The guard's mouth set grimly. "She was with someone else, a male we couldn't identify as a fellow student. Would she have any friends among the resident non-mages?"

"I suppose she might." The Adept frowned. "I really don't know."

"She seemed willing to be with him, whoever he may be."

"A friend, then. Not Ba'tvian." Oknare gave a humorless smile. "She wouldn't stand for what he's done. Will your men continue to keep an eye out for her? Ba'tvian is the priority, I know…"

"That we can do."

"Then let us go," Hamal said, drawing everyone's attention. "We have a trap to bait."

46

The College of Magery,
The Red Tower of The Trinity

THEY entered through the seaside terrace. Nerisse no longer led the way. Ba'tvian had pulled her back, using the Shadows as scouts to check what lay ahead. He was not surprised by what they'd found. No students. No staff. Guards in plenty, and in the room Oknare called his office, his former master waited with the High Judge who had damned him.

Yes, he could what they intended.

He forestalled the inevitable conflict in favor of another goal, seeking out the library. The college hadn't changed in the time he'd been away. His memory was a map, one he knew so well that he didn't have to think about using it, or the torch he'd brought with him. He knew things about the building that its keepers never knew or told, the secret nooks, the hidden crannies, the loose building blocks in the back of a maid's closet.

Despite the lack of faculty and pupils, the halls were still a danger zone. Twice, he had to detour around armed patrols before he got into the closet. Once there, he set Shadows as lookouts so that he could inspect the back wall. Nerisse hovered nearby, chewing her bottom lip distractedly. His questing fingers found the block edges, felt them shift when he pushed. Satisfied that the way in hadn't been sealed off, he turned to the rest of his Shadows. They slithered up to him, their eyes gleaming in the darkness of the room.

"Go," he commanded, gesturing to the wall. "Look."

They glided to the loose blocks, their bodies seeping through the stone work.

"Where did you find them?"

He looked up at her whisper, debated his answer. Finally, he shrugged.

"They found me."

"What are they, exactly?" She flushed a little under his gaze, her blue cheeks showing a faint blush of purple. "They don't seem to be evil or particularly violent, and they don't fit any description I've ever heard of before."

"They are Shadows – the Shadowed Ones." *They are mine. They chose me.*

A Shadow slipped out from between the block in the wall to swirl around his feet.

There is no one. The way is clear.

"Good. Now…" He bent to the wall and pushed. The stone gave way, hesitantly at first. He crawled through, then reached a hand back for Nerisse. "Come."

She obeyed.

47

The College of Magery Library,
The Red Tower of The Trinity

NERISSE didn't know what it was that Ba'tvian was looking for until they came to the library vault. It stood in a hidden alcove behind desks of archivists who maintained the books, with its narrow double doors of bronze facing away from the shelves and tables. Though she had never seen it before, she that inside were the forbidden texts on the higher forms of magic. Curiosity ensnared her immediately. She'd always wanted to look through them, see what mysteries they contained. Hadn't she?

I've never really thought of it before...perhaps that desire was there all along...

She was pulled out of her reverie by the frustrated slamming of a fist on the heavy doors in front of them. Ba'tvian cursed under his breath, the anger so keen in his voice – so like intense grief – it made her heart ache. Reaching out, she lightly touched his shoulder.

Emotion swamped her. Grief, fury, despair, anger, hate, that ever -present sense of looming failure. It swept through her mind like a raging storm. They'd taken his magic – he couldn't get through – if he couldn't do this, he would never succeed – She felt her eyes sting with the tears that he wouldn't shed.

"You can't work through the warding on the doors," she murmured, wiping those tears away. "Perhaps – perhaps I can, if you tell me how."

His head angled away from the door, towards her. His eyes were black with the same storm that she now experienced. When he spoke, his voice was low, harsh.

"Why?"

"I don't want you to fail." Her eyes welled up again; she fought to keep it in. "If you fail, you die. I don't want you to die."

He stared at her, through her, for a long moment. Shoving himself away from the vault, he stepped up to her, grabbed her chin. Her breath caught at his touch. A warm thrill traveled from belly to sternum. He nodded once, slowly.

"Reach into my mind, let me in yours. I will show you what needs to be done."

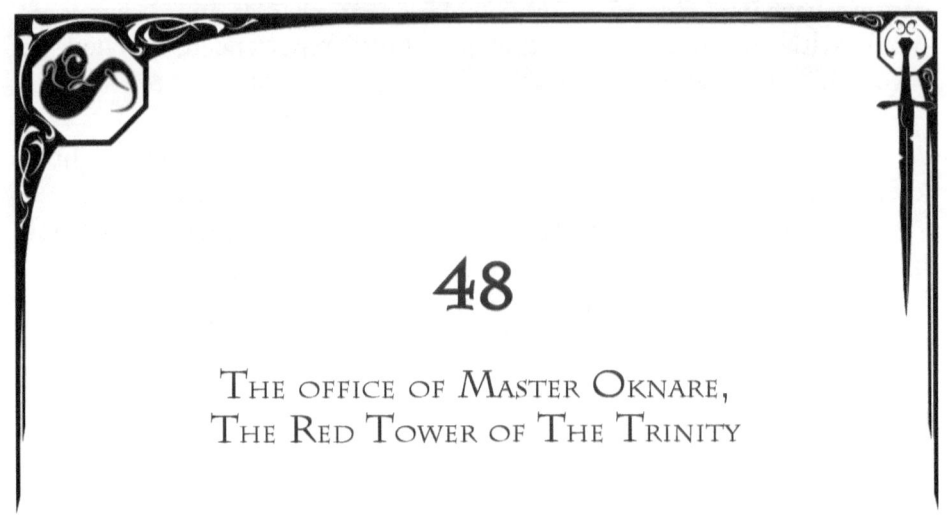

48

THE OFFICE OF MASTER OKNARE, THE RED TOWER OF THE TRINITY

"T HEY'RE jumping at shadows out there," Hamal commented when he entered the room. He had ventured out to check with the patrols and take a turn through the nearby halls himself. Though not a mage, he was a trained warrior, having risen through the ranks of the guard before becoming a Judge. As experienced as he was, however, Oknare had fretted over his friend's absence.

"Wouldn't you? Good God, Hamal, you saw what he did to the crew of the *King's Folly*." He shook his head at himself, rising from his desk to pace around the room. "I'm turning into an old woman, my friend. Why did I choose to be closed in my office for this?"

"There's only one way in, one way out. We know his direction of approach here. I just wish we could say the same of his current location."

The adept huffed to himself. No one had gleaned so much as a hint as to where Ba'tvian – *the fugitive; I must keep that in mind* – was. The trap had been set for hours now. Despite the long days he'd spent in this office, the moments on enjoyment that had cropped up there amid the collections of books, scrolls, and papers, it was becoming more like a prison cell with every second that passed. The wait was getting to him.

"Why don't you make yourself some tea?"

"Yes. A good suggestion." He smiled weakly as he puttered around, gathering his implements. "It seemed so easy on paper and in discussions. I hadn't thought about what it would feel like."

"You're holding up well enough, Oknare." The Judge cocked a chair towards the door as he settled into it. "I'll admit that I'd hoped to be done with this before nightfall, though."

"The Shadows…" He paused in his measuring of the tea leaves. "You said that they're jumping at shadows?"

"They know what to look for. The descriptions you gave us were quite clear. It's just that mind plays tricks when there's nothing but fear and waiting while on guard duty." Hamal grimaced.

"I can imagine." The mage poured water into the kettle, then hung it over the small fire going in the hearth. "He'll show. Eventually. Has anyone thought to check the library? It occurs to me that he might detour there."

"Would he be able to get into the vault? It's rather heavily protected, isn't it?"

Oknare hesitated, then shrugged.

"I honestly couldn't say what his capability is now. We stripped him of his magic, yet blood mages tend to find ways – "

Stars exploded behind his eyes. All went black.

49

The College of Magery Library, The Red Tower of The Trinity

B A'TVIAN hit the bookcases lining the wall hard. He fell to the floor, momentarily stunned. He shook himself aware as the Shadows began to drift in around him. They hummed in his mind. The melody conveyed approval, a kind of joy. His thoughts cleared, the aches from the bone-deep bruising he'd received vanished.

Climbing to his feet, he took stock of his surroundings. Books, papers, and odd burn marks were scattered about him. The marks emanated from the two bronze doors of the vault. They now sagged on their hinges, the metal warped and glowing with the familiar patterns of magic that had once warded them. Ragged lines of blood red fractured the designs, the color having taken the master pattern over.

A few feet away, Nerisse lay.

"They would have heard that. Oknare may have felt it. Guard the entrances. Kills are permitted." He felt their eager pleasure as they flowed away from him. Their interference would buy him time – time he needed to take what he wanted, and decide.

He glanced at the elf girl. She was a tool, a good one. With her inexplicable predisposition towards him, it might prove wise to keep her. Remembering her willingness to submit to his mind, the surreal experience of feeling her attraction for him, he moved towards her. There may yet be other benefits to be reaped at a later point.

He knelt beside her, checked her pulse, found the rhythm strong. Sensing that the door to her mind was still open, he slid inside.

Having had little practice at this, he wasn't gentle. One command was forced into sub-consciousness: *obey.*

"Wake up."

She moaned. Her eyes fluttered open. He waited until they focused on him.

"You did well." Strange, he thought. How strange it was to say those words to someone else. "Come. We must hurry."

Helping her up from the floor was an afterthought. He did it almost reflexively, then led her into the vault, still holding her hand. The cramped space inside looked very much like the rest of the library. Surrounded by the forbidden texts, he pulled her forward. He took out the torch, gestured for her to light it. She wordlessly raised a hand, a spark flying her fingertips to ignite the brand.

She looked so pale and fragile in the firelight.

He felt an inner prompting. He didn't question it; none of these near-instinctive urgings had led him wrong before this. Taking a small dagger from his belt, he pricked his finger, watched the blood bead. Then, looking into her eyes, he drew his sigil, the one he had chosen for himself in the months during his exile, on her forehead. The blood gleamed eerily.

We will change the world, his mind murmured to hers. *With you by my side, I can do anything.*

"Yes." The word was a breathy whisper, barely audible.

His finger smeared his blood on her lips. His mouth took hers. As she yielded to him, he knew that her life was his.

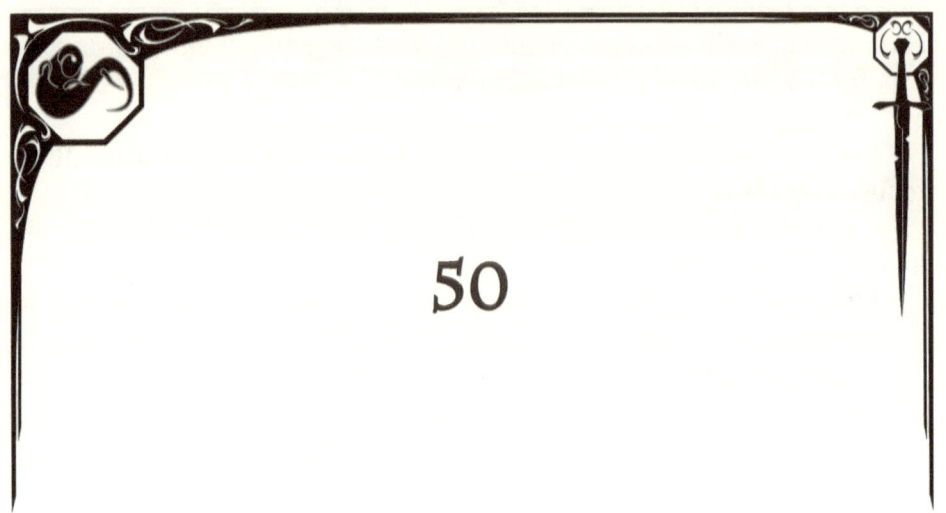

50

"YOU know what must be done now."

She nodded as she took up the next stack of tomes they were taking. Her mind seemed to drift through a fog. The unraveling of the wards, the explosive force of it, then the kiss – she couldn't think. It blurred her thoughts, overwhelmed her senses. So she did as she was told, gathering the tomes to be gated out once the deed was done. She turned to collect more and found him watching her intently. Wordlessly, she went to him, taking the books he held.

He grasped her wrist with one hand, her chin with the other. His eyes searched hers.

"Too much for you, is it, Nerisse?" He said it softly. "Would you rather remain here, prepare the way for us, while I deal with matters?"

"Yes." Relief pervaded through her. Had she really dreaded seeing it that much? Of course, she had. She was fond of Master Oknare. He was wrong, so much of what he believed was wrong, yet the man himself had been pleasant, father-like.

"Needs must, Nerisse."

"I know." A tear welled up, overflowed. He brushed it away, his face determined, intent. There was no disapproval, only…purpose, she thought. He was right. It needed to be done.

"Stay then. You have made your choice. For now, that is enough."

She nodded again. Watching him leave, she silently wished him luck and success. She knew what choice she'd made. She wouldn't be a priestess of her people. She wouldn't be a student to one of the foremost adepts of the Trinity. She wouldn't be a woman left yearning for something she couldn't have.

She'd chosen her lord – and a different future.

51

B A'TVIAN moved through the library to the corridor without hindrance. In the hall, he found three bodies, their faces contorted in terror, their skin slashed to ribbons. He took a moment to admire the work. The Shadows, he mused as he stepped over the corpses, were quite skilled by now. He hadn't heard the kills being made.

As if he had called them with the thought, they appeared, sliding over the stonework of the walls and floor to cavort around him. Their anticipation hummed in his blood. His own excitement was rising within him. He kept it in check. He knew he still needed to think, to plan.

Mentally, he directed his daemonic escort to fan out ahead of him. They had cleared the way. The knowledge of that slithered into his brain. Even as it did, they understood what he meant for them to do. With an uncanny lack of sound, they fairly flew away and out of sight.

Even as he moved through the school to the staff offices, Ba'tvian reached out with his awareness to touch the minds of those he'd sent here months ago.

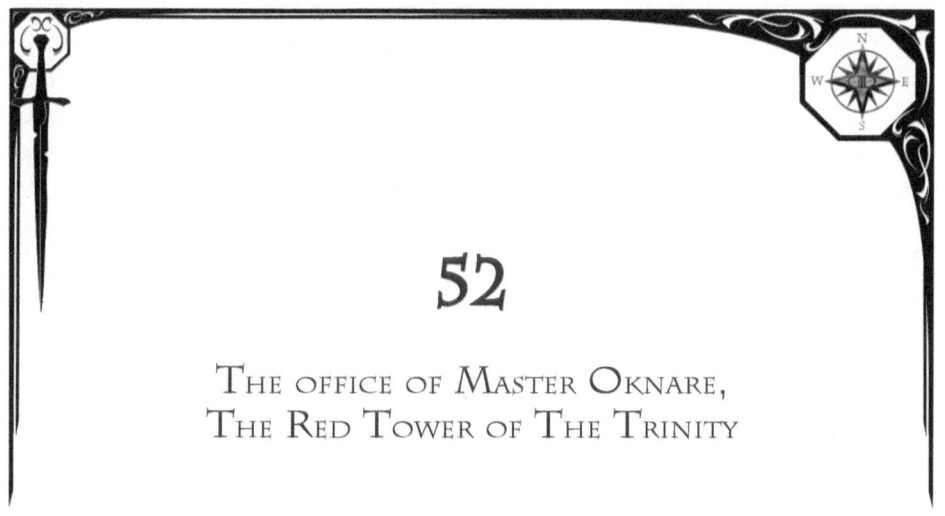

52

The office of Master Oknare, The Red Tower of The Trinity

"THE halls are empty. I can't find anyone else about."

Grim worry edged Hamal's voice. Oknare massaged his throbbing temples, cradling his head as he listened. They were alone in the college. The trap had been sprung, with deadly results. Hadn't Absol once told him that Shadows consumed the dead?

"Perhaps it is best that we left, Oknare."

He looked up at his friend, shoving the pain from the forefront of his thoughts to respond.

"It wouldn't stop him, my friend. We can end it now. The preparations are in place. Running will only prolong it, kill more people." Running might endanger Nerisse. He prayed that she was far away from Ba'tvian's path of destruction.

"If you're certain you wish to finish this…" The judge looked resigned, the lines around his eyes telling of his mental fatigue and growing anxiety. When had he started to show his age? He didn't remember him looking quite this old, gray hair aside.

"I am."

He straightened in his chair behind the desk, closing his eyes in concentration. Stubbornly disregarding the nasty headache the breaking of the vault wards had given him, he checked the magically elements of the trap. He'd augmented those wards after discovering Ba'tvian's practices, he remembered. He should have known, should have anticipated, that he would find a way to break them.

One of the other adepts could have reset wards on the vault. I wouldn't have this bloody pain wracking me, if I'd only thought of it.

The magical triggers were ready. He would trip them once Ba'tvian entered the room, then the "cage" would snap into place around him. Once that happened, it didn't matter what the boy did. Oknare could die and it would still hold him long afterwards, deflecting any power he cared to use directly back at him. The mage-born construction was of his design, yet not his making. The adepts who had built the trap under his supervision were now at the Gold Tower, awaiting its activation.

"All's ready, Hamal."

There was no response.

Frowning, he opened his eyes, on the verge of asking his old friend if he'd heard him. Shock hit him hard, stole his breath.

The judge sat in his chair. His head lolled back. His eyes bulged, his mouth gaped. The expression was one of surprise and horrific realization. Blood trickled from a gash at his throat.

Too little. It was too little blood for a wound like that, Oknare thought distantly. He got jerkily to his feet, fumbling for a handkerchief. He knew it wouldn't do any good. He couldn't seem to do anything else. Stumbling to Hamal's side, he pressed the cloth to the wound.

Two leprous white points of light glimmered in the air just about the neck. Falling back, Oknare stared as a Shadow materialized, it's maw fastened to his friend's throat. It stared at him with its gimlet eyes as it suckled the injury. Then it lifted its head. Blood spilled freely onto the floor, soaking the rug.

"By the One," he murmured in a hoarse croak. "You –"

We. The voice slithered into his consciousness like a viper made of razors. Fresh agony exploded in his mind. It was blinding. *We are here. To serve, to guide, to follow. His time has come.*

Clutching his head with one hand, he scrambled up from the floor. He staggered back, hit the desk. Blinking his vision clear, he saw them. They were everywhere. Some were wisps of darkness on the grain of the stone, the spines of his books. Others were large, bloated, not nearly as transparent as their smaller brethren. Fear gripped him.

"Shadows."

Frantically, he began to call up shields, magical defenses. Something brushed against his legs. He looked down. The sight of four of the things coiled around his calves had his mind stuttering.

We are many, they murmured. *We are legion.*

The door creaked open.

Oknare looked up. Former master and student regarded each other. In that moment, nothing moved. Then the adept flung his mind at the trap's trigger, gathering power to activate it.

"My Shadows have your Nerisse."

No.

Shock reverberated in the older mage. The swelling magic hesitated.

Shadows swarmed up his body. Teeth sank into flesh. Blood fell in tiny rivers and droplets on the floor. Instinctively, he called on his power. Raw, wild magic arced like lightning around him. It struck his enemies relentlessly. Black bodies smoked, cooked, degraded. Still, they hung on, bleeding the mage from dozens of wounds.

Suddenly, the pain faded. The magic display vanished. The Shadows glided calmly away from him as he felt his body slump in slow motion to the floor. His gaze tracked their departure, his own descent. Gradually, his eyes drifted down to the dagger hilt protruding from his chest.

Footsteps echoed in his ears. The sound of them pulled his face upwards as if on a string. Ba'tvian crouched in front of him.

"I lied." He smiled as he said, his dark eyes cold and filled with hate. "She's safe. Isn't that nice to know, Oknare?"

*He...lied...*His thoughts were beginning to slur. His body felt chilled. He knew what they meant yet clung to those words. Ba'tvian had lied.

The younger man leaned in close, grasped the handle of the knife. He pushed it deeper. The adept barely felt it.

"Here's something else you should know."

His vision was graying at the edges. He struggled not to black out.

"She's mine."

Yours...? The thought formed the word. The lips refused to.

"Yes. She chose me, Oknare." A maddened light glinted in the dark eyes. It was the color of fresh blood. "She chose me, knowing full-well what I am. I'm keeping her. If it hadn't been for you, she would not have been here. She wouldn't know me. She wouldn't be *mine.*"

His vision failed. He heard the suction of flesh on the blade as it was ripped free. Despairing grief consumed him as death claimed him.

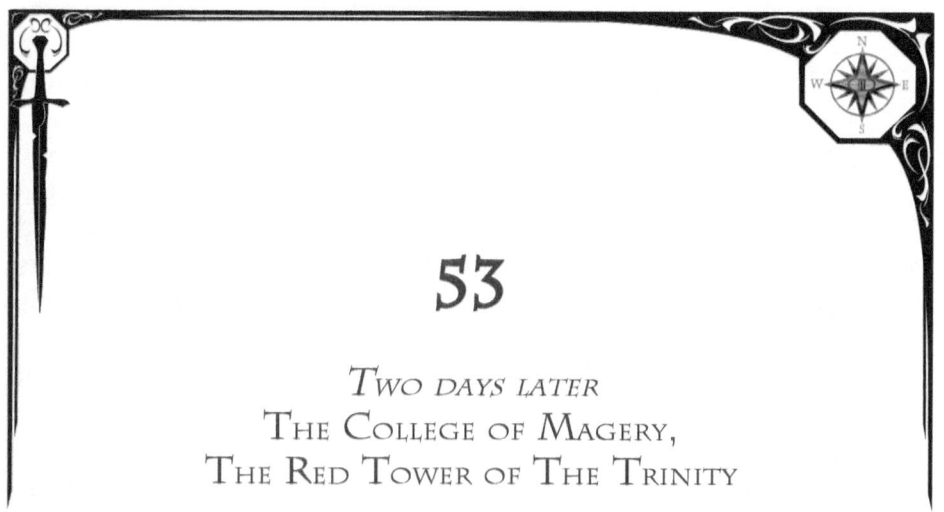

53

Two days later
The College of Magery,
The Red Tower of The Trinity

M ANCER Absol Omine stood on the terrace, at the back of the
crowd. On a raised platform at the terrace wall overlooking
the ocean, was a long row of caskets. The lids were closed. The
standard of the Trinity Guard covered all but two. One was dressed
with the colors of the college. The other bore the flag of the Red
Tower.

Arrayed in front of him were the faculty, guards, students, and
residents of the city. Some wept, some prayed. Most just listened as
the Red Tower's Council gave the eulogy. As for himself, he could
only stare at the boxes containing the men he had known all too
briefly.

He hadn't gotten here soon enough. His initial message of
warning had somehow gotten lost; he'd been told that they had not
received a sending from him prior to his embarkment on the *Fisher's
Delight.* No one knew what had happened to the message. Because
of this, good men had died.

Part of him blamed himself.

He wasn't the one to blame. Ba'tvian had slain these men. He
had already been committed to the hunt as a Mancer. Now he
wouldn't rest until the blight had eradicated.

Of course, it isn't that easy.

He had a young charge to care for, one he hadn't seen in months.
The monks of Destiny's Way wouldn't be able to raise or train the

boy. Time would have to be carved out for that. He'd promised young I'k'Nole, hadn't he? Promised that he'd be a Mancer, his apprentice. Well, he would find a way to keep both commitments.

One of the school elders stepped up to his shoulder as the eulogy gave way to prayers offered up for the dead. Neither spoke as the final death rites were given. One by one, the caskets were pushed from the platform, over the wall, to tumble into the sea. Mourners congregated at the terrace's edge, throwing flowers and farewells scribed on paper after them.

"We believe he took Master Oknare's apprentice with him when he left."

The words confirmed a heavy suspicion. Absol nodded.

"As a convert, slave, or bargaining chip, probably." He turned to the grave man beside him. "Do you have reason to believe that she's a convert?"

"No." He sighed. "Her friends tell us of a curiosity she had. She wanted to know more about him, his circumstance. Some of them felt that she didn't altogether agree that he was evil or malicious, yet she didn't say anything to that effect."

"He's never taken a prisoner before this." Sacrifices, yes, and tools. All were discarded in a permanent fashion once their usefulness had expired. "He might well have taken her to turn her. I understand that he escape through a gate?"

"Yes. He managed to erect a portal – a gate – and pass through it. This indicates that all the blocks on his mage abilities have been broken."

"He is an adept then." Only mages of that degree of power could create gates.

"With proper training, he would have been an adept." The man sighed. "He will be a most formidable foe now."

"Yes, he will."

"You will still hunt him down, Mancer Omine?"

"Yes." Absol's eyes locked with his. "Or die trying."

INTERLUDE 10

ELSEWHERE...

LABIYAL Biyalban watched the mirrors in the dark. He had dismissed his servants, given his reports to both his sire and master. Now, he could enjoy some of the results of his work as he dined on fruit. Sipping from the goblet of red wine he held, he saw the funeral at the Red Tower draw to a close in one silvered pane. Its neighbor showed the sleeping forms of the boy and the elf girl. They were on the mainland of Orthanor now, sequestered in the wastelands of the dead Spirlan Forest. They lay in a tangle of cloaks in a den hollowed out of earth. Above them, was a roof made of the trunk and branches of a dead spire tree. The Shadows glided in deceptively lulling patterns around their bodies.

He allowed himself a small smile of satisfaction. Ba'tvian had done well thus far. He had studied hard, learned quickly, and proven his worth by producing his first gate. As for the girl... His lips stretch thin, continuing their upward curve. Her dreams, those little secret desires, made her malleable. She would be excellent as both Ba'tvian's helper reward.

He made a note to contact the boy under his guise as a fellow blood mage. The younger mage would want more information regarding the Mancers soon. It was also time for his fee to be paid.

Appearances had to be kept.

Now he needed to return to his other projects. Ba'tvian was the largest of the seeds he had planted along this road, but not the only.

The next era would be years in the making; those seeds needed tending in order to survive long enough to bear fruit. Until then, he would observe and guide.

Descent Into Darkness

Part 3

His Beast

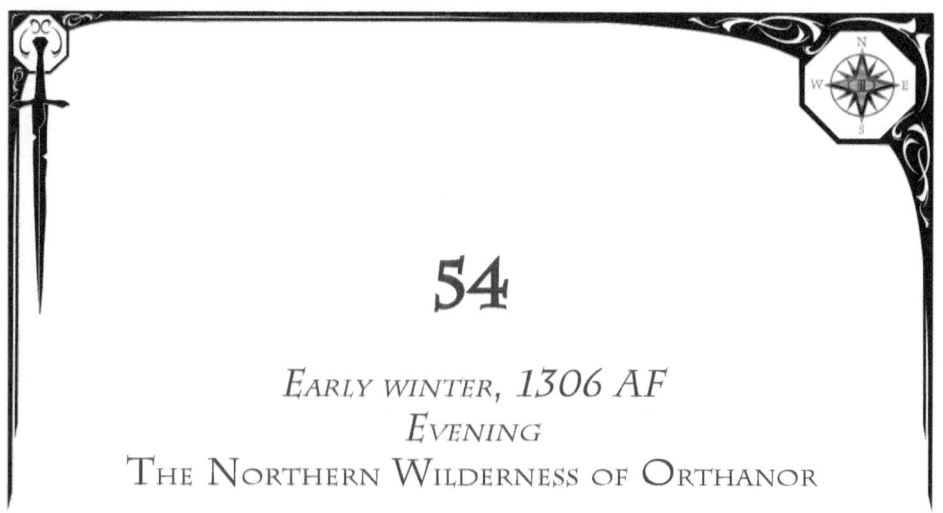

54

EARLY WINTER, 1306 AF
EVENING
THE NORTHERN WILDERNESS OF ORTHANOR

I T was a small cabin, the family crowded into the largest room for warmth. A hearth stood at one end of room, embers smoldering in the ash. On the opposite side, two braziers were eating through their portion of firewood. They, along with the thick bedding cocooning each person, provided heat to stave off the bitter cold outside.

Amongst the mounds of blankets and people was a dog. In the night time gloom, it was hard to make out the breed. The size, however, indicated that it could be one of those used for hunting or protection.

A silent order was sent out. Something began to slither in the dark.

The canine woke first. It roused with a snuffle, its bi-colored eyes darting around the room for whatever it was that had disturbed it. It clambered to its feet, shook itself, then began to inspect the murk-filled room. Working its way around, it paused by the window, stared at a semi-transparent shape bathed in moonlight. It resembled an over-large salamander, with broad flat head and no legs. It opened eyes of leprous white, its body bunching in on itself. The dog growled low.

It leapt. The canine lunged, jaws agape, a harsh sound reverberating in its chest. Behind it, the floor of bedding began to move.

The creature dove into the dog's maw, stretching thin. The

animal choked, hit the sill, coughed, yelped. The hind end of the creature, a vague shape of blackness, thrashed as it hung out of its opponent's throat. The canine flung its head about, still coughing, choking. The noises, the motions, became more frantic.

Blood ran in rivulets down the shadow's length to pool on floor.

Awakened by their pet's distress, the family scrambled out of their bedding. Three adults and five children gave cries of dismay as the dog collapsed in a puddle of moonlit crimson. The creature wiggled out of the carcass, looking more substantial that the ether it had resembled before. As the adults went for whatever weapon they could find, as the children screamed, it opened its flat, lizard-like jaws. With a sickening crunch of bone, it bit through the dog's head.

In the gloom around them, the rest of its ilk moved in for the kill.

55

B A'TVIAN Delthanurk stared into the eyes of the man as his knife cut symbols into his chest. He saw the grief, pain, mindless fear in the glassy depths. In a few short hours, this northern trapper had been stripped of reason, of hate, and filled with loss, with suffering.

He was, he reflected, getting better at it.

Around him, his Shadowed Ones slithered in an accompaniment dance. Light from the lanterns, fireplace, and brazier gilded their outlines, illuminating the corpses that littered the room. They lay waiting for his creatures which had not yet begun to feed. They would stave off their own hunger until he finished.

With the last rune drawn in living flesh, he drew back to check his handiwork. The placement was precise, the lines clearly defined. He was ready for the next step.

Up to this point, he had taken his time with his victim. Now he quickened the pace. Chanting the words to capture the life force as it was released, he cut into the body just below the ribcage. He thrust a hand inside, shoving his arm up into the chest cavity as the man screamed, and closed his fingers around the sacrifice's beating heart. A deft twist, a hard yank tore it free of its moorings.

He felt it, the beginning of death, the ending of life. It filled him, coursing through him like a drug, euphoric, erotic, exciting.

He brought the heart out, the body twitching, the vital organ still pounding in his palm. Life force, blood-born magic – *power* – was gathered in as he raised it above his head, chanting. Crimson liquid dripped down his arm.

He ended the chant with a triumphant phrase in a long forbidden tongue. The heart flared with a red glow before turning black. The ritual ended, he deposited the heart in a leather bag for later, motioning his shadows to take their reward. While they swarmed over the dead, he looked for a wash basin, found one in the corner of the room. He did what he could to clean himself up.

Ba'tvian didn't bother with gore lying around. He stepped around it, searched the larder, then the simple chests against the wall. He took food and clothing; what the trapper family had possessed was warmer than what he wore. With that in mind, he took the time to change out of his bloodied garb for the cleaner, heavier garments.

One of the chests had clothing of better quality than the rest. They sported fur-lining, more ornamentation, a finer weaver in the fabric. Trade goods, probably. He had no desire to trade, but knew the value of having such items in the region they were in. They could be a key into a settlement, if need be.

Coming upon a woman's embroidered cloak, he glowered at it. It was a beautiful article, colorful embroidery on brown velveteen with rabbit fur for lining and trim. Nerisse would want it. She wouldn't ask for it, wouldn't expect him to give it. Yet she would want, would hope. Then she would be disappointed when he didn't give it to her.

It was one of her more obnoxious traits.

The elven chit had her uses, however. She had been his first taste of sex, served to slake that thirst when the need arose. She was pretty, a little shy, an outward innocent. People trusted her. As bait, a lure, she did well. Her Empathy, her ties to the earth found them game and shelter in the wilderness. Her herb lore meant that their food was flavorful, their wounds or ailments treated.

In the two years since his old master's death, Nerisse had proven her devotion, her convenience. As his tool, it wasn't enough. He wanted more from her.

She was trying, however. He could not say that she wasn't. Still, she failed frequently. It galled him to find that flaw, that weakness, in a tool of his choosing. He didn't bother to hide that from her. It spurred her on, made her try harder to succeed, to please him.

He had to admit that her growing desperation to be what he wanted was something he enjoyed.

Perhaps...perhaps it was time to give her more incentive, however illusory it might be. He had been very careful not to make a commitment, though he demanded one from her. He slept with her, used his attentions as reward or punishment. There had been no gifts. Calculating, he considered the cloak. It might serve the purpose. He stuffed it into a satchel along with the other trade items he'd selected. Another bag held more ordinary, practical clothing as well as the food. Having pilfered what he wanted, he deposited his loot in the snow a ways outside the cabin, then went back inside.

The shadows had finished their meal. They turned their pale white eyes to him as he scanned the interior. There was only one thing left to do.

"It will burn."

Yes, lord.

The sibilant voices sounded sated, pleased. Those nearest the lanterns turned them over. Glass shattered, oil spread. Ba'tvian scattered the clothing he hadn't taken about the floor, soaked blankets with oil stored in one of the chests if they weren't already drenched in blood. Once done, he led the way out into the cold.

He paused by the satchels, looked back. A bare moment's concentration, a wisp of freshly harvested magic, and the interior lit up like the sun. When the glare faded, flames were consuming everything left inside.

Should a Mancer find his way here, there wouldn't be much left to tell him what had transpired or who had done it. One day, he thought, he wouldn't need to be so careful. He had plans.

He hefted his loot and left.

56

NERISSE shivered in the cold, the two cloaks she wore pulled tight around her. In the snowy woods surrounding the trapper cabin, she tried to ignore the icy gray, white, and black of winter even as she tried to once again to please him.

Pain lingered in the snow, the trees, having absorbed it from aura Ba'tvian had generated. If she pushed her consciousness past that, to the dwelling itself...

She did.

A thousand cuts – fear – bile – bitter tears streaming – lust – a blow, hard to the face – hate – the feel of the blade plunging in – shock – elation – a hand digging around in her chest –

A strike to her shoulder brought her out of the spiral before the scream could claw its way out of her throat. Dazed, she looked around her. The snow was clean, the cold not quite felt. That wasn't a good sign. She was in shock. Even as she realized it, her gaze tracked to the tree beside her, the one she'd fallen against when her legs had given way. That was what had brought her back. Numbly, she patted the bark, saw the purple tinge to her slate blue skin. She needed warmth.

She needed to pull herself together before he got back. He would not be pleased to find her like this.

The thought of Ba'tvian, her lover, her mentor, returning to find her in such a state galvanized her. She mentally reached deep into the ground, past the frozen soil, the organic strata to the fiery heart of the world. She fumbled a bit yet got a link established, one that allowed her to draw a minute portion of that heat into herself. She had done this several times in the past when temperature had dropped too low. Was it her, or was it more difficult this time? Perhaps, she thought, perhaps it was the shock.

As she watched, the skin of her hands, the only exposed body parts that she could see, gradually lost their purple tint. In the dim recesses of her mind, she heard the earth call to her. She always heard it, yet, in the last two years, its voice had become increasingly less intelligible to her. She didn't understand why. It was something to discuss with Ba'tvian when he was in a good mood.

Hauling herself out of the snow, she listened to the earth as it told her what he was doing. It told her of the blood, the death...the sex. That was humiliating. Weren't they lovers? Didn't they love each other?

She knew what he would say, that he'd taken another female because she couldn't be there. He had needs, and it wasn't as if there was any attachment between himself and the 'chits', as he termed them. He would have claimed her, if she had been there. He preferred her. That was what he said.

So I have to get past this.

It was the Empathy. That was the problem. She needed a way to blunt that ability, temporarily, in order to accompany him for the rites. There were herbs that could be used for that purpose. How long the effects lasted varied widely, however. At any rate, this far north, the only herbs that she would find to experiment with would require theft or bartering, and traveling to a town or village. She wasn't aware of any nearby.

She wished for a proper library to research. Ba'tvian had one, a small one, sequestered away in a sea cave along the coast. They were miles away from there, though. It was unlikely that he would want to turn back...

"Nerisse, what are you doing?"

The harsh question jolted her out of her thoughts. She looked up to see her lover standing a few yards away, his shadows gliding over the ground around him. He was wearing different clothes, she noted, with two bulging sacks slung along his back. She supposed he'd raided whatever stores the trapper family had possessed.

"I tried. I'm sorry, I tried." She saw the flash of irritation in his eyes, winced inwardly. The feeling of shame, of inadequacy, inched in, weakening her link to the earth. As the tie loosened, the warmth began to fade. She shivered in reaction. "Maybe another variation of shielding, an anchor shield –"

"Shielding has proven useless in solving your problem." The flat tone his used made her drop her gaze. "Anchor shielding cannot be moved once set up. The moment it comes down, you will be... afflicted."

She hadn't thought that through. By his expression, she should have. Silence fell between them as her mind searched for another option, a possibility that he might approve of.

"Is there a settlement anywhere?" she asked finally.

"I have already said that we will not go into any village, Nerisse."

"Yes, but – please, hear me out." She lifted an imploring hand when she saw anger cross his face. "I ask because they might have a healer or herbalist. They may know of a way to stymie my Empathy. If it can be rendered dormant for a short time..."

She let her voice trail off. She couldn't read his face now. He stared at her without a word, his narrowed eyes hard. Recognizing the signs of temper, her heart sank.

"I'm sorry. I shouldn't have questioned." Tugging at her cloak, she turned away from him, heading back towards their camp. She hadn't gone far before several of the shadow creatures blocked her path, watching her glinting white eyes. She stopped, shivering from the cold, and wondered what would happen this time.

There was soft thump behind her. His hand tugged her hood off, then fisted in her hair. She didn't fight him when he pulled her back against him. It wasn't violent, almost gentle.

"Your Empathy is of great use to me." He spoke the words into her ear. "I will not have it shut off completely."

"No, lord." She felt his hold loosen at the honorific.

"The nearest village or town is some distance southeast of here. You do realize that you have to deal with the healer yourself?"

"Yes." Was he agreeing to the suggestion?

"You are a woman of note, Nerisse." His free hand came around to draw the cloaks open, to run a possessive path over her breast, her stomach. "There can be no witnesses." He gripped her hip, his body rubbing against her backside. Heat and arousal began to simmer in her core. "Which means what, Nerisse?"

"I have to be careful. I have to be discreet." She let her eyes close as the sensation spread. He nipped her earlobe. He released her hair to fondle her breast through her bodice.

"And?"

"The healer. I'd have to kill the healer." It was getting hard to think. She felt hot wetness pool between her thighs. "Ba'tvian –"

"You've disappointed me, Nerisse." The soft tone he used was like a caress. "Do you want to earn my forgiveness?"

"Yes." She didn't have to be able to think to give that answer.

"Yes, what?"

"Yes, lord."

"Then we'll do something different this time, you and I."

He spun her around, kissed her hard as he grasped the neckline of her bodice and yanked down. She gasped as the fabric tore, as the chill air hit her exposed breasts. He kneaded one roughly as he broke the kiss.

"Kneel."

Her eyes didn't leave his as she obeyed. Around them, the shadows drew closer, intent, watching, waiting. He gestured toward them.

"Whatever they wish of you tonight, they will get."

She swallowed, shivering as she gave his followers an uneasy look. He had never shared her before. Always, he expected loyalty, fidelity. Faithfulness. This – was unexpected. Her gaze returned to his. In his eyes she saw darkness, anticipation, a wealth of knowledge – as if he knew everything she thought or felt, as if he understood more than she ever could.

It was one of the reasons why she loved him, why she'd do anything with him, for him.

Something touched her knee. She looked down as a shadow slithered over her lap, raised its lizard-like muzzle. Its tongue flicked out, rasping the underside of her breast, as Ba'tvian reached down to cup her chin, making her look up at him.

"You will think of me all the while. They will tell me if you don't." She licked her lips, gave a slight nod. The words settled her nerves. It wasn't sharing so much as feeding another need, wasn't it? He needed to test her again. Test her loyalty. She couldn't prove it – not yet – by participating in rites, but she could prove it with this.

"First, however," he began, tracing his thumb over her bottom lip as he unfastened his trousers. "You will please me."

It was hours later before they returned to camp.

INTERLUDE 11

ELSEWHERE...

WASN'T it interesting, what children learned?
    Within the austere confines of his study, Labiyal Biyalban watched Ba'tvian's domination of Nerisse in the mirror, thinking of how well the young man manipulated his pet. Of course, the methods he used could be turned against him easily enough if the girl ever managed to pull herself free of his will. Sex was a double-edged sword, as sharp as it was cunning. Yet Ba'tvian was being careful with her. For the most part.

It was remarkable that someone who had looked like anyone else, had grown up as a serf, could turn out to be so more. Brown eyes, brown hair, a body hard from work and wilderness survival. He was so similar in appearance to the poor man who had raised him – and unlike him in all other ways.

Thankfully, hiding his heritage was an easy affair.

"Observing your playthings, spawnling?"

His sire stood just inside the room, having been ushered in by a servant. Well-groomed, dressed in the dark robes of a Camen Desert noble that contrasted the almost white blonde hair he sported, the Daemon Lord Biyal had changed his appearance again from their last meeting over two years ago. Labiyal made a mental note to find out what his father was doing in Camen, if anything. He preferred to keep track of all daemon activity when possible.

Dismissing the mirror image with smallest movement of one

finger, he rose from his seat to greet him.

"Yes, Lord Biyal." He waved a languid hand to a table, set with food, drink, and a *chesra* game. "Would you like a report?"

"On a plaything?" The tone was condescending, a sneer visible in the black irises he'd affected. They seated themselves at the table as he continued, "No. Our King wants a report on the boy you've been nurturing."

"He has grown strong in his power." The half-daemon studied the *chesra* board as he spoke. "Though he is human, he has shed himself of most of humanity's morality. He isn't greedy as much as ambitious. He has plans for the future – plans that will benefit all of daemon-kind and our King in particular when the time comes for him to crossover."

The Daemon Lord's eyes narrowed.

"Beneficial in what way?"

"He will remove the obstacles, forge us a path, hand us a world that is beaten." Labiyal selected a minor game piece, moving it to another square. "The Mancers are his first test."

"The Mancers are strong in Orthanor, spawnling," warned his sire. "Do not risk our most promising opportunity needlessly."

"Strong they are, yet so is he. More, he thinks. Few do." He watched his father move one of the pieces, then countered it. "He has turned an Elvaraen earth priestess into his willing apprentice. He will gather others before he acts upon his plans." *I will see to it.*

"He remains ignorant of us?"

Labiyal thought of the Shadowed Ones, the ethereal brethren that were once his sire's daemon siblings. They followed Ba'tvian. Protected him, encouraged him, approved of him. What would Biyal say should he be told of it?

"He knows nothing of us." It was a kind of truth.

"How soon will he be ready to act?"

One, then two pieces shuffled into new positions on the game board.

"That depends on the course he takes now. An...opportunity will present itself soon." It was another of his many projects. Other daemons might think it a waste of effort. With the boy maturing into the 'key' their King sought over a period of years he could ill afford not doing all he could to ensure his success.

The more time is invested in him, the more my continued existence hinges on him.

"The first steps have been taken. The next will not be far behind," he assured his guest. Ba'tvian Delthanurk is not one to let opportunity pass him by."

57

The Northern Ice Fields of Orthanor

A fox trotted over the white expanse, heading for a cache. It sniffed at the snow, circling around the area, then stopped. It began to dig. Once the hole was deep enough, it rooted around, bringing up the frozen leg of a *dersti* calf. It dragged its meal out on the hole, before proceeding to fill it back in.

A nearby snowdrift heaved up.

The scattering of white made the fox leap back from its food. It barked a warning as a second drift exploded into the air, much closer to the animal. The fox bolted.

The barbarian known as Ibestor climbed out of the snow he'd been hiding in, barely noticing the fox's escape. Clothed haphazardly in layers of furs strapped together with leather thongs, with his dark hair and beard matted into rope-like locks, he looked like nightmarish bear. He trained his hazel gaze on the meat the animal had hauled out of the ground.

On the other side of it, another hulking form rose to shake snow off its pelt. It looked like a strange, twisted amalgam of several different creatures. It had the deer-like body and head of a *dersti,* the mouth of a wolf, and the paws of an ice bear. The places where the pieces came together looked oddly melted. As the man watched, a bit of hide from the thing's nose slid off. It left a glistening trail of yellow fluid.

It wouldn't last much longer.

He picked up the leg, sniffed it over, licked the stumpy end. Satisfied, he examined the fox's cache place. He gestured, muttering something intelligible. In response, the composite creature dug into the ground. It unearthed another frozen leg. Ibestor collected it. He came around to the side of the thing he had created. A pad of furs was strapped around its middle, with leather thongs threaded into to hold crude bags made of hide. One was full of booty similar to what he now carried, another held cooking or eating wares carved from bone. A third bag hung empty. He stuffed the legs into it.

Dogs barked on the edge of hearing.

The beast beside him twitched, angling its head away from its owner toward the sound. Ibestor peered over its back in the same direction, grunting when he saw the sleds headed their way. The local tribe had clued in to his presence. Even from this far away he could see the spears mounted with skulls – a symbol of war. If they closed in on him, they would do their best to kill him. It was time to move on.

He hauled his bulk onto his beast, wheeled its head around to face the south. Ahead of them lay the mountains of the Northern Ring, the single barrier standing between the polar region and the rest of the world. He had always known that he would have to cross them eventually. Having heard no tales of others who had come this way, he didn't know what to expect, only that it would be different from the endless ice, the wind, the snow storms. He wondered what kind of food he might find there.

With tribal calls echoing behind him, he goaded his mount into a gallop and set off for the unknown world.

58

THE moon is almost full.

Ba'tvian glanced up at the luminous object in the sky, more out of reflex than a need to double-check what he'd been told. He trusted his Shadows more than anything else living or dead. The reminder, however, hadn't been necessary. He had been contemplating his contract fee for some time now. It was something that was best done alone, which meant that his companion would have to be given a task.

It was a situation that he had long ago termed the 'monthly issue'.

He shifted the weight of the sack on his shoulder as his eyes slid sideways to the elven girl who trudged beside him as they traversed the frozen wilderness. She carried the rest of the goods he'd looted from the trapper's cabin. Her slate blue skin held a rosy tint from exposure to the cold, her silver eyes clear.

She had taken her punishment well, he thought, better than he'd anticipated. There had been no tears, no pleading, only obedience. Since then she has made more an effort not to be a disappointment or burden.

Still, that sort of…activity should probably be kept to a minimum. He had plans for Nerisse; he didn't want them spoiled because she'd taken interest in someone or something else. He remembered reading somewhere that sex with daemons could be addicting. Shadows were close enough to daemons that he didn't want to risk it.

She hadn't shown any attraction to them, however. Instead, she'd become skittish around them and made an effort to keep her anxiety from him. That stoic effort could warrant approval, he supposed. He considered rewarding her with that cloak he'd taken. No. It would be best to hold off on that until after his errand was complete.

He stopped walking, letting his burden slide to the ground. Nerisse drew to a halt as well, glancing at him curiously. Around them was desolate forest. A day's journey eastward lay a village according to his Shadow scouts, a settlement with a healer.

"It is that time." After two years with him, she knew what that phrase meant. "You will continue to the village alone. You will go forward with your plan as we'd discussed while I take care of this. Understand?"

She looked anxious at his words yet didn't protest the order. She tugged at her cloak, a thick, utilitarian one stolen from the dead trappers, before answering.

"Yes." She glanced up, meeting his eyes. "How long will you be gone?"

"As long as it takes." His reply was dismissive. One thing he would not tolerate was keeping her abreast of single thing he did. "I will need to make a portal to travel the distance. I need you to mask it."

She nodded, closing her eyes.

As she started to delve into the earth for whatever it was she was able to conceal his arcane signature with, he studied the surroundings. To travel anywhere through a gate, portal, crossing, whatever term people bothered to use, a mage had to know the destination. It wasn't a matter of noting the number of trees or committing a mental sketch of the place to memory. It was the feel, the unique signatures of life, of death. It was the season, the history that a place had witnessed, the things that it had experienced. A person could not see what truly mattered about a location with his eyes or a map. It took a mage of great power and knowledge.

Which was why, Ba'tvian supposed, absorbing the winter dormancy of the land, only adept level mages could cross the portals.

As he finished cataloging the imprints and impressions of the area, he saw that Nerisse was beginning to sweat. Frowning, he took in her expression of concentration, the tenseness of her body. She should have been done by now.

Abruptly, her features went lax. She sagged on her own frame, still standing as she took a shaky breath. A moment later, a tiny cloud puffed out when she released it.

"What happened?" If her abilities had been compromised then he would have to alter his plans. It wasn't a possibility that he was pleased with.

"I – I found it. What we needed. I –" She breathed in deep again before straightening. When she did, she seemed more herself. "I'm sorry. It was more difficult than anticipated. It – the link I have to establish with the earth didn't take root right away."

"Why?" Under his harsh stare, the elf wilted a little. Biting back a sound of frustration, he said in as careful, neutral, a tone as he could manage, "I am not...angry, Nerisse. I am...concerned. Why was there trouble with your link to the earth?"

"I'm not certain." She hesitated. "It – it might have something do with my people's beliefs. We – they – are devoted to the earth. It sustains them so they give thanks and praise. There are ceremonies, rituals that are performed that affirm that relationship. I have not taken part in them since leaving ho – them."

Though his face didn't give evidence to it, he noted the corrections in her speech with disapproval. Part of her was still attached to her race, to that subterranean cavern they called home. If his plans were to move forward, that tie had to be cut and cauterized.

Now was not the time to address it, however. There was something of more immediate importance.

"Links can be forged in many ways, Nerisse." Ba'tvian had crafted several through blood and sex to bind her to him. Who knew better? "Pay attention. I will instruct you in what to do..."

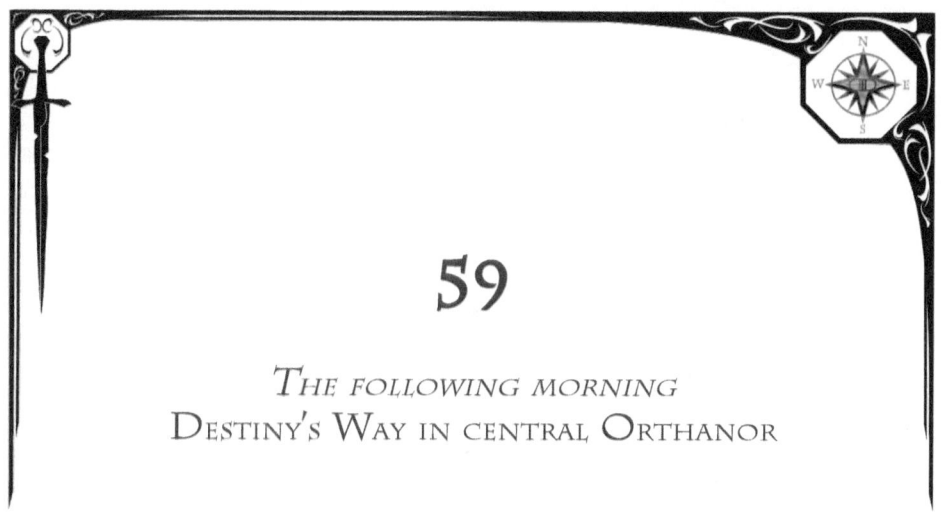

59

THE sun was just peeking over the horizon when the Mancer Absol Omine rode into the small village of Destiny's Way, his ribs aching. Most of the village-folk were already up and about their business: tending to kitchen gardens, opening shop, seeing to the livestock. When he was noticed, they stopped to give him a wave of greeting before going back to their chores.

He nodded back at them, not stopping to chat. His last hunt had left him with several fractured ribs. With them throbbing as they were, all he wanted was to get to the shrine, stow the horse in the stables, see young I'k'Nole, his friend the Abbott, eat, and sleep.

It was a small community yet far from insular as most small communities tended to be. They didn't hold much, the people of Destiny's Way: small plots of land, small houses, a few milk cows, goats, chickens. There were three barns, all communal. No large individual farmsteads, but a few fields that were worked by everyone.

Absol had never quite understood how it all worked, the sharing. In his forty-two years, he had seen anything quite like it. If there were hitches in the way things were handled, he hadn't heard of them. As often as he came here, he should have gotten at least a rumor about them.

He put it down to the Master Abbott's doing. The Abbott, Dannon, would put it down to the grace of the One.

As his horse took him down the only road that ran through the village towards the shrine that stood between the Wood of Destiny and settlement, he reflected on his old friend. Dannon was a devout monk, dedicated to the people around him, to his duties, to the greater good. They'd known each other since childhood – since the orphanage on whose doorstep they'd both been dumped. Neither knew their parents. At this point, they didn't care to.

That orphanage, a strict place of squalor and charity in the city-state of Chalbrooke, was no longer there. He wasn't sure what had happened to it. While it was in operation, it had served as a source of recruits for monastic orders as well as the Mancers. Dannon had gone to the Order of On'Desae. Absol had been taken by the Mancers.

They'd kept in touch. The Order worked closely with the Mancers in any case, providing shelter or provisions when necessary. When Dannon had been posted at the Wood's shrine two decades ago, he had opened his new home to his old friend.

It was the only place Absol called home.

The shrine's outer wall loomed ahead. Beyond it was the courtyard, the stable, the wing of rooms that served as the local inn. He rode through the open archway, wondering – again – why they bothered with the wall when there was no gate to bar passage. The one time he'd asked about it, Dannon had shrugged.

"It's always been this way," he'd replied. "From the day the shrine was first built after The Flood."

The courtyard was empty of anything except a few well-kept shrubs and flowerbeds. To the left was the stable, to the right, the inn. Straight ahead lay the shrine itself, joined to the stables by the laundry building and to the inn by the kitchen.

The Mancer dismounted with care as a slim monk came out from the stables. He looked like a willowy reed of a man, garbed in the un -dyed robes of the devout, a stark contrast to Absol's own gear of dark leather and chain mail.

"May I take your horse, lord? Your bags, as well?"

"Brother Filtan, you don't have to call me 'lord'," Absol returned with exasperation. The older monk only smiled at him. With a resigned sigh, the Mancer let the subject go. It was a longtime argument, one that he always lost. "Yes, you can take him. How are things?"

"Quite well. Your boy's been a joy to have around the place. He helps me out in the stables most every day."

The corner of Absol's mouth quirked up in a smile. The monk had said the same thing every time he came for the last two years.

"Good. He's with Dannon?"

"Yes, lord. They're breaking their fast in the kitchen. The cook made plenty. Baked fresh bread this morning, too."

"Then I'd better make haste before it's all gone. Thank you, Brother Filtan."

"No trouble at all, lord. I'll just see to your steed and deposit your bags in your usual room."

As the monk led the horse away, Absol entered the shrine's kitchen. It was a wide room, with most of the cooking space occupying the far side. Nearer to the door, three eating tables with benches had been set up. Two people sat at the middle table. One was a heavy set monk whose back was to him. The other was a raven-haired boy with violet eyes who sat opposite, facing the door. The scent of fresh bread, sharp-tasting cheese, sliced onion, and fried sausages filled the air. His stomach growled loudly in response.

The child looked up, gave a shy grin before dropping the slab of bread piled high with food onto his plate. He scrambled off his perch to run to him.

"Absol!" The boy stopped just shy of embracing the man, looking a bit uncertain. It had been a few months since his last visit, so he wasn't surprised. The Mancer solved his dilemma by pulling him into a loose, friendly hug.

"Mind the ribs, lad. By the One, I'k'Nole, you've grown." Absol pulled back to study his ward. The boy's head was at his chest now. "Your wardrobe will have to be replaced soon."

"Yes, that's always the case with youngsters, isn't it?" Dannon turned in his seat, amused. "Well, come in, come in. Eat something. Then tell us why we must mind your ribs."

"Some fool tried to resurrect his wife as she died in childbirth," the Mancer began as he took a seat. "Raising the dead always causes trouble. What he got wasn't his wife. It was a ghoul using his wife's body. It put up one hell of a fight when I was brought in to put it down. As payment, I have the guild fee, plus a couple of fractured ribs that have to heal."

"So you'll be staying some time to recover," Dannon said as more food was served.

"A few weeks, at least." Absol began to pile sliced cheese and onion on a piece of bread. "What has been happening here?"

They spoke of everyday things as they ate: the communal harvest, the shrine's visitors, I'k'Nole's latest achievements, anecdotes of traveling and people. When the food was gone, mugs of strong hot tea sweetened with honey were passed around the table. The conversation turned more serious. I'k'Nole listened quietly, drinking his tea as the men talked.

"What news have you of Ba'tvian Delthanurk?" the Master Abbott inquired, sipping.

The Mancer gave a snort of disgust.

"Found his trail in Iverness a few months back, as I'd been told I would." A traveling merchant had passed that rumor on during Absol's last visit to Destiny's Way. "I tracked him from there to the Relds," he continued, referring to the boggy marshes to the north-west. "I lost him there. Followed a few leads, rumors mostly. Still, the trail had gone cold. I left messages for the other Mancers in the area, then came back." He sighed.

"I've been hearing nightmarish tales from people who have travelled northward." Dannon studied the contents of mug grimly. "Rumors. You may have heard them already."

"I've heard – and verified – attacks on remote villages, farmsteads, way stations. He leaves a bloody mess in his wake."

"I heard that the last hostelry on the Sradieen Trading Route was turned into a charnel house." His friend looked up at him, troubled. "Is it true?"

"The last hostelry?" He frowned. "That one escaped me. Timbrel is in that region. I'll see if I can't contact him tonight."

"Is there still no sign of the Elvanaren girl he kidnapped from the Trinity?"

"No." That worried him, frustrated him. It was as if the Lady Nerisse se li Astorae had vanished. "The blood, the death, the rites – they are all Ba'tvian's. No one else participated in them. We'd have seen the traces of their arcane signatures at the scenes, else-wise. He's done a good job of avoiding people, except for when he needs victims; he doesn't leave witnesses behind." Absol shook his head, set his mug down, lean back in his seat. "There's nothing to go on. For all we know, he's killed her, stashed the body out of sight, thrown her into the sea."

"He wouldn't keep her?" This from I'k'Nole. He watched the Mancer with eyes that understood more than a child of eleven should. It wasn't a youngster's gaze.

"It's possible, I suppose, but why?" Absol countered. "A prisoner would be too much to take care of all the time. What purpose could she serve?"

"What if she isn't a prisoner?" The boy's eyes went thoughtful, curious. "I mean, when Kurk and Elli got married, everyone thought it was his idea, but it was really hers."

Now he was baffled.

"Who are they?"

"Two of the local younger set. They ran off to Veltan to be married without a word to anyone, came back two weeks later." Dannon gave him a wry smile as he answered.

"Couldn't she have gone with him because she wanted to?" I'k'Nole persisted. "Maybe it was his idea, killing Master Oknare and all those people. She could have still gone with him if she liked him enough."

"From all accounts, she didn't know him. They'd never met before her disappearance." Even as he said it, Absol wondered if he needed to revisit the Trinity. There might have been something he'd missed. Nerisse had been sixteen at the time. Sheltered. Naïve. Could she have developed feelings for the blood mage? Was it possible in so short a time?

He had no idea.

"Never thought of it, have you?" Dannon rose to get the tea kettle from its hook at the hearth, then the honey pot from one of the counters. He brought them back to refill everyone's mugs.

"No. There didn't seem to be a reason to." It was an unlikely new angle. Still, it was much better than the nothing he'd had before. "I'll look into it." He noted the lad's pleased smile at the words, thought of his quick mind. He considered his age, the ambition I'k'Nole had intimated not long after he'd been found. Thought, too, of the future. "Are you still keen on following me? Becoming a Mancer?"

He nodded, his face becoming solemn, his eyes hopeful.

"I'll speak with the Headmasters. We'll see what they say. In the meantime, keep up with your good thinking."

The boy grinned in response.

"How long were you on the road this morning?" Dannon changed the subject as he spooned honey into his tea.

"Since well before dawn. A little after midnight, I think."

"You'll want some rest, especially with that injury." The Master Abbott stood, mug in hand. "We've chores to see to in any case. You finish your tea and take to your bed, my friend. I'k'Nole, take your drink with you. We're off to the vestibule to see to a few things."

Absol watched them go, absently sweetening his tea. Now that they'd left, he felt the weariness settling in. He decided to obey Dannon's order, taking his mug with him as he went to seek out his bed.

He would review the hunt for Ba'tvian from a new angle after he woke.

60

The Maltek Mountains,
on the edge of The Northern Ring

IBESTOR watched as the creature he'd made out on the ice struggled to live. The things he made rarely lasted for more than a few months. He felt no sorrow as the beast stumbled, as the hide split where the animal parts had been melded together. The fluids it oozed from its wounds had gone from yellow to red in color. The look in the eyes it turned toward him was one of confusion, pain, misery.

From where he sat in the crude camp he'd made the night before, Ibestor let out a sigh. Unsheathing the long knife at his belt, he rose, went to it. Grabbing hold of one antler, he tilted the head away from him. With a deliberate motion, he sliced the blade across the creature's throat. He watched the body collapse, shudder, then die with a detached curiosity. When it finally stilled, he hunkered down beside it to poke and prod. There was decomposition at the merging points. He studied them, thinking.

His creations usually held together better than this. He wondered if the flaw was in the selection of animals. Predators and prey didn't mix well on the Ice Fields. Until this past year, he had not even been able to meld them into a single beast.

He stood up, looked around. His mount's demise had left him with a quandary. He was in unknown territory, in the mountains. Somewhere in this vicinity could be another tribe. There was a ways to go until he reached the southern boundaries of the tribal lands. Beyond that border was a different world, one he knew nothing about. There'd been tales told of those who dwelled in the mountains, at least.

He needed another mount. It meant staying in the area longer than he wanted. He acknowledged the danger inherent to that necessity yet saw no way around it. He would have to be careful. Perhaps this time he would be able make a new companion that was all predator, something that could fight back as well as run. He just had to set his traps.

His gaze landed on the dead thing at his feet. He had bait for his snares, food for the night. He wouldn't waste anything.

Kneeling down once more, he began to carve up the carcass.

61

IT was already getting dark. Ba'tvian drew the cloak tighter around his frame as he stared at the stockade. Standing two stories high, the hewn trunks lashed together with thick ropes and pitch, it surrounded the entire village. There was only one point of entrance, a gate portcullis guarded by two interior men.

The village sat in the middle of a mixed forest; half the trees were bare for the season, the other half evergreen. Most of the Orthanorian north was covered with trees of one type or another. The variety of wood here was reflected in the barrier – the shades of color, the texture of the trunks. The villagers had taken notice of it, erecting the shaven trees in such a way to form a regular pattern. The artistic touch was lost on Ba'tvian.

He scowled at the barrier from his camouflaged position amongst the barren trees. This wasn't optimum as a target – too many risks, too few escape routes. Entry would be difficult, likely complicated. A portcullis gate was easy to shut, not so easy to open; the guards were not readily accessible; the bloody wall was too damn high. Each thick pole would have been sunk deep into the ground so digging under it was out.

He needed to get them to let him in…

Well, I might just have a way to accomplish that.

"Find out what they expect of a single traveling trader. Scout out the inn, if there is one, or whoever might be amenable to taking in a stranger for the night. Watch the guards, identify any potential threats." His orders were whispered to the creatures that skulked in the shadows, were part of them. "Return to me when you have what I need."

His Shadowed Ones crept out of the dark crannies of the forest around him, emerging seemingly out of nowhere to obey his commands. Retreating from his position, he returned to the evergreen in which he'd cached his belongings. He retrieved his things, dug into the loot sack, pulled out a woolen scarf. Doffing the hood of his cloak, he wrapped the scarf around his neck so that it obscured the bottom half of his face. Then he replaced the hood. He checked the rest of the contents, taking inventory. The more essential items – things that any traveler might carry – had been left with Nerisse. He had taken all the luxury items with him. Satisfied that he knew what he had, he counted what little money he had before gathering everything up.

He turned to find several of the dark lizard-like creatures waiting for him.

There is no inn, only a small tavern. They might allow you to sleep by the fire in the common room. The leprous eyes of one blinked slowly at him before it continued in a more disdainful tone. *The tavern is serving vegetable stew and bread.*

He sneered at the dinner. He preferred something with meat. Still, he could pretend gratitude for the meal so long as he kept his end-goal in mind.

There is one who would do well as payment, lord. This came from a second Shadow. Ba'tvian narrowed his eyes as the choice was described to him. The victim could be more difficult to transport, but not as likely to fight him. He considered all angles before nodding.

"That one."

By this time, the others came in with their reports. He took them all in, mulled over logistics, outlined another set of commands. He hefted his possessions to make his way toward the snow-covered road that led up to the gate of Winede.

His heart rate kicked up as he approached the portcullis. Doubts began to niggle their way into his mind. He ruthlessly squashed each one. He couldn't doubt himself. The Shadows would see it, know it. More, a leader that doubted himself was a leader doomed to failure.

If he failed now, only more failure would follow.

He concentrated on controlling his breathing. His heart slowed its beat. He was starting to feel the near drunken euphoria of anticipation spiking his blood. That was much better. As he walked, his mind cleared, the thoughts came fast.

He stopped at the metal grid blocking entry to the village. On the other side, the murmured conversation of the guards ceased. He could see them clearly now, rough men wrapped in wool, fur, and leather. They wore scarves as he did – dressed much in the same way he was dressed, in fact. The only differences were that their cloaks lacked hoods and they sport fur-lined helms with flaps that came down to protect their ears.

One of them came forward, placed a gloved hand on the bars.

"A bit late in the season to be traveling the north," he commented. "What's your name and business, then?"

"Cedane Harvier, originally of Menie Port. Been I need provisions, maybe a bit of floor space to spend the night. I've a little money. If that's not enough, I've goods I'm willing to trade." Ba'tvian watched the guard's brows rise.

"Well and good, but brings you this way? It's past the time for traders."

Ba'tvian suppressed a surge of annoyance.

"Though my wares are good enough, my profits have been lean. There was a blizzard over by Carter's Rock," he explained, referring to a small town to the east, "that caused me to over-extend my travel time. Lost some opportunities from that." He made a frustrated sound; he didn't have to feign it. "The rumors running around the north haven't helped any."

"Oh?" The second guard had come to gate now. Curiosity lit both their faces. "What rumors might those be?"

"You haven't heard of Ba'tvian? The blood mage that was exiled from the Trinity, the one that the Mancers have been hunting for the last couple of years? They say he's somewhere in the north."

"We've heard of him." The first guard's voice was grim. "Heard about what he leaves behind. What has he to do with you?"

"I'm a stranger." He shrugged, affecting a helpless air. "It's my first season trading up here so my face isn't known. People get spooked by what they aren't sure of when there's a known blood mage on the loose."

"True enough. You've a Trader's Guild chit?" the guard queried.

"I do." He un-slung the loot sack to free his hands so he could open a belt pouch. He took out a carved wooden disk the size of his palm, held it up to show them. On the face of it was seal of Trader's Guild, a quartered circle ringed by the guild's motto 'Provision of Goods to All, For Fair Trades or Barter'. Each quadrant presented a symbol of the business: the scales for fairness, a book for accounting, a wool bundle and a candle for general goods.

Ba'tvian thought the design mediocre at best.

"That's in order. We'll raise the gate."

He waited until the guards had lifted the portcullis well above his head before stepping inside. As they brought it down again, he scanned the village. Every building had been built much like the stockade: with shaved logs, thick rope lashings, and pitch. He turned back to them as they left the windlasses mounted on either side of the gate.

"There's the tavern over that way," one of them said, jerking a thumb to one of the central buildings. "No rooms to rent but you can sleep by the hearth there for eight pence. For twelve pence, you get an evening meal with the space. Breakfast is two pence, as it's usually what's been left over from yesterday's dinner."

"Thank you." He tried not to think about where the leftovers were stored overnight.

He left the guards, heading for the tavern, a windowless structure in the long cabin style. With every step he took, he analyzed his plans, went over his steps. He would blend better if he paid for the night and evening meal. He had the twelve pence. Besides, he could make sure to get it back before he left.

The tavern was empty when he stepped inside. The floor was more or less free of grime, which was always a good sign. The tables were also neat, well-tended, despite being scuffed or scarred. A fire burned in the hearth; it was the main source of light. It heated the room, chasing the cold he'd become accustomed to from his extremities as it did so.

A rotund man was at the bar, polishing its surface with a semi-clean rag. Bat'vian went over to him. The man looked up, gave him an appraising once over as he ran his cloth over the counter.

"New to these parts," he observed. " Just come through the gate?"

"Yes."

"I be Silmon. This is my place." He gestured with rag at the room. "What will be your pleasure, friend?"

"How much for a mug of something hot?"

"Hot tea is half-pence, hot ale is one pence." Silmon gave him a smile. "It's thick barley ale and the tea's brewed strong here. Honey for the tea is extra."

"Tea's fine. No honey." Ba'tvian produced the money, handed it over. Silmon filled the order from a kettle kept on an iron wood stove behind the bar. "Guard said you might rent the floor by the hearth."

"Yes, I do. He give you prices?"

"Yes." He took out the coins, left them on the bar. The large man swept up the money with one hand as he delivered a steaming mug with the other.

They spoke of trivial things as Ba'tvian sipped the tea, doing his best to stifle impatience, to play the role. When asked, he gave the same false name and story he'd given at the gate. In turn, he inquired about provisions.

"Don't often trade for provisions. More tea?" At his customer's nod, he took the mug, wiped at the spot where it had sat out of reflex. While he refilled it from the kettle, he continued. "I usually don't need whatever there is for barter. Now, I can do some asking for you around supper time, see if there's someone interested in sparing something from their larder. It's likely that someone will. What have you to trade?"

"Some cured hides, a few fur-lined cloaks. There's a nice lady's cloak, lined, embroidered. For that one, I'd want jerked or dried meat as well as bread and cheese." He took the mug when Silmon brought it back, made himself inject a little gratitude into his tone. "I appreciate the help there."

"We do what we can. It's vegetable stew tonight, good and hardy. It'll be ready in an hour." The man gave Ba'tvian another smile. "People will be coming in about then."

The blood mage's lips curved in response.

"I'll wait."

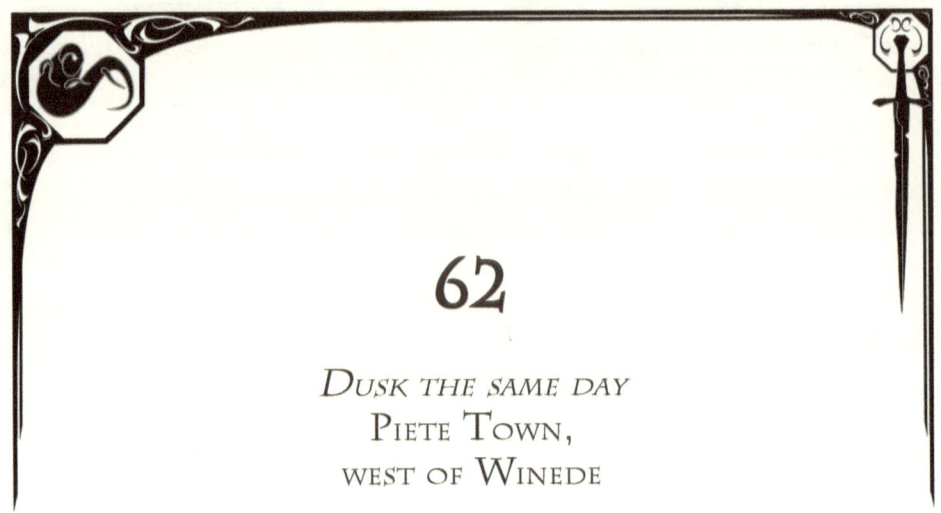

62

THE town was a hive.

Like most northern settlements, it was surrounded by a wooden stockade made from local trees. Unlike the other villages she'd seen, the earth had been mounded up high inside the barricade, with another row of erected trunks had been planted on that. Peeking out above the jagged points of the second set of thick poles were dramatic peaks of buildings.

The entrance was guarded, as one might expect. Two heavy doors were open at the first wall. At the innermost entry was a second set of doors with a mid-section consisting of a metal grid; these were kept closed. Between them lay a corridor hemmed in by earth and logs. Beyond the outer town barriers, the gloom of dusk, lit by torches the unpaved street bustled with carts, wares, animals, people. The traffic had churned the snow on the ground into a muddy slush.

The Shadows darted unseen amongst the townspeople, dodging feet, hooves, wheels. They flickered in the dark corners, slid into buildings through cracks. They listened to gossip, bartering, conversations between neighbors and friends. What they heard was not altogether pleasing.

Only one person spoke of the rogue mage killing in Orthanor. The man didn't even know the mage's name.

The people of the north would have to be educated. They would have to learn. Once they had, they would never forget Lord Ba'tvian's name.

Eventually, they drifted out of the town as silently as they'd drifted in. They left no sign of their presence behind. They found their master's pet in the woods, watched by several of their brethren. The elven chit glanced uneasily their way, then returned her gaze to the lone cabin she'd been looking at.

It was a small thing, built far enough away from the bustle of the town to be peaceful, yet near enough to be handy. Painted on the exterior walls were emblems of a healer. As most healers would tend to any wounded, regardless of who they were, one living in a lone cabin such as this was safe enough from most man-made threats.

It was full night now. The only light to be had came from the cabin windows. The temperature was dropping low enough that not even the winter garments the girl wore was enough to ward off the cold.

As they waited, the Shadows moved restlessly around her. Nerisse was dithering. If she did not move tonight, do as she'd promised their lord, they would have to do as they'd been ordered to do. A double punishment – one from them, and a worse one from him. The tool would break. That would be a waste for all.

Finally, shivering, she took in a deep breath, then walked toward the dwelling. The creatures ceased their restlessness to trail after her in the dark. Melting their ethereal bodies into the snow, they observed as she knocked on the door. A man opened it, a woodcutter by his dress, and the healer's husband. They spoke briefly before a pretty brunette woman garbed in green came to the door.

"I need help," Nerisse explained, her voice holding the faint edge of desperation. "I'm an Empath, and my ability is such that I sense most anything despite my shields. It's gotten so bad that I can't bear venturing into the smallest of villages to buy provisions or a bed for the night. Is there anything you can tell me, anything you can give me that might help?"

"I might. Come inside where it's warm. We'll talk. What's your name?" the healer asked, stepping back to let her inside. Nerisse didn't hesitate in her answer.

"Asha." Nerisse answered without hesitation. "Asha se li Vedeaea. Thank you so much…"

The Shadows glided in with her, slipping under the door, around the hinges, as it closed shut.

63

B A'TVIAN waited until well after the moon had risen, until the patrons had gone home to crawl into their beds. He had endured the cacophony of the dinner hour, the boisterous of the late night drunks. As Silmon had commented to him, there was little else to do on a winter night other than drink, talk, and making love with their women.

Ba'tvian, under his persona of the trader Cedane, had held his scathing opinion of the activity choices. Instead, he had calculated, watching the town's people interact, listening to their gossip. He spoke only when spoken to, suppressing the irritation he felt at their friendly overtures. His dislike of people in general, especially after having been on the run for the past two years, was something that gnawed inside him with teeth as sharp as razors. Yet he had done as needed to be done. Now none of them thought him to be a threat of any kind.

Silmon had mentioned a few people who might be willing to stock his provisions in trade for a cloak. He'd pretended interest in the names, had spoken to one of them during the evening meal. Arrangements had been made for them to meet in the morning to make the transaction.

By morning, Ba'tvian would be well away.

He shifted on the bed roll he'd situated by the hearth, opening his eyes to stare at the tavern ceiling. It was barely illuminated by the glowing embers in the fireplace. No one else shared the floor with him. It was a small piece of good fortune. Silmon was in his rooms above the tavern, and was the only other person in the building. One of the Shadows watched him.

All save the gate guards are asleep, lord. The sibilant voice slid into his mind like a ghost sliding through water. *The large one will not wake.*

What of the woman? Ba'tvian responded in kind.

Not far from here, said another. The transparent, lizard-like figure brushed lightly against his leg. The contact wasn't usual. They tended to keep a respectful distance. He frowned over it, wondering what it meant as it continued. *There is a back door, a way to be unseen by those still awake.*

Scout, watch, warn. They've dogs about. Take care of any that might sound an alarm.

He rose, his movements quiet in the near dark. He rolled up the bedding, packed it away. He might have preferred not to have the bulkiness of his possessions with him as he skulked through the town yet he had little choice. There was no place to stow it, and his exit would be have to be from the site of capture. Before leaving the tavern, he slipped behind the bar, into the kitchen. He took several food items, some seasonings, some dried meat. Then he snuck out the back.

He couldn't see his Shadows in the night gloom. He could sense them, was aware of the position and activity of each one. They had spread out around him as he had ordered. Their obedience was gratifying. No one else, not even Nerisse, made him feel like the lord of power he was destined to be.

That would change. It had to. So long as the world saw him as contemptible, as dirt, he wouldn't know true success.

One of his smaller creatures led him through the byways to a house in the middle of town. It whispered to him about the occupants: two adults, one child, no animals. The dwelling had only one way in or out. He had his minions drift through the home, relaying its layout, the locations of the residents, the state of the door hinges.

With eyes narrowed, he stood in the darkness just off the stoop to think it through. The more noise there was, the narrower his window of time. A full rite wouldn't be possible here. Disappointment mixed with disgust at the necessity to forego it. There were other ways, however, to leave his mark.

He delved into his belt pouch for a bit of thread he kept there. He ran it through his fingers, drawing it taut as he concentrated. The colored string began to glow a ruddy red. A faint wisp of smoke spiraled up into the air. He crouched down, holding the thread out to two of the Shadows as they crept forward. Each took an end almost reverently.

"The boy. Take him as your reward. He is to be shared with the others."

A child was a rare treat for them. They murmured their pleasure at the prospect as they eased through the cracks around the door.

Ba'tvian tried the latch, found it unlocked. He curled a lip at the complacency. They had to be a gullible indeed if they thought that the evil in the world wouldn't come to their door in the night. The sneer turned into a cold smile. That was about change.

He opened the door slowly, refusing to wince at the slight squeak in the hinges. Once inside, he shut it, locked it, then looked around. The house was small, consisting of three rooms. One was a common room with a small kitchen area in the corner and the bedrooms off the right side. The adults slept in one of the rooms, the boy in the other, the doorways blocked by hung quilts rather than actual doors.

He left his things on a small table in the middle of the room. As he stalked past the doorway nearest the front of the house, he heard the quiet frenzy of his followers, the gasping of a dying young thing. He paused to tweak the blanket aside. A window let in enough moonlight for him to make out a writhing black mass cocooning a struggling figure on the bed. The glow of the ensorcelled thread could be seen through the dark ethereal bodies, through the boy's throat where it had been wrapped tightly around. Hanging in the air was a whiff of burning flesh, the heavy scent of blood.

Pleased, he let the blanket drop back into place. He moved to where the parents slumbered in their bed. They lay side by side, the woman with her bulging belly facing away from her husband. Both wore sleep clothes. With silent steps, he approached the bed with his ritual knife drawn. Chanting words of power in a whisper, he sliced the man's throat open with one quick stroke. The man's eyes flew open, a gurgling sound coming from him as his mouth gaped open. Blood gushed out onto the bedding as the heart pumped. A hand reached up to the wound. The eyes unfocused, glazing over in death.

Ba'tvian didn't watch him die. The wife began to stir. He touched her forehead, seeking her mind with his. He found her open, very little in the way of natural defenses. Though he wasn't as adept as Nerisse, he implanted the compulsion to sleep. She mumbled something, fighting the command for a moment, then went limp as she capitulated.

The man's life energy hung in the air over the bed, a faint red haze seen only by a mage's eyes. The spell he'd woven as he'd killed the victim had prevented it from dissipating. Ba'tvian gathered it in. That done, he searched for something to bind the woman's limbs with.

He came up with a long scarf. He ran the knife down the middle of its length and used one piece to tie up her hands, the other her feet. Delving into the chest at the foot of the bed, he found a shawl. Again, he used the knife, fashioning a gag. Once the wife was trussed up to his satisfaction, he turned his blade onto the body of the husband.

He was precise in his butchery, in the carving. The runes he made on the corpse held only a fraction of the power they would on living flesh. The diagrams he sketched with the blood would retain nothing, unlike when they were drawn before the kill was made. Their purpose was to make a point, a statement.

Ba'tvian Delthanurk was to be remembered and feared.

By the time he was done setting the stage, his creatures were finished with their feasting. They came to him, fat and sated, their movements lazy. They waited while he brought his things the bloody bedroom, while he used the power from the fresh kill to open a portal that would take them elsewhere. Through the rift he'd opened in the fabric of the world, he could see the rocky precipice at the ocean's edge. Already, Shadows had gathered there to greet him.

He tossed his possessions through first. Then he gathered up the pregnant woman. He stepped through, allowing just enough time for his minions to follow. Behind them, the portal closed.

It was warmer here. Though winter could still be felt in the air, it lacked the biting ice of the northern climes. The ground was barren as far as the he could see, leading him to believe that he wasn't on Orthanor. Two years ago, after Ba'tvian had slain his mentor and regained his powers, he'd been taken here by his contact, told that they would meet here when possible. In the years since, Ba'tvian had not been able to ferret out the name of the place.

Setting the sacrifice down gently, he walked the few feet that took him to the cliff's brink. Far below him, waves crashed into the rock. It reminded him of his studentship at the lauded Trinity College of Magery. His exile. His vengeance.

There was still a debt for them to pay. The interest was building up.

Brooding now, he turned away from it to find his contact waiting for him. Dressed in the fashion of nobility, his hair and neatly trimmed beard the color of fresh blood, the newcomer watched Ba'tvian with golden eyes. He was an older blood mage. The Shadows vouched for him which was enough for Ba'tvian. Though the man's real name had never been given, they'd long ago settled on a use-name to make things simpler.

"I've your payment, Red." Ba'tvian gestured to the woman as he strode forward. "Your report?"

Red's lips curved slightly as he studied the sleeping woman.

"That's more payment than our contract requires. Do you seek a boon, Shadow Master?"

"It will depend on your report." Ba'tvian kept his gaze trained on the other mage. They might be contracted, the Shadows might have his back, but he couldn't bring himself to relax around the man.

"The Mancers have learned of your presence in the north. A few have caught the scent of your trail, though they haven't been able to maintain it for long. Timbrel Jodrek has come the closest to you. He is, however, several weeks behind. Absol Omine has returned to Destiny's Way." Red paused, his eyes flicking over the captive's rounded belly. "Would you like something to draw them off for a bit?"

Considering, Ba'tvian tilted his head. Around him, he could feel his loyal followers watching. The weight of their expectation lay heavy on his shoulders. Deflection, more running, would not win their approval.

It's time for a more direct course of action.

"No. I've something else in mind." Behind the scarf he'd kept twined around his neck and face, he smiled grimly. "I'll let you know when I want the boon."

INTERLUDE 12

THE EASTERN CLIFFS OF EXILE'S PERIL

LABIYAL Biyalban, called Red, watched as Ba'tvian Delthanurk opened a gate to take him back to northern Orthanor. His Shadow escort drifted after him. A few of the local Shadows went with him, he noticed. Interesting. The rest melted away into the night.

It was fascinating, how they seemed to know when and where he'd be. He'd watched them in his mirrors, knew that they had to communicate over long distances. If the boy figured that out, realized that he could gain his information from them, he might cut off their association. Labiyal hoped that he remained unaware.

He walked over to the woman, examined her carefully. Save for the mental compulsion that kept her in sleep, Ba'tvian had done little to her. The compulsion would fade in an hour or two. The bonds were secure yet didn't bruise. She was clean, garbed in a long nightshift suitable for the winter. There were no bloodstains on her clothes; nothing married her skin. She was, he thought, as pristine as any pregnant female could be. A sacrifice that was more than fitting for payment.

Ba'tvian tended to find victims that were more than fitting.

The boy was planning something. Labiyal, as Red, had given him more details as to where the Mancers were located, what they were doing, what they had found, before the boy had taken his leave. The younger mage had asked questions, rooting through the information for particular nuggets that could prove useful. Labiyal had to approve of the thoroughness. If, as had been indicated, Ba'tvian was going to do more than avoid, it would be a good change of pace. It would also segue seamlessly into Labiyal's plans for him.

The wind began to pick up, sweeping in from far out over the sea. As it ruffled his crimson mane, he reached into his jacket to bring out a small hand mirror. The ornate, golden frame seemed to glow under the moon, the silvered glass at its center shining with an inner light. The light dimmed, the scene of a mountain trail with traveler fading into view. The fur-wrapped barbarian was astride another monstrosity. It vaguely resembled a small dragon, though only in outline.

Labiyal took a moment to puzzle over the beast's components. He could identify only pieces of the thing that Ibestor rode. He supposed that what comprised it didn't matter. It would serve its purpose before it inevitably fell apart.

He considered the progress of this current project. The barbarian's route would bring him close to Nerisse, as Labiyal had intended. As for the elven chit...

The mirror's image swirled into another, showing him the girl in question. She lay on a bedroll by another fireplace, not unlike her master had done early that night. As he watched, she sat up, taking a long, careful look around the room. A Shadow drifted into view, its dull white eyes never leaving her face as it stopped in front of her.

Labiyal allowed himself a thin smile. Ba'tvian had almost completed what Labiyal had started for him two years ago. The boy had definitely come along nicely.

A low moan at his feet drew his attention. He glanced down at the woman as he tucked the mirror back into his jacket. He would keep her alive for a bit longer, he thought, save her for the task that Ba'tvian would give him later on.

He made a negligent gesture with one hand. A portal opened and two servants came through, their eyes cast downward. No orders had to be given. They gathered up the woman, then followed their master through the portal to his den.

64

The Healer's Cabin
just outside of Piete Town

THE healer's cabin was quaint, tidy. It was rustic, like most of the dwellings in the north. There were feminine touches here and there: a pretty table cloth, a few decorated vases, curtains at the windows, the woven rug in front of the hearth. The colors were warm, welcoming. The earth on which the home was built felt happy.

Nerisse regretted that what she was about to do would shatter that happiness. She hoped that the earth would understand.

Arrayed around her, half-seen in the faint light of the banked fire, were the creatures of which her lover was so fond. She tried to ignore them. They made her uneasy – always had – but since that night, she found herself more anxious around them than before. Especially when they watched her as they did now.

They won't touch me. He promised that they wouldn't touch me.

The Shadows never disobeyed Ba'tvian.

She had been right about the healer. The woman had known what herbs to use to dull the Empathic ability without interfering with any other talents; more, she had stocked them. During their conversation, she had educated Nerisse as their use, when and where the herbs grew, how to brew them into a tea.

The healer had also given her a warning. If used too often, the body adjusted to it. The draught would inevitably lose effectiveness over time. The elven girl hoped that between them, she and her lord could find a way to prolong or duplicate the effects in before the medicine was rendered useless.

The wood of the ceiling creak, settling in the cold. She stilled at the sound. Slowly, she relaxed as nothing happened. Moving quietly, she got up. From the kitchen, she fetched a tea kettle, a mug. She filled the kettle with water retained in a barrel standing in the corner, then brought it back to the fireplace. With a little coaxing, the fire was brought back to life. She hung the kettle on the hearth hook, swung it over the blaze to heat the water.

She found her hostess' still room just off the kitchen area. Scanning the shelves, she took what she needed. After a brief hesitation, she added several other items that to her collection. They were things that could treat minor injuries, or had the side effect of lowering a person's natural psychic defenses. Nerisse had a vague idea as to what she could use them for. She also took the healer's herbal, a book filled with herb lore and recipes.

Depositing them in her satchel, she sat on her blankets to wait for the water to finish boiling. She didn't think about what she planned. If she did, she wouldn't be able to go through with it.

Once the tea was prepared and poured, she drained the mug. The medicine took effect more slowly than she'd have like. It gave her too much time to think. She concentrated on Ba'tvian, what he'd instructed her to do, the intimation that he might have something special for her if she succeeded.

Finally, the emotional feedback from living things that was always there faded to nothing. It was, in a way, like being rendered deaf. That was something else she tried to ignore.

She arranged herself more comfortably on the bedroll, using the flames for her focus as she dropped into a trance. She extended her mind, noting the dulled edge of her awareness. There was only a dim sense of other minds around her. Thoughts echoed faintly from the Shadows, their patterns too foreign for her to interpret. Past them, she could just barely pick out the human thoughts that drifted in the bedroom of the healer and her husband.

Reaching for them, she identified the slumbering mind of the man, the restless dreams of the healer. The woman was not sleeping well. Intrigued, Nerisse touched her, skimming over the healer's defenses until she saw the minute fissures that were inherent to any

Empath's psychic shields. Choosing one, she teased it wider, slipping through it into a morass of anxiety.

There were no true images, just flickering impressions of what she could sense: watchful eyes, whispered voices, movement on the periphery of sight. There was suspicion. Nerisse couldn't experience it – a first for her – but she could recognize it. It saturated the upper layers of thought. Deeper down was a growing realization, one that played out in snatches of dreams.

The healer's guest had brought evil to her door.

Nerisse's heart gave a hard thump before she willed it steady again. She tamped down on the fear of discovery. If that got out of control, the woman would wake, would *know*. Then her failure would be Ba'tvian's downfall. She couldn't – wouldn't – be the cause of his fall.

He was meant for great things, her lord. It was her job – her duty as his leman, his lady – to help him achieve success. He would be heartbroken, hurt, if he failed. If he failed, they'd kill him.

No one was going to kill the man she loved.

With grim determination, she began to weave the fragmented dreams into a new pattern.

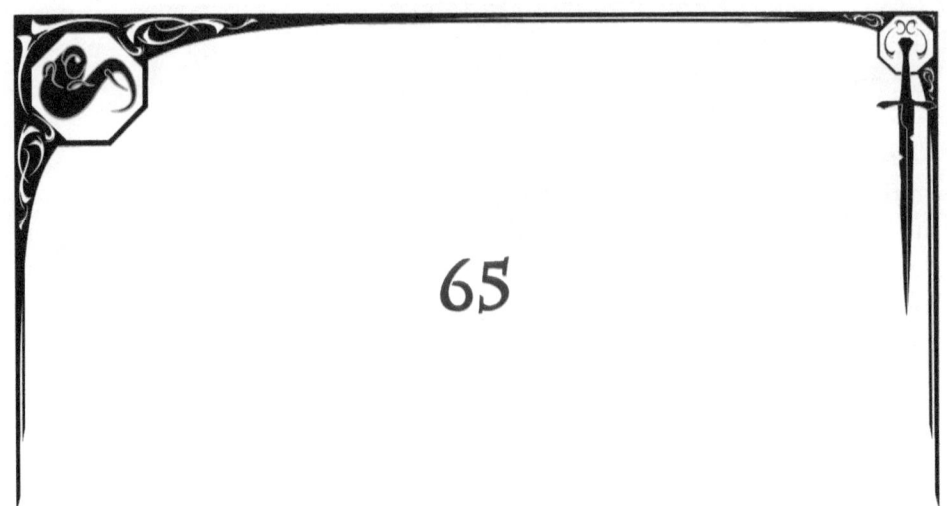

65

IN the bed, the woman's eyes opened.

Something was wrong. The healer could tell that something wasn't right. There were eyes watching her in the dark, things in the recesses of the room. Moving with care, she sat up, looking around her.

Everything felt surreal, disconnected. Part of her floated in the darkness, still asleep. She was dreaming. That knowledge flowed in from somewhere deep inside. Dreaming…

In the dream, her gaze tracked blankly around the room, settling on the covers of the bed. She wasn't alone. She was rarely alone in her marriage bed. Yet in this seeming of reality, she couldn't tell if it was her husband or not. The healer reached over, peeled the covers away to look at the face of the man sleeping on his back beside her.

It wasn't right. It was…she couldn't say what. It was wrong. It looked like the man she loved, but wasn't him. Her heart tripped in her chest. A panic began to rise from her belly, though it felt as if it were happening to someone else. It wasn't him. For all that it looked him, it wasn't.

The figure shifted in the bed, his eyes fluttering open only to close again as he stilled. His eyes had gleamed white in the dark. For the second that they had been open, his skin had flickered black.

Someone began to babble in the back of her mind. The detached part of her, the dreaming part of her, wondered who it was. Hysteria wasn't the way to deal with this. She was a practical woman, a healer. She did what needed doing, no matter how bloody it was.

She knew what to about strange things in her marriage bed.

She slipped out from the underneath the covers. Clad in her nightgown, she crossed the room to open the door. She didn't look back at the thing in her bed. She didn't pay heed to the other things in the dark corners of the house as she made her way to the rack by the front door. Her husband's logging axe was there, the blade glinting in the firelight from the hearth. Her hands lifted to take the axe down.

Deep inside, the babbling turned to wails. Annoyed, she slapped that part of her mind back to quiet it. It was only a dream after all.

Turning, she walked back into the bedroom, to the side of the bed the thing slept on. She raised the axe over her head. As it swung down, the voice inside her began to scream.

The blade hit the creature's arm, slicing through the flesh and bone. It woke with a yelp, disoriented. It spoke, pain in every word. She couldn't understand what it said to her. She didn't care. It was a dream.

Even in dreams, monsters had to die.

It rolled away, calling out her name as she raised the weapon to strike again. She couldn't allow it to get away. She hit one knee, then the other. The second leg was severed clean through. As the thing writhed in the bed, the amputated limb rolled onto the floor.

Her husband would have proud to see her wield his axe this proficiently.

She cut into its stomach with axe. The stench of blood and bowel filled the air. The thing bellowed in agony. She swung again, fluids spattering her face as she hit bone. Again. Its good hand lifted in a beseeching gesture. She hacked the arm off. The sounds it was making had devolved into whimpers now. It stared up at her as she swung the axe for the final time.

The blade lodged deep into its face.

She let go of the handle, breathing hard. Inside her head, the part of her that screamed wouldn't stop. She stumbled back as someone opened the bedroom door to step inside the room with a lantern. Its light flickered into the room, dispelling some of the darkness that crowded her.

Blinking, the healer stared at the elven girl with slate blue skin and alabaster hair. Memory trickled in.

"Asha…" Her name was Asha. She'd taken her in as a guest for the night. The girl was an Empath. Still, she was confused to see her in the doorway with such a cool expression. "Did my nightmare wake you?"

"No, you didn't wake me." Asha's eyes landed on the bed. "Lady, what have you done?"

"Done?" Bewildered, she followed the girl's gaze.

The bed was soaked with blood. Crimson streaked down the headboard, the wall behind it. It dripped onto the floor. In the center of the mattress lay a man. He'd been hacked to pieces. Though the axe had been buried in his face, she could still recognize him as her husband.

"No. No, no, no, no…" She stepped forward, almost fell as her foot came down on something unexpected. Looking down, she saw the bloodied leg. "No!"

She'd killed her husband. She whispered it over and over, collapsing to the floor to rock. Asha came to kneel beside her.

"Let me in, lady. Let me help you." Without waiting for an answer, Asha took the healer's face in her hands. In her shocked grief, the woman didn't resist as the elf began to unravel her mind.

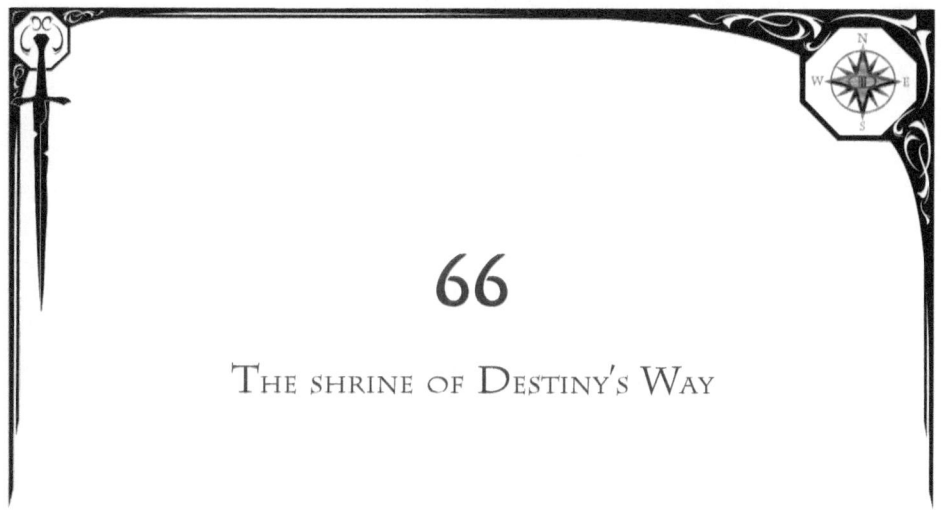

66

The shrine of Destiny's Way

ABSOL Omine sat in the small room holding the shrine's archives, flipping through notes and chronicles. It was well past midnight. The monks had long ago sought their beds. Even young I'k'Nole had succumbed to sleep not long before; Absol had sent him off to his room when the lad had started to doze.

The Mancer himself didn't feel tired, having slept for a good portion of the day. His ribs twinged a bit, yet didn't bother him over much. Dannon had brewed him a tisane that took care of the pain for a time. So long as he didn't move too abruptly or lift anything heavy, he was fine.

Not long after rising from his bed, he had sent off a request to the Trinity Council, then contacted his northern colleague, Timbrel. The communication hadn't taken long. Both Mancers were low-level mages, capable of establishing a link that allowed them to speak to one another despite the distance. It was one of the few magical abilities that Absol used regularly.

The conversation had confirmed the rumor Dannon had heard about the hostelry.

"It wasn't the only massacre I've come across up here," Timbrel had said, his voice echoing oddly through the mage link that had connected the two of them. "There was a trapper's cabin only a few miles from the hostelry. The family had been killed, right down to their hunting dog. He's escalating, Absol. More, some the kills bore the signs of the Shadowed Ones. If they are making kills, not just participating in what he's doing, then the problem is much bigger than we thought."

Absol shoved away from the desk he was using to pull more manuscripts off one of the bookcases. What he was looking for was more likely to be found in the libraries kept by the Mancer Headmasters, but the Master Abbott had amassed a treasury of information on his own. Absol had added to it over the years. The object of his search was, in fact, one of his contributions.

He brought the stack back to the desk, cleared away the one he'd already gone through. As he opened and scanned the pages of each chronicle, he thought hard. It was there, the knowledge a wiggling minnow in the sea of his mind, darting out of reach each time he sought to pull it to the fore. It had to do with the Shadows, the killing.

As he set aside one document to look over the next, a name caught his eye – I'k'Nole's name. Stopping, he read the page.

I found the child wandering the ruins of the Spirlan Forest in the aftermath of the Great Earthquake. He did not seem to remember what had happened. Yet this boy gives evidence to hidden talents. He can see them – see the Shadowed Ones that feed on death and destruction.

"I remember this," he murmured, tapping a finger on the passage. "The Shadows were strong in the area. All that death – many of them had glutted on it, manifested physically…"

That wasn't unusual, though. Granted, the amount of death needed to allow them to manifest in such a way wasn't commonly found. Battlefields, disasters – those served the creatures a banquet. Still, Timbrel's report had indicated that the creatures might have been solid in form *before* the killing started, not after.

He discarded the notes he'd written after finding I'k'Nole. Then there it was, what he'd been looking for. Several years ago, snippets of legend, rumor, and proven information had been woven into a theoretical treatise. When Absol had come across it during one of his visits to the Trinity, it had intrigued him enough to obtain a copy for Dannon's library.

Reading through it, he frowned over the implications. Blood rites were not enough to cause the physicality of the creatures that seemed

to follow Ba'tvian's every move. The amount of death the boy –
young man, now, he supposed – generated wasn't even near the scale
required to achieve it. Was it something that the mage was doing or
was it a hitherto unknown facet of the Shadowed Ones themselves?

He wasn't certain.

The treatise lent weight to the idea that the slithering things were
able to build up blood- or death-born power within them until they
had enough for solid manifestation. All they needed was a link, a
conduit, through which to glean what they needed. As if, he thought,
they could only sip at that power otherwise, not glug it down by the
gallon. No human could do serve that purpose.

A Daemon Lord, however, could. That begged the question of
why.

67

THE HEALER'S CABIN
JUST OUTSIDE OF PIETE TOWN

S HE hadn't gotten it right.
  Nerisse studied the mind of the healer, re-tracing the new pathways forged in her psyche. She had started working with the idea of making the woman into a tool of sorts. What kind, she hadn't been sure. Her lord required sacrifices, needed blood, death, and sex the same way he needed food, water, and breath. As she'd worked, teasing the innermost workings of the mind apart, she began thinking that they could use the woman as a lure. Her face wasn't known in the same way theirs were, could go places that they couldn't.

What the elf had gotten at the finish was an obedient woman, mute and unthinking. Well, on the surface, she was unthinking. She couldn't act without instruction. Yet the healer's personality, hadn't been completely destroyed. Her identity, her Empathic self, had been preserved, contained. Inside that cage deep within, she screamed.

Nerisse could hear the whispers of it echoing in the vaults of her own mind.

A bit of darkness slithered to her side, it's blunt nose nudging her thigh. Jerking, she mentally withdrew from her victim to see the Shadow glide toward the bedroom door. There it paused, glancing back at her.

It was time to go.

Hesitating, she looked at the healer. She couldn't leave her alive. Perhaps...yes. Perhaps her lord would appreciate the woman as a gift. An offering, she thought, to make up for her failures.

"Stand." Nerisse paused as she obeyed. "Get dressed to go outside."

The healer did so, the movement lacking the grace she had exhibited when Nerisse had first encountered her.

"You will follow me. You will keep to my side. You will not trip, not fall. You will not make any noise."

Orders given, the elf walked out into the main part of the cabin. All that she would be taking with her had been packed earlier. She barely heard the shuffling behind her that indicated obedience to her commands. Movement on her periphery drew her attention as she bent down to gather her things. Peering behind her, she saw the human female standing vacant-eyed, her lord's pets drifting around her. They seemed…curious. Almost puzzled.

One of the larger creatures peeled away from the rest to blink white eyes at her. Though it didn't speak, she answered as if it had.

"She belongs to Ba'tvian."

It flicked its tail, turned, let out a low hiss. Its brethren slipped away from the woman. Wondering if she might have gained some measure of approval from them, she straightened, shouldering her overstuffed satchel, the bedroll strapped to its top. Gazing thoughtfully at the Shadows, she left the cabin, her offering trudging after her.

Now that it was over, the world felt surreal for Nerisse. Had she really done that, caused one person to kill another? With the herbal brew in her body, she hadn't experienced the pain, the death, the horror. There were twinges of regret, the faintest aftershocks of adrenalin, of fear. What she held deep in her heart for Ba'tvian outweighed them.

In a few more hours, she would begin to feel again. In a few more hours, she would be reunited with her lover. She hoped that he would be pleased with what she had accomplished.

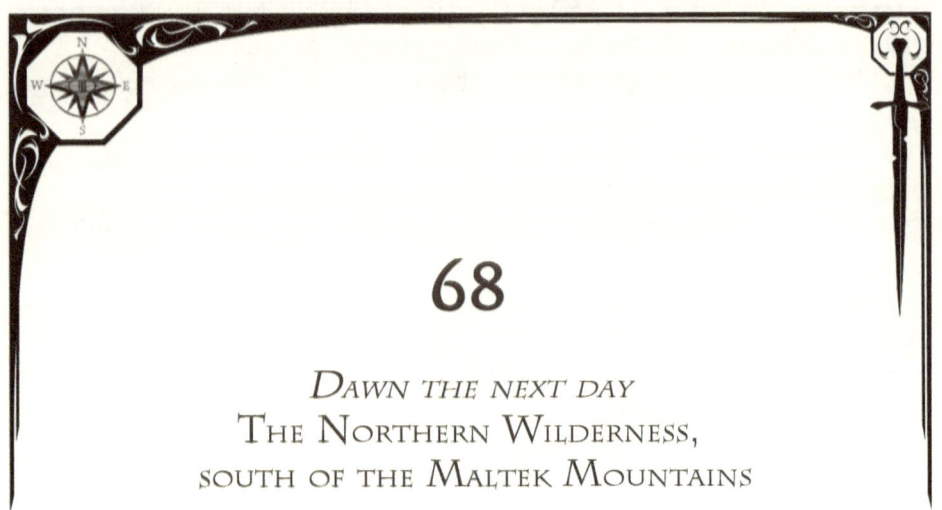

68

BESTOR rode his new beast, rocking with the uneven gate as it half-trotted, half-walked along the ground. He looked at the snow-laden countryside idly as the creature traversed the terrain at a fast clip. It was much different here than the frozen wastes he was used to. With the mountain at his back and the land dipping into a broad forested valley at his front, he thought of the air. It was warmer here. His beast would begin to fall apart much sooner than in the severe cold.

He accepted the fate of his creation much as he had everything else in his life: with only faintest hint of resignation. A replacement would have to be built in a few days. Until then, he would make the most of the one he had.

He had gotten a good look at the landscape as he'd descended. There had been a strange feature winding its way through the forest, a strip of barren land cutting through the trees much like the giant eels he'd sometimes fished out from under the ice in the Northern Snow Fields. It had ended at a point only a few miles to the left of where he was. He pondered what it was, what it meant. In the mountains, he had seen trails scored through the wilderness by animals but nothing of this size. Perhaps it had been made something big. A large animal, a creature that he could use to make the next mount.

With a series of guttural grunts, he pointed the thing he rode in the direction of the trail's end. If he could track a beast through the

Frozen North where the snow fell and shifted every few hours, then he could surely do so here. He would see what he found.

69

THE NORTHERN WILDERNESS,
WEST OF PIETE TOWN

NERISSE flipped through the herbal she'd stolen as they trudged through snow. They'd veered away from the road, wishing to avoid anyone who might know the woman ambling with them. Around the two women, the Shadows roamed, weaving through the trees like the predators they were. The largest of them glided next to their captive, keeping a cautious eye on her.

For her part, the elf ignored them. The herbal was a boon she hadn't anticipated. It was filled with things she hadn't known, sketches of fungi and plants that had all kinds of uses. There was a blue shelf mushroom, for instance, that could be distilled into a potion that eased pain, but too large a dose would cause hallucinations. The patient's mental barriers would also weaken, if not crumble, for the duration that draught was in effect. The fungus only grew in winter and Nerisse had spotted it growing on several trees as they traveled. She'd collected each growth, careful not to the get the mushroom's juice on her skin.

The possibilities were endless.

Hissing broke through her concentration. Pausing in mid-stride, she looked up to see the Shadows swarming around them, all of them agitated. Branches snapped in the distance. Something breathed out hoarsely enough to be a muted roar.

The healer continued to march on.

"Stop. Come here and stay with me."

At Nerisse's command, the woman shuffled to her side. Hardly sparing her a glance, the elf knelt in the snow, digging through it with her gloved hands until she uncovered a layer of dead grass. Taking off the gloves, she sought the soil with her fingers, closing her eyes, seeking with her mind.

What comes this way?

She let the whispered question seep into the earth. There was a feeling of reluctance, as if the earth wasn't sure if it should answer her. She asked again, imploring it. Finally, it showed her.

...a beast that is made not born, a mixture of living things melded into one; a man draped with furs, more animal than man...

...from the north, down the mountain, they came from the ice beyond the earth...

...the bloodied bedroom, the mangled corpse...so much blood...it stained the earth...

...such death...foul death...

...why?

"He needs it. I need to give it to him. He's mine, you see. He loves me. Why can't you understand?" Nerisse heard her own husky voice, felt unexpected tears prick at her eyes. The earth was part of her, she was part of it. It had to understand her need.

The earth did not respond.

Suppressing the hurt that twinged in her heart, she let go of her connection to rise to her feet. Was the earth rejecting her? No, no it couldn't. She was tied to it. It was tied to her. Yet...if it was...

Ba'tvian would know what to do.

She took a deep breath, feeling a detached calm settle inside, and noticed that all the Shadows were staring at her expectantly. Giving herself a mental shake, she relayed what the earth had told her. They milled about, as if trying to decide what do with the information.

It was strange to see them so disconcerted. She looked at the healer, thought she heard the faint mental screams grow louder. The woman would be of little use. What should she do?

She cupped one hand, forming a ball of mage energy in its palm. It glowed with the silvery white light that was the color of her magic, but there was something on the edges of it, a new tinge of red that was barely visible. It reminded her of the Ba'tvian's power, which held the color of blood.

Blood for life, he'd said once.

She inserted her thoughts, asking a question that she might not have a few weeks ago, then sent it off to her lord. It flew from her hand, fading into the air as it went. She waited, as the noise in the trees came nearer.

Yards away, she saw snow cascade from an evergreen. The largest Shadow hissed. The rest of the black shapes darted forward at the ungainly beast that lumbered towards them. As they wove between its legs, halting its progress, she got her first good look at it.

The main body might have once belonged to ice wyvern, a creature she'd heard about but hadn't seen before. The scaly hide, the coloration, and the direction from which he had come seemed to match what little she knew of them. The claws seemed to be an amalgam of wolf and wyvern. The head was that of a bear. Patches of fur were scattered all over it. The eyes – those caught her attention – were milky, sunken, empty.

It seemed to be oozing all over the place.

The man astride it, a northern barbarian clad in light colored furs, leaned over to one side to gaze down on the slithering things as they moved. He studied them as if trying to decide if he could use them in some way. His face…there wasn't much expression there. It wasn't as if he was trying to hide what he thought or felt. It was as if he didn't know how.

She let herself fall into a half-trance as she stood there, probing cautiously with her mind. She found brittle shields, things that were battered, worn, ill-made. There were layers, like an onion, each easily peeled away. He didn't seem to notice as she worked her way into his mind.

What she found there was as primal. She wasn't certain that she could call it barbaric, let alone human. He lacked human experiences, hadn't been taught the value of emotion, morality, or complicated thought. Though he had power – a great deal of power – he had no training. What he did with his magic was use it the way he would use any tool: bluntly, forcefully. Even the shielding around his mind had come about because he needed to block out the world, yet no natural shields to rely on. Despite all of this, he had managed to create things, biddable creatures. They were companions, meals on legs, transportation, protection, anything he needed them to be.

It was intriguing.

A flash of red light entered her field of vision. Withdrawing from the stranger as stealthily as she'd infiltrated, she held out her hands and her lord's mage sending settled into them. The sending gave her his answer.

She smiled.

70

The Northern Wilderness, south of Piete Town

B A'TVIAN sat on a fallen tree trunk at the southern end of the huge valley, waiting for Nerisse to return. Her sending had been…interesting. The chit had her uses, he knew. She had skills he lacked, serviced his lust as he needed. This, now…he hadn't expected this from her.

He sent out a tendril of power, summoning one of her escort to him. The Shadows could travel quickly when they wished to. He spent the next hour nibbling on rations, considering what he had to do. The Mancers were becoming more of a problem. As Red had indicated, most of the dratted order was hunting him. Running, hiding, evading – it would only get him so far. It was time to begin hunting back.

Various scenarios played out in his mind, each considered, then discarded. Whatever he did, it had to make a statement. He'd grown strong since the confrontation with Oknare. He could achieve much. Still, there was one chink in his success: Ba'tvian had never bested a mage before, not directly, not without help.

He would have to sometime. His loyal ones had to know that their master was not weak. So the proving ground would be with a Mancer, this Timbrel Jodrek. All Mancers were mages, to one degree or another, were they not? And they were enemies. They hunted *his* Shadows, among other things. Because of this, the world listened to them, watched them.

It was something to keep in mind.

He smiled to himself as the creature he'd summoned glided up to him. It slithered up onto the log, came under hand to be petted. He stroked its blunt head.

"What has Nerisse done?"

She has found a way to quiet her mind. She caused the healer to kill her mate and now brings the woman to you as a gift.

"She didn't mention that in her mage sending," he murmured with a frown.

She wishes to please you.

"Hmm." She tried, persisting in the face of failure. He mulled over whether or not he should allow her to succeed this time. Perhaps he should. He wanted her to keep trying. "What else?"

She attempts to think as you want her to think. The white eyes blinked slowly. *Her mind is more malleable when it is quiet.*

Interesting. He stored that bit of information away for later use.

"What of this...encounter?"

The barbarian has power but little intelligence. The creature's mental tone was scornful. *He may be of some use. She is chaining him.*

"Chaining?"

In the mind. She tried with the woman. She broke her. The elf has learned from her mistakes. The man will be yours.

"Good." If nothing else, he could kill him. Or, he mused as a glimmer of an idea began to shine in his thoughts, there may be another purpose for him. "Return to her. Keep watch."

He gave the Shadow one last stroke, then gestured to others who loitered around the log, barely visible. They came, their bodies darkening, becoming more solid as they came nearer.

"Find the Mancer Timbrel Jodrek. I would know where he is, where he is going, and what he knows. I do not have to tell you to be careful of him."

Most of them left. The largest three remained. Two curled around his feet. The third settled beside him on the log.

What will you do, lord?

"Kill him, as the world watches."

INTERLUDE 13

ELSEWHERE...

LABIYAL looked up from the report he was reading as the door to his study opened. Putting it aside without any hint of irritation, resignation, or surprise, he rose from his seat to welcome his sire as he strode into the room. The Daemon Lord Biyal had chosen to use a form of masculine beauty this time, with a black mane pulled back in a waist-length pony-tail. He'd left his eyes their true color of reddish -gold, as it matched the silk robes he wore. It was the form he favored when spending time with his concubines.

The Lord took in the antique desk, the array of mirror stands around it, and gave his son a condescending smile.

"Playing again, spawnling?"

Labiyal gave him a slight smile in response to the jibe.

"What brings my lord here? I did not believe that we were due to meet." He made a polite gesture for the Daemon to take a seat in the chair in front of his desk.

"We weren't." Biyal lounged in the chair, watching his son like a lazy cat. "Our king has a few questions. I am here to get answers."

Labiyal went to his drinks cabinet, coming back with two goblets of wine. He gave one to his sire before taking his own seat to wait.

"This elf girl – Nerisse. What is her purpose, exactly? The king believes she may yet prove to be a liability."

The half-Daemon felt only the merest prick of impatience at the question. He had answered it several times before. This time, at least, he had more promising news to combat it with.

"She is a tool, one whose corruption is now virtually complete."

"Oh?" Biyal's elegant eyebrows rose. "She is an Empath. It is general knowledge that they cannot be corrupted."

"There is a way around it." Labiyal allowed himself a cool smile. "She has slaved herself to him, a position of which he has taken advantage. Of her own free will, she has sought for a way to negate her Empathy. She has succeeded. She killed for him."

"She hasn't performed any blood rites." The elder man scowled. "The king would have known if she had."

"She will. Ba'tvian will see to it."

"We will watch for it, then." The Daemon Lord's tone indicated that it had better be soon. "We have waited nineteen years, spawnling. Do not test our king's patience."

"I have no wish to. However, these things do require time." Labiyal sipped his wine. "What other questions does our ruler have?"

"The barbarian is essential to your plan? He is of little intelligence."

"Sire, the barbarian is another tool. Ba'tvian will make great use of him."

"Ba'tvian has still to prove himself." The Daemon leaned forward, locking gazes with his son. "Our king remains trapped; the Mancers continue to hunt us down, while you waste time and resources on a human boy for nearly two decades. We must see that our investment is worth its expense."

It took little effort to suppress the surge of irritation he felt at his sire's words. It had cost their race nothing. Labiyal had been careful to see that it wouldn't. The fact remained, however, that their king wasn't known for his patience. They needed something; he would have to give it to them.

The price of failure in this venture was death.

"One month," he replied with smooth calm. "In one month's time, perhaps a bit less, you will have your proof."

"If we don't, spawnling," Biyal stated, his eyes turning crimson. "Our king may well demand a piece of you."

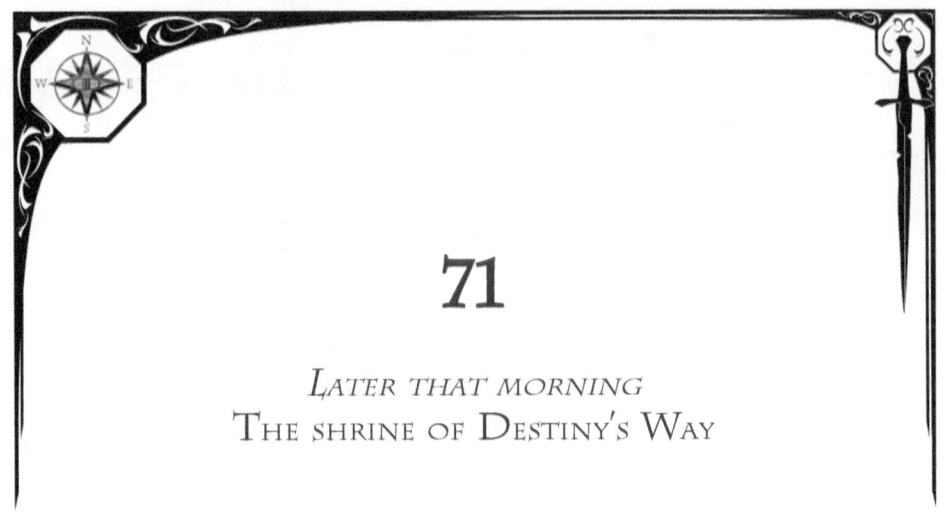

71

ABSOL woke with a start as a hand touched his shoulder. His ribs protested with a painful throbbing. With a groan, he shoved away from the desk he'd slouched over, holding a hand to his side until the throbbing subsided. Beside him, Dannon gave the Mancer a critical look, then proffered the mug of painkilling tea he'd brought with him. Absol took it gratefully.

"How late were you up last night?" The monk pulled up a chair, looked over the papers, scrolls, and books strewn all over the desk. "Did you find what you were looking for?"

"I don't recall when I fell asleep, but I did find what I needed." Absol took a deep swallow of tea before continuing. The cobwebs of sleep were already clearing from his mind. "Unfortunately, it leaves me with more answers than questions. There are indications that a Daemon Lord may be involved. Where's I'k'Nole?"

"Attending to morning chores," Dannon replied. "So, does that make Ba'tvian a puppet?"

Absol took his time answering as he drained the mug. It was a possibility, one he'd considered in the night.

"I don't know. It doesn't make sense. Daemon Lords are notoriously self-serving. They must benefit in some way. I don't see how Ba'tvian's activities do that. As near as I can tell, the boy's wandering around Orthanor, almost as if he's looking for something. Yet if he is doing so in service to a Daemon Lord..." He shook his head. "They aren't patient. He's been at it for over two years now; they'd have killed him by now. Daemons are hard on their tools as a rule."

"That's not the only thing bothering you," the monk observed, taking the empty mug from his friend. "Is it the missing girl?"

The Mancer frowned as he thought of Nerisse. Again, he gave a shake of his head.

"She's part of it, certainly. Still, it's the Shadowed Ones that present the most irregular piece in puzzle. They swarm around Ba'tvian; they turn up in high numbers wherever he's been. No Daemon Lord has ever worked in conjunction with them in so far as I've seen or heard."

They sat quietly for a moment. Finally, Absol sighed.

"There's little anyone can do at this point. Ba'tvian's in the wind, Nerisse is only-the-One-knows-where, and there's not enough documented encounters with Daemon Lords to explain what's going on."

"Then let us break your fast." Dannon rose, helping his friend to his feet. "Perhaps your fellow Mancers will discover something that will shed light on the hunt."

"Timbrel's in the north," he murmured half to himself. "I hope he finds the trail – and is careful. Ba'tvian has already killed one Mancer – a young, inexperienced one. Tim's cautious but I can't help feeling that we haven't seen the worst of what Ba'tvian is capable of."

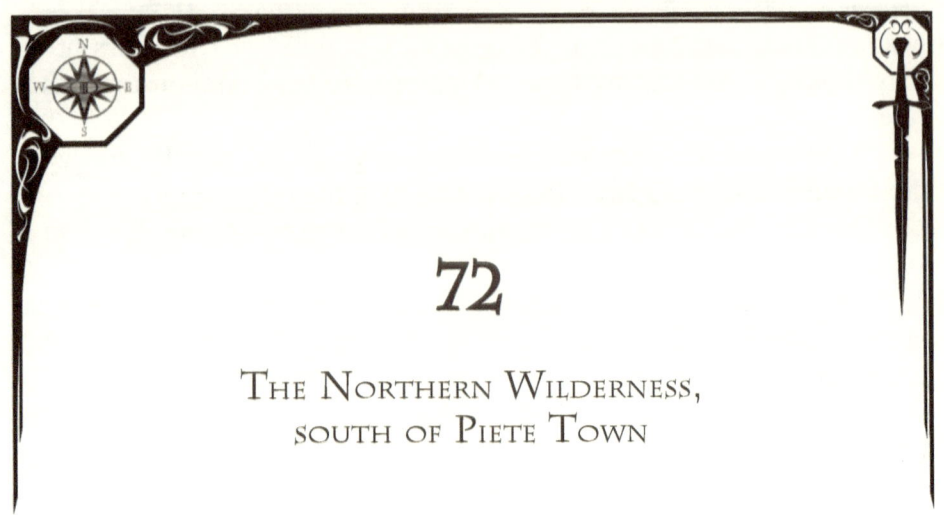

72

The Northern Wilderness, south of Piete Town

NERISSE had outdone herself.

Ba'tvian had expected her to find the healer, perhaps find a cure for her so-called malady. He had ordered her to leave no witnesses, had expected her obedience there. He had not expected gifts.

Since the Shadows' report, he had debated over his reaction to the news. Part of him wanted to discourage the behavior, yet she had chosen people – victims, potential tools – as her offerings. It was a practical choice, one worthy of positive reinforcement.

The woman she had brought him was chained within her own mind. The prison fascinated him. When he had touched her mind with his, he had heard the screams, felt the fear, the grief, the horror – the knowledge that death would come soon. It would have been amusing to toy with her, to give her hope, then dash it. He wondered how much of it the healer would take before she broke completely. As it was, she was a fractured being. Nerisse's handling of her mind had not been as careful as it should have been.

No matter. She would serve another purpose.

Now he gazed at the barbarian with interest. The fur-clad man was docile, sitting cross-legged beside his grotesque creation. The eyes were vacant. As a mage, he had considerable power – it took a great deal to meld living things into a single entity – but his training was non-existent. His shields were weak, brittle things.

He glanced at Nerisse as she rose from their small campfire. Nestled in the flames was the cast-iron teapot she'd procured at the healer's house.

"How long did the effect last?"

"Half the night and a little past dawn. It's not a permanent solution. She said that I'll grow immune to the draught's effects over time." Nerisse came to stand at his side. They both looked at the barbarian.

"What do you know of him? Is it safe enough for me to touch his mind?"

"His memories are...basic. Though his mind is human, it functions at a level that is more primal, more animal." She pulled her cloak more tightly around her as a breeze began to blow gently through the trees. "His name is Ibestor. He is from the Northern Ice Fields. He was cast out as a child; the barbarians have superstitious beliefs about magic. He managed to survive the wastelands up there by using that magic."

"What made him come south over the mountains?"

"The tribes. They've been hunting him for years, driving him out of the Ice Fields. Give me a moment with him, and you will be able to touch his mind."

She stepped forward, laid a hand on the Ibestor's shoulder. The barbarian's head turned towards her.

"Ibestor, this is Ba'tvian. He is your friend, as I am. Are we not friends?" She waited for him to give a jerky nod, then looked intensely into his eyes. "Our lord Ba'tvian wishes to see your mind, Ibestor. You will let him do this, because we are friends." He gave another nod. She straightened, turning back to Ba'tvian. "He is yours, lord."

He leaned forward, touched the man's forehead. He saw differences in what Nerisse had done within his consciousness as opposed to what she'd accomplished with the woman. The frame work was the same. The artificial structures she'd put in place were greater in number. They re-routed thoughts, altered patterns of thinking. More than that, he couldn't determine. This was not his kind of magic.

"Link with me. Show me what you've done."

They had never linked minds or magics before this. Beside him, he sensed her rising pride, the pleasure she took in the offer. It implied trust. As for himself, he was not convinced that he should trust completely. Still, for this moment, he would play the odds. She had already done much in an effort to gain his approval.

He felt her thoughts sync with his. The weight of minds holding the ends of a mental connection was a familiar one, though he hadn't experienced it since his exile from the Trinity. He had managed to conceal his inner self from his old master then; doing so with Nerisse was effortless.

She took him deeper into Ibestor's mind. He found himself studying the lines and patterns that made up the human instincts. There were faint after images of what they had been, with new silver lines overlaying them. He touched one, identified Nerisse's arcane signature. She took him through other centers of thought, saw infantile foundations of trust, loyalty, faithfulness. The man hadn't had much of a personality to begin with; now he had even less. It had been stripped down, rebuilt. At the center of the newly established pattern was…Ba'tvian.

They surfaced a few moments later, disconnecting from each other the moment they'd left the barbarian's mind. Ba'tvian gave Nerisse a long, thoughtful look. The longer the silence between them stretched, the more uncertain she became.

"I, ah, I thought that anchoring him to you as his leader would be appropriate. There – there is an incentive." Anxiety crept into her eyes. "I had to put in an incentive. I'm sorry that it places an obligation on you, lord, but –"

He held up a hand to cut her off. Obligation he didn't care for. If he deemed it too much, she would change it, or they would kill him.

"What incentive?"

"Protection." She spoke the word in a small voice. "Acceptance. He has had neither."

He nodded. For now, that would do.

"Your work with him is not finished."

"No, lord." Her body relaxed, her tone returning to normal now that she knew he wasn't offended at her initiative. "I was only able to do as much as I did because his shielding is –"

"Worthless," he interjected. "That will need to change, Nerisse. I will not risk your hard work being undone. You can teach him to shield? With provisions in place that you and I can access his mind as needed?"

"I believe so, yes."

"Good." Sparing a glance for the vacant-eyed man, he gave another order. "Send him to sleep, then drink your tea."

Leaving her to it, he strode over to the woman huddled in the snow. The Shadows circled her in lazy passes. Reaching out, he tugged her head up by the hair, staring into eyes as dead as the grave. At the edge of his awareness, he heard the faint echoes of her screaming.

He hauled her to her feet when he heard Nerisse coming stand once again at his side. With one hand still gripping their captive's hair, he used the other to trace lines along the elf's jaw and down her neck. His fingers settled on her pulse. It began to beat faster.

"We will make the most of your gift, Nerisse." He indulged himself for a brief moment, savoring her anticipation, the woman's fear, his own desires. "It's time for your first lesson, and your reward."

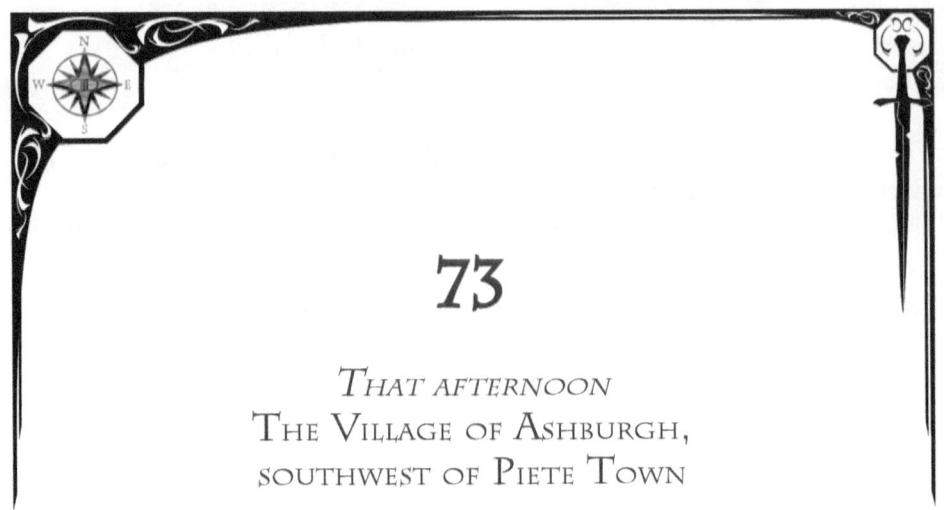

73

TIMBREL Jodrek was headed west of the Sradieen Trading Route when he decided to stop in Ashburgh for a hot meal and whatever news the tavern had. The village folk had heard of Ba'tvian, yet none had anything to say about him that he didn't already know. They spoke mostly of his last known endeavor. The fate of the trapper family had already made its way here, riding on the lips of traders. A few people had already approached him to verify what they'd heard, recognizing the garb he sported as belonging to a Mancer. He had seen little choice in confirming their worst fears: a blood mage was loose in the north.

The initial hubbub that had burst out over that had finally calmed enough that he could eat the stew he'd ordered with few interruptions. As he finished his meal, he found himself the subject of many covert looks and whispers from the tavern's clientele. It was aggravating, though not unexpected. The Mancers had been a few steps behind Ba'tvian since the beginning of their hunt for him. It was beginning to damage their reputation in some parts of the continent.

Of course, it doesn't help at all that there aren't that many of us to begin with.

Being a Mancer was dangerous work. A man was lucky to see his fourth decade, what with all the daemons, the ghouls, the blood or black mages they had to see to. Their life was one on the move, either on the hunt or patrolling a region. Few Mancers saw retirement, or kept a place they could call home.

That was the dream, of course. Retiring to a small farm, or becoming a monk in the Order of On'Desae – that was a Mancer's reward if he was very, very lucky.

Overall, though, a Mancer's life wasn't one that most people found appealing. Recruits were hard to come by. Of those they did get, about half of them died within the first five or six years out of training.

Timbrel had come close to being one of the dead. He'd been twenty-two when he'd encountered a pack of minor gremlins and made a crucial miscalculation in his own abilities. He'd triumphed in the end, he recalled, absently fingering the claw marks on his face – his reminder to be cautious. It had cost him in pain, blood, months spent in a healing house. It had been a high price to pay, though not as high as it could have been. The scars he'd been with were his trophies, as well as his reprimand.

Ten years later, he still found himself tracing the marks, remembering his folly.

He spooned up the last of his meal, then picked up his mug of steaming tea. As he drank, the air in front of him began to waver around a single point the size of a man's thumbnail. The point began to glow, heralding an incoming mage sending. He set the mug down, held out a hand just below the glow to catch the ball of light as it appeared. His fingers closed around it and he heard a voice – a Mancer at the Guild in Chalbrooke – speak in his head.

A healer is missing in Piete Town. Her husband has been murdered. You must confirm if this is the work of the blood mage Ba'tvian Delthanurk. There is evidence that he has been in Winede and may be traveling west. Inform the Guild and Absol Omine of your findings. Use caution; Delthanurk may be working with or for a Daemon Lord in some way.

As the voice faded from his mind, Timbrel became aware that all sound in the tavern had ceased. Taking a deep breath, he sent a reply, acknowledging the receipt of his orders. He drained his tea, signaling to the bartender. The man hurried over. Timbrel pressed a few coins into his hand to pay for the meal as he rose to leave.

"Has there been news, lord?"

Everyone's ears strained to hear his answer. Timbrel hesitated for only the briefest of moments before replying.

"Be careful who is let through your stockade. If you've anyone living outside the town, have them brought inside." Timbrel pitched his voice to carry throughout the room, though it was unnecessary. It was quiet enough that a mouse could be heard sneezing. "Piete Town has lost its healer. More than that, I do not know. I must go. Be safe."

He pulled the hood up over his head as he exited the tavern.

Interlude 14

Elsewhere...

IN a mirror set up on his desk, Labiyal watched the Mancer depart from the tavern. Cupping one hand, he produced a tiny ball of light. It hovered an inch above his palm as he filled it with thoughts of what he knew. He set it free with an economic gesture, then sat back in his chair to consider his next move.

Ba'tvian needed to begin proving his mettle. As head of this particular project he had to facilitate that. Wasn't it fortuitous that he'd already begun that before his exile?

Long term planning was the key to any project like this. Most of the Daemon Lords had little patience for it. It was why, he mused, they so often failed. There might be immediate payoffs, yet in the years to come, everything inevitably fell apart. The only part of that Labiyal had difficulty comprehending was that even they had failed in the end, their punishment was lenient. He supposed the early successes, no matter how small they had been, were the reason.

Labiyal Biyalban, half-breed that he was, had no leniency coming to him. No half-breed did, regardless of what methods they used. It was a source of amusement for the rest of the Daemon race.

It will come together. It must. Once it is all said and done, it will be my plans, my efforts, which will set our king free.

His life depended on that.

So he had been careful in orchestrating this current project. Using the guise of a rogue blood mage, he had laid the foundations on which Ba'tvian Delthanurk would build. There were others of like minds. Their potential would give his chosen pawn the capabilities he needed to act.

He was already in contact with them, these pawns that would feed Ba'tvian. They knew Labiyal by different names, different faces. The only common thing between the encounters was the promise – a debt that they were bound to fulfill. Soon, he would collect those debts.

He turned his attention outward, gazing at the large mirrors placed on stands around the room. Most were dormant. One showed Ba'tvian rewarding Nerisse, their bodies entwined on the bed roll while Ibestor was slumped in sleep against his make-shift mount. The ruined shell of the healer lay nearby in a huge patch of snow stained red.

Was it ironic that Nerisse truly loved the man she called her lord? Some might say that loving Ba'tvian was forgivable, but she had killed for him. There would be no coming back from that. Now the only thing left was to break her ties to her people, to corrupt her link with the earth.

Labiyal had plans in place for that as well.

A second mirror lit up as he shift eyes over to it. The image that coalesced within the frame depicted three other blood mages engaged in a rite of their own. It was depraved, almost decadently so, by his standards. Ba'tvian would curl his lip at most of the trappings they used. Still, he wouldn't miss the opportunities that presented themselves there. He would even improve on them, make the power collection more efficient. As it was, half the power generated was being lost as they indulged themselves in sadistic pleasures.

They would meet soon enough, this trio and the Master of Shadows. Once they did, none would ever be the same.

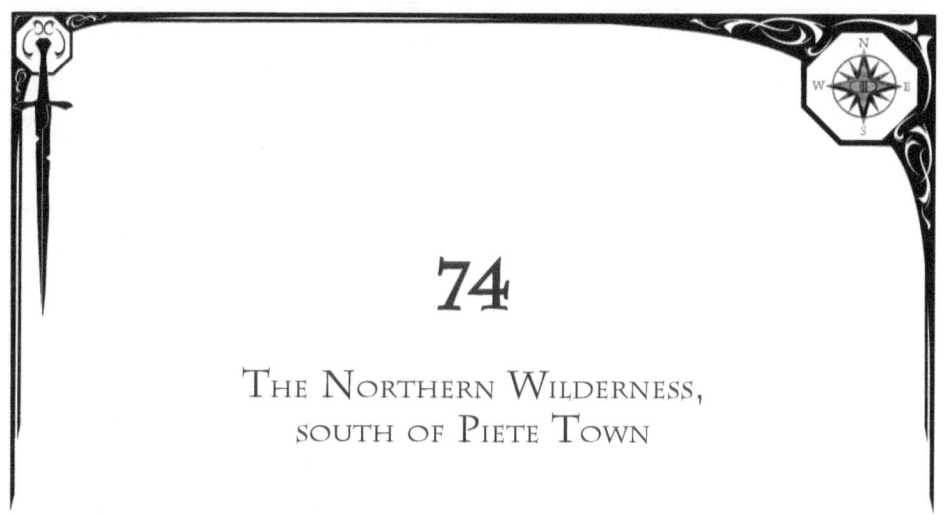

74

The Northern Wilderness, south of Piete Town

D RESSED, Nerisse combed her white hair in the aftermath of their lovemaking. She felt loose, languid, content. Her lord had given high praise for what she'd accomplished, had even given her a gift. The thought of it made her lips curve in a dreamy smile. Their time together on this day would become one of her most cherished memories.

It had ended as all their trysts had, with the real world beckoning for Ba'tvian's attention. This time, it had been a mage sending from that mysterious informant of his. The Mancers, or one of them, had picked up their trail again.

More specifically, her trail. Ba'tvian hadn't been displeased over this, however, which puzzled her. He hated the Mancers, hated being hunted. This time, he seemed to be looking forward to it.

Who am I to question how he feels? I should be happy that he wasn't upset by it.

As the glow from his attentions began to fade, the cold started to seep in. She donned the ornate cloak he'd stolen from the trapper's cabin, reveling in its warmth, admiring its embroidery. He had waited for the right moment to give it to her, he'd said. His thoughtfulness brought a flush of pleasure to her cheeks as she remembered.

Ibestor remained asleep across the campfire from her bedroll. The Shadows were clustered around the corpse, having been allowed to feast on it once Ba'tvian had risen from their blankets. When they were done, only the bones would be left.

She averted her gaze from them and scanned the area for her lover. She found him communing with more of his Shadows a short distance away. He was fully engrossed. She watched him for several minutes before rousing herself to action. He had asked to see to the barbarian's shielding, and there was still work for her to do in his mind at any rate. Checking her empathic ability to ensure that the medicine she'd drunk was still in effect, she left her warm seat by the fire to settle down next to Ibestor. She placed a hand on his forehead, studied him with her mind's eye, then slipped inside his crude protections to work.

Hours passed unnoticed as she re-aligned mental pathways, teased instinctive patterns into new shapes. She decided to place a compulsion deep within, using her training as a psychic healer to embed it. She designed it with care, forming barbed roots that delved into his psyche in a tangle. It was complex, too complex to remove without permanently compromising the man's mind. Its purpose, though, was simple. As she finished its creation, she said the words that would mold Ibestor in a telepathic whisper.

Obey Ba'tvian at all costs. Protect him, his belongings, his dreams. You will obey him, and you will obey me.

The last thing she did before withdrawing was instruct him on how to shield. When Ibestor's subconscious fumbled with it, she fashioned a secondary compulsion for the purpose. Each step had to be outlined with painstaking precision in order for it to work. Allowances had to be made for her and Ba'tvian to pass through the protections. She used arcane signatures as the identifiers. Specific words or phrases would have been easier but anyone who knew them could use them. Her lord wouldn't care for the risk.

Finally, she climbed back into her own mind, feeling the weariness weigh heavily on her bones. She opened her eyes with a sigh, breaking physical contact with the barbarian. When she looked up, she found Ba'tvian watching her intently.

He was crouched in the snow beside her, the lizard-like forms of his Shadows crowding around them. He was petting the largest of them with an idle hand as he stared at her.

"My lord?" she asked, uncertainty in her tone.

"What have you done?" His face was unreadable.

"His mind – I needed to work on it, make him more…" She searched for the right phrasing. "Yours. I also saw to his shielding."

"I can still get in?" The question was almost a demand. She nodded.

"I made certain that you could with ease."

"Good." He seemed to relax a little. "There is a Mancer on the move. He is headed to Piete Town. That is where you got the woman, correct?"

"Yes, lord."

"Is he…" He gestured at the slumbering figure. "Ibestor – is Ibestor well enough ensnared that he will do as commanded?"

"I believe so, yes."

Now his dark eyes took on an anticipatory gleam. She felt her pulse pick up speed in response to it.

"Then you will take us back to Piete. This Mancer would hunt us. Let us instead hunt him."

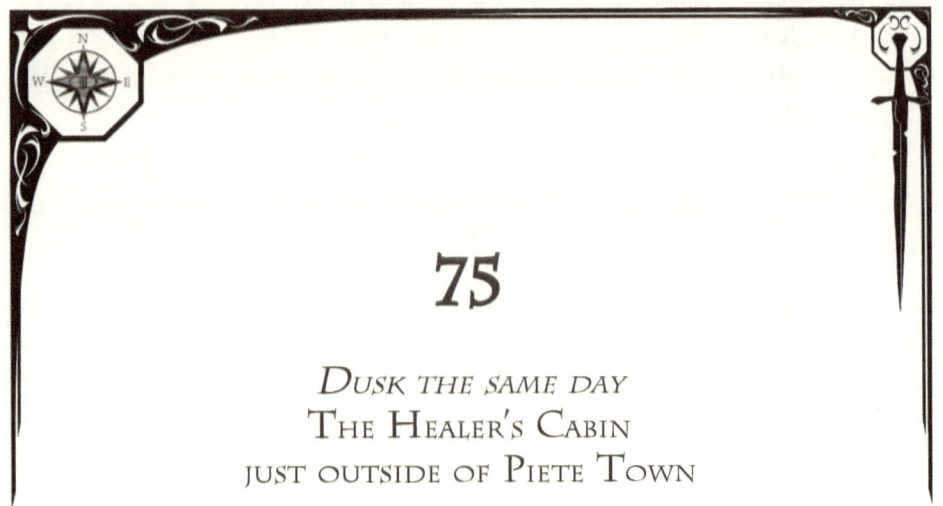

75

Dusk the same day
The Healer's Cabin
just outside of Piete Town

THE door was wide open when Timbrel arrived at the healer's cabin. New snow hadn't fallen, so he could still see the tracks leading away from the cabin. It looked like two people had left, with one set of prints leaving traces of blood on the snow. Kneeling down beside the ones nearest the cabin, he studied the crimson stains. Smears, he concluded. The blood traces became fainter as the tracks moved farther away from the cabin. Whoever had left was likely not bleeding.

"Lord?"

The Mancer turned to see the guard who'd escorted him there hovering a few yards away. The man was staring at the tracks with some apprehension.

"Yes?"

"Do you think she's alive? The healer?"

Timbrel glanced at the tracks, weighing the odds. If this was Ba'tvian's doing, he doubted the healer would survive long in his company. Regaining his feet, he gave the best answer he could.

"Anything is possible, but you have to understand that the odds of that are small. Stay there until I'm done here."

The guard nodded morosely as he turned away to study the cabin front. The porch bore traces of blood – again, just smears, as if whoever had left them had walked through a spot of blood as they shuffled along. The door itself wasn't damaged. Whoever was responsible had likely been let in by the healer herself.

Being careful to touch as little as possible, he entered the dwelling to begin his search. The coppery scent of blood was strong. Ignoring it, he searched the main part of the house. There didn't seem to be anything out of place in the main common room, save for more bloody foot prints. The prints were coming out of the back room, being more distinct the closer to the room entryway they were.

The door to that room – a bedroom, he saw – was as open as the one leading outside.

Leaving it for last, he found the healer's kitchen and still room. Most of its still room shelves were empty. The pantry wasn't been fully stocked either, he saw as he went through the kitchen. Whoever had taken the healer had first raided the stores here. He had seen similar evidence of theft at a few other places that Ba'tvian Delthanurk had raided.

He didn't find blood in either area.

That left the bedroom. Timbrel ventured toward it. He was within a few feet of the entrance when he spotted the rusty sprays on the far wall. The scent of death was growing more intense as well. He stepped inside, took in the spatter laden room, then focused on the bed.

He had to suppress his rising gorge. His eyes latched onto the ax handle sticking up in the air above what had been a man until he was sure he wouldn't be sick. Breathing as shallowly as he could, he made himself study the gruesome sight. The body had been partially dismembered. The torso had been hacked at, the head cleaved nearly in two. The blade was still buried in the victim's face.

There were no overt signs of ritual. No rune drawn with blood, no symbols carved or chalked on the floor. There wasn't even a residual shimmer of dark power in the air. The scene was...not arcane in anyway. It appeared as if someone had gone mad, lost control, and killed him with might have been his own ax. Yet the healer was missing, having gone with a person unknown.

Whatever this was, it hadn't been done by the blood mage that was on the Mancer's most wanted list.

Half an hour later, he exited the cabin and took a moment to savor the crisp clean air. After drawing in several deep breaths, he continued on to where the guard still waited for him, a small bundle at his feet.

"This…atrocity was not accompanied by blood magic. There were no rites performed here." Timbrel watched the relieved expression suffuse the man's face. "That does not mean that a blood mage is not responsible. I know that one is in the north somewhere."

"That Delthanurk boy. We've heard." He sighed. "Can we bury him, at least?"

"Have you seen him?"

"No." He shook his head. "I've heard from those who have that he died badly."

The Mancer looked back at the cabin. "If it were left to me, I would burn the whole thing as his pyre. No one needs to see what's inside that house." He returned his attention to the guard. "Has anyone begun tracking?"

"No, lord. It – we thought it might have been the blood mage." He shuddered. "None of us wish to face the likes of that one. What we've heard, he can kill several people with a thought."

"I doubt it." Timbrel recalled what Absol had passed on to him recently. "Even if a Daemon Lord was helping him, I doubt he had that kind of power."

"Will you track him then?"

"Yes, and I'd best start now if I've any hope of catching up."

"You'll want this." The man bent down to retrieve the bundle. He handed it over. It was a small burlap sack. When the Mancer looked inside, there were several wax paper packets of food. The guard continued. "Our thanks for coming. If you get the bastard who did this, you won't need to pay for meals or lodging whenever you come to Piete."

"It's appreciated."

The two shook hands. As they went their separate ways, Timbrel tucked the bundle into his pack. He couldn't bear the thought of eating right now. Perhaps when the image of the healer's husband had left his mind he could manage it.

In the twilight between dusk and night, he set out, following the tracks through the forest.

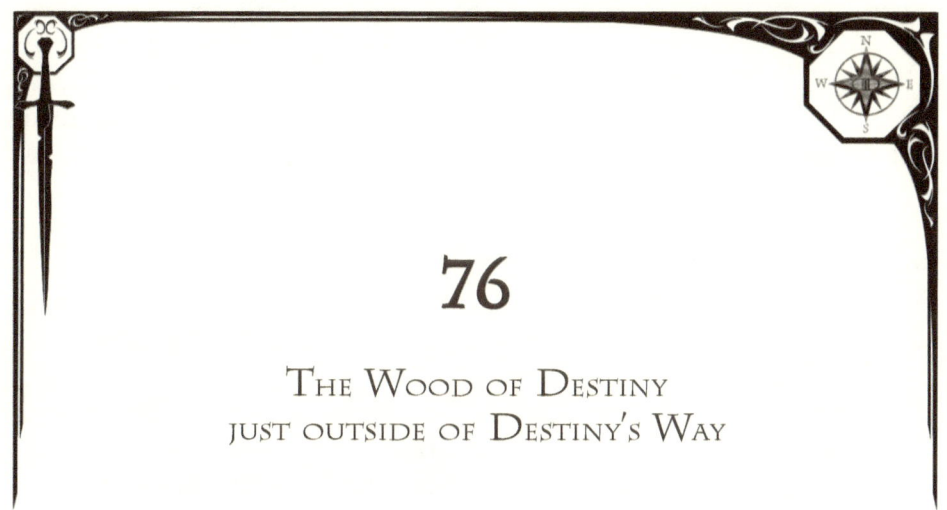

76

The Wood of Destiny
just outside of Destiny's Way

ABSOL frowned as the he cupped Timbrel's mage sending in his hands and its message unspooled in his mind. There were not just words. The Mancer's memories of the scene he had witnessed were unfolding to the sound of his voice detailing the find. When the sending was spent, the small glowing ball of light that carried it faded.

He sat on his moss-covered rock, staring at nothing. Around him, the trees of the Wood of Destiny rustled their branches. He looked up at them, using the sight of them as a way to quell the images that had yet to leave him.

It was a magical place. The flora had an inner vibrancy that shown through the bark, the leaves, the ground. It gave everything a jewel-like, ethereal quality. What grew here, what dwelled here, saw and felt. They sung, as well. The constant sound was akin to a harp's music, faint voices whispering lyrics in a language no one knew. That song wove through the Wood touched everything that heard it.

It told people things. It showed them futures, presents, pasts. That was why people called the place 'Destiny'. It had, Absol knew, driven men mad, which was why the shrine had been built here. Yet he had been coming here to walk the Wood for many years now, finding a serenity that didn't exist elsewhere in his life.

He had never troubled himself with the future. He knew he

would die. Odds were that he would die badly. That was the way of Mancer. As for his past and present, he had always accepted them. There was nothing he truly regretted. The Wood had responded to this by showing him nothing of what may happen through the time of his life.

Now, as he studied the Wood around him, the song took on a somber tone. The landscape seemed…anxious. Though sunlight still filtered in through the canopy, the shadows gathered, darkened, deepened. For the briefest of moments, he saw the Wood aflame.

He blinked.

There was no fire, no dark figures standing behind the flames. Still, the peace of this place had gone. He stood up with slow deliberation, bracing his legs as he addressed the world around him.

"What would you show me?"

The song stopped for the first time in Absol's memory. A wind blew in, whipping through the trees to thrash his cloak, stirring up fallen leaves and dust. With it came the vision, a ghost-scene that played out in front of him. Most of it was blurred. People came, people went. Some were killed – or so he thought – while others fought. At the end was the only definite image. It lasted the time it took to blink an eye.

The wind died. The shadows receded. The song resumed its eternal whisper.

Absol stood quietly there for most of the evening. It was well into the night before he returned to the shrine. Once sequestered in his room, he began to makes plans for pain-filled future.

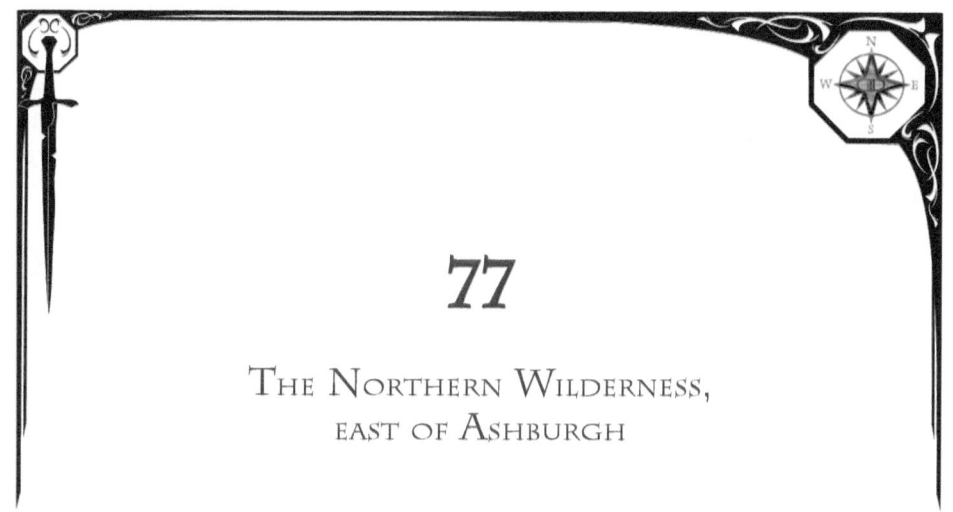

77

The Northern Wilderness,
east of Ashburgh

TIMBREL followed the tracks, thankful for the full moon that lent enough light to see them by. He had taken a few hours of rest early on the night. It wouldn't be long before doing so again. Just three or four hours, he thought. He didn't want to be exhausted when he caught up with whoever had done the killing at the healer's cabin.

There was the snapping of branch somewhere off to his right.

He froze. Easing closer to the barren trunk of a nearby tree, he drew his sword from its scabbard at his waist. Another loud crack ricocheted through frozen forest. He tensed. Something shuffled through the snow. There was a loud exhalation of breath.

Whatever it was, it was big. There were ice drakes in the mountains. Had one of them come down into the lowlands?

Silence descended as he waited. When nothing more happened, Timbrel left the tree to investigate. He moved carefully, stopping frequently to scan his surroundings. A few hundred yards away from the trail, he found trampled snow. He couldn't make out defined prints, but there were drag marks, as if whatever had come there had been dragging its tail behind it.

As he studied the snow, a faint sound caught his attention. It sounded like weeping. The hairs on the back of his neck rose.

In the middle of the northern woods, where there seemed to be no one around for miles, Timbrel felt eyes on him. The trees seem to close in without moving. The crying was coming closer.

A low growl rumbled through the trees. The weeping turned begging. A woman's pleas to…the earth. Timbrel's eyes narrowed. The earth wasn't worshipped in this region. Yet if Ba'tvian was in the north…

There was one person that this woman could be.

Moving with as much stealth as he could manage, he crept along the snow, skulking among the mix of dormant trees and evergreens until he spotted the…thing.

It was massive. At first, he took it for an ice drake. The body looked like one, but the rest of it – what in the name of the One was it? It was as if a children's animal puzzle set had been mixed up and put together wrongly. It was unnatural. A mad man's creation, he thought. A quick probe proved the point; the thing was being held together by magic.

Which meant its creator was around here somewhere.

The creature faced away from him, hunched in a predator's crouch in front of a distraught woman. She was garbed in the attire of northern native. He couldn't see her face, as she had her hands raised to ward off the thing, but her hair was too light in color for her to be the healer.

The animal amalgam slunk forward a step. The woman tried to rise. One leg wouldn't support her in the even snow. She fell back, clutching at her ankle. The thing growled low, advancing again.

The Mancer made a split-second decision. He darted from the behind the creature, leaping up to scramble onto its back. It jerked in surprise, roaring defiance. It whipped its head around, snapping at him as he straddled its shoulders and thrust his sword into its spine. It squealed in pain, twisting onto its side to dislodge him. Timbrel leapt down before it hit the ground, then ran as it began to roll.

The body wasn't moving right. Only one side seemed to be functioning; the other just twitched. It tried to right itself. There was the sickening sound of flesh tearing as it managed to roll back onto its belly. One of its limbs was left in the snow beside. It labored for breath, not seeming inclined to move.

Timbrel kept an eye on it. It had three limbs now, yet two were still fully functional. Staying wary, he approached the woman.

"Come on, before it decides to try for us again." He bent down to help her up. That was when he saw her face.

Her skin was slate-blue, her slanted eyes silver. Her white hair barely hid the slight points of her ears. She was a young Elvanarae, and there was only one matching her description that he'd heard of.

"You – are you the lady Nerisse se li Astorae?"

She hesitated for the barest moment before giving a jerky nod. Then her eyes flicked over his shoulder.

He whirled raising his sword as a hulking, fur-clad man charged at him from behind an evergreen, bellowing like an enraged bull. The Mancer met the barbarian halfway. He slashed, spun, kicked out. His foot caught his opponent in the chest. The man grunted, grabbed his ankle as he stumbled back a step. Pulling on the captured foot, he sank his teeth into Timbrel's calf.

Cursing, Timbrel lashed out with the sword, catching the other's arm. The blade bit into the furs draped over his shoulders with no effect. The barbarian chewed on his leg, breaking through the leather breeches. The Mancer reached for a throwing knife as his flesh was torn into.

Sharp steel slipped into his spine. Feeling below his waist fled. The leg he stood on collapsed beneath him. He landed on his side, blade still in hand.

"Release him, Ibestor."

The command was given in a soft, female voice. Nerisse – she'd been bait. This had been a trap –

The barbarian dropped the leg. Blood stained his beard, his eyes shining like feral stars. He bared his teeth at the Mancer and growled.

If he was going to die, he'd be damned if he wasn't going to take at least one of them with him. He threw the knife.

It was caught in mid-air. The nimbus of magic that surrounded it was the color of old blood. It bore an arcane signature he knew, one that he'd been tracking for weeks now.

The others – they need to know –

Ba'tvian Delthanurk stepped into view. Dressed in the drab, warm clothing of a trapper, he reached out to pluck the knife from the air. He shoved his hood back just enough to fully reveal the coldness of his dusky face, the bright hate in his dark eyes. He didn't look like a young man of nineteen years. He looked older, angry, powerful.

Behind him, all around them, living bits of darkness began to appear. They slithered over the ground, gathered together in a ring that encompassed the humans. They were Shadowed Ones. Timbrel realized with a dawning horror that they had physical form. All of them.

By the One...How many had they consumed to give them material bodies?

Ibestor muttered something, made as if to come at the Mancer again. He froze as he took the first stride toward him. Nerisse, moving gracefully over the snow, came up alongside the blood mage, one hand raised in the barbarian's direction.

"You will have your chance with him again." Ba'tvian's words hung in the air with promise.

Their uncouth companion protested his restraints. Ba'tvian turned slightly, snapping something at Nerisse. The Mancer made use of the opportunity. He poured everything he knew, and what little power he had, into a mage sending, then released it.

Ba'tvian sensed what he was doing. Delivering a vicious kick, he barked a few arcane words. Magic slashed through the air. It felt like being slammed into the ground from a great height. The breath was knocked out of him. He coughed as he gasped. Wet warmth trickled out of the corner of his mouth.

The pain hit a moment later.

The world spun, then went black.

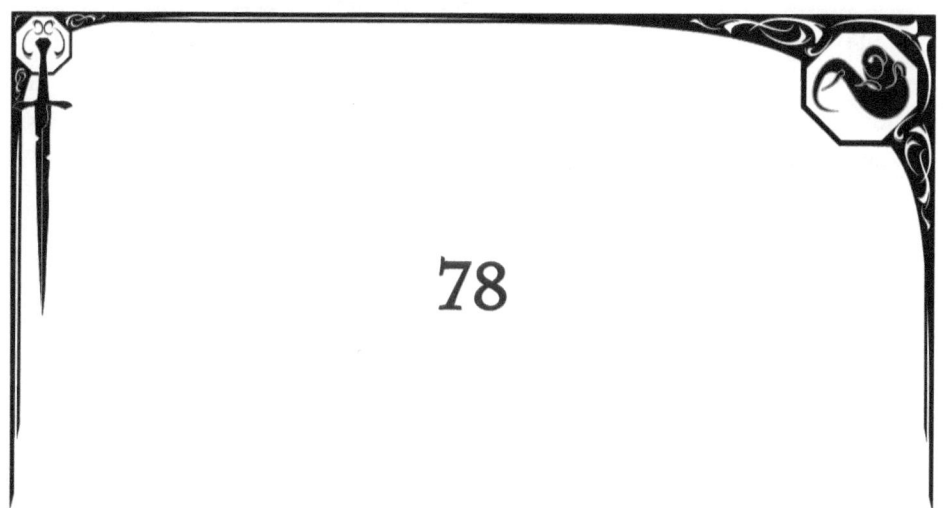

78

B A'TVIAN watched their captive slump onto the snow. With a curse, he gave his Shadows a sharp look.

"Did that sending get out?"

Yes, lord. The largest of his Shadows twitched its tail in agitation. *The Guild of Mancers will soon know what has happened here.*

He scowled at the reply, indulging in another kick at the prone Mancer. Ibestor grumbled. The uncouth man was still showing his bestial side. Seeing it, Ba'tvian reigned in his temper. Losing it would only encourage the barbarian's feral behavior.

There would be a way to make this work, to play the mage message into his favor. He just had to think of it, to plan for it. First, though, Ibestor needed something to do. He was a distraction as he was now.

"Go see if your creation can be salvaged," he ordered the barbarian. Their new 'friend' was released. As he shuffled off obediently, Ba'tvian gave Nerisse a measured glance. "They will now know that you are not only alive, but that you are with me."

"Yes." She looked troubled. "It may make things...difficult."

"What will the Elvanarae do when they find out?" The Mancers would tell them.

"I don't know." She gave him an almost desperate look. "I'm sorry, lord."

"Hmm." Glaring at Timbrel, he considered. "We will wait and see what your people do. As for the Mancers…" He crouched by the fallen man at his feet, running a gloved finger along the flat of the blade he held. "…it is time that we took the fight to them."

INTERLUDE 15

LABIYAL Biyalban sat with his sire as they watched the mirror. They were in his study, a small table set with food and drink standing between them. The only illumination was provided by two candelabra floor stands that bracketed the large oval shaped mirror they were using for scrying.

The image displayed was in the north, focusing on the blood mage that was Labiyal's gamble. The Mancer had lost consciousness. The barbarian Ibestor, upset over the damage done to his mount, was being allowed to tend to it under Nerisse's supervision. As he inspected it, Ba'tvian began preparing their latest victim for a blood rite.

He had invited the Daemon Lord Biyal to witness this event once the Ba'tvian's course of action had become clear. The Daemon Lord was uncharacteristically quiet. His son wondered if it was due to the Shadowed Ones. This was the first time Biyal had seen them working in concert with Ba'tvian – or anyone, for that matter.

In the mirror, they saw Ibestor kill his beast, then proceed to carve off pieces of it.

"For what reason does the barbarian take the meat?" Biyal did not take his gaze away from the glass.

"For consumption, by either himself or to use as bait for trapping creatures to use in making another amalgam."

They fell silent as Ibestor and Nerisse joined their leader. Nerisse roused the Mancer to wakefulness. The rite began, the Shadowed Ones gathering around the trio in anticipation.

"Do you know what they are, the Shadows?" Biyal's voice was subdued.

"Yes, lord. I do." They were his sire's brethren, the first generation of Daemons fathered by Hell himself. They had been reduced to Shadows by the One's curses in an era that most of Einlienn had forgotten about.

"I have never seen them gain substance, not since their curse began, though I have heard stories of the rare instance. Even then, the stories told of it happening with only one or two. Not dozens. Not like this." He paused as the Mancer's blood began to run. "How long have they worked with him, spawnling?"

"I have seen them in his presence off and on," came Labiyal's careful answer. "I know that he occasionally gives them leavings from his rites."

Biyal nodded. Again they fell quiet. This time, nothing was said until the rite was finished, the scene fading from the mirror's surface.

"Our king will approve of this Ba'tvian Delthanurk you have chosen." He rose from his chair, then turned to look down on Labiyal. "You will see to it that this act will continue. The Mancers must be eradicated if we are to have any hope of success – if you are to have any hope of staying alive."

"I am aware, sire." Labiyal bowed his head. "I have already set that in motion."

"Excellent. I will give our king this favorable report." He glanced back at the mirror, an arrogant smile playing on his lips. "He will be pleased with this progression."

Labiyal stood to see his sire out. Once he was alone, he walked over to where his desk sat shrouded in gloom. The oil lamps that hung from sconces on the wall behind it flared to life.

There was, he thought, a great deal yet to do.

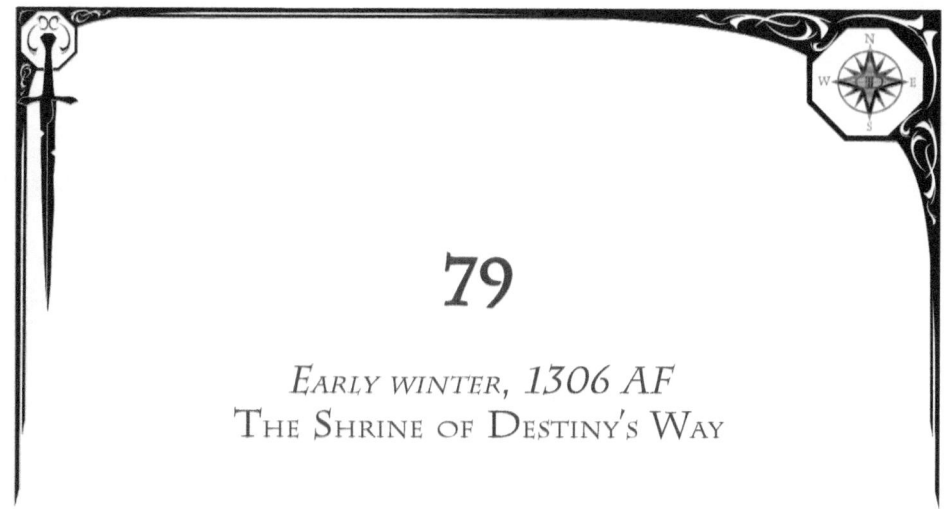

79

ABSOL awoke in the early hours before dawn, a sense of dread permeating his sleep fogged brain. He stared at the ceiling, seeing only darkness, as he waited for his mind to clear. In the air above him, a ball of light coalesced into existence.

He sat up, reaching out for it with one hand. The light settled into his palm. The memory exploded into his mind.

– Nerisse se li Astorae was alive – she was bait – he'd been trapped, waylaid – Ba'tvian Delthanurk – she was working with Ba'tvian and an unknown barbarian – so cold – he'd fallen for it – the others must know –

Timbrel Jodrek was dead, or worse.

Absol Omine sat on his bed, heart numb. In his mind's eye, Timbrel's memory played through, then repeated. As he grieved the loss of a friend and brother Mancer, he resolved to avenge him. Ba'tvian Delthanurk, those who followed him – they would fall. If not by his hand, then by someone else's.

No matter how long it took, they would fall by a Mancer's hand and no other's.

THE
APPENDIX

AF – "After Flood". The calendar for Einlienn places year 0 at the point when the global flood receded.

ABSOL OMINE – a human male serving as a Mancer in Orthanor. In his forties, he travels a great deal and is highly proficient in his work. He is also well regarded within his field of expertise. Absol is the Mancer hunting Ba'tvian Delthanurk.

ADEPT – the third of the four classes of magery. As the fourth class, sage, is an extremely seldom seen caliber, most people hold the mistaken belief that the mage-rank of adept is the highest.

ANNIA – (pronounced *Ah-nee-ah*) the second largest of the three major continents of Einlienn. It is situated to the west of Orthanor on the other side of the Capil Ocean.

ASHA SE LI VEDEAEA – (*pronounced Ahsh-ah seh lih Veh-day-ah*) the alias Nerisse se li Astorae uses when she visits the healer of Piete Town.

ASHBURGH – (pronounced *Ahsh-behrg*) a town of the Northern Wilderness of Orthanor. It is situated to the southwest of Piete Town and to the west of Winede. Like most other towns in the region, its residents are loggers, trappers, and small-time traders.

BA'TVIAN DELTHANURK – (pronounced *Bah-t-vee-uhn Dehl-thah-nehrk*) a young human male from a serf family living in squalor on the estates of the Lord of Menie. He was given the chance to attend the Trinity College of Magery on scholarship, where he later became interested in the darker arts of magic. At the time of his exile from the Trinity, he is sixteen years of age.

BARBARIANS – any one of the rough, often volatile tribes that live on the edges of the Northern Ring and Northern Ice Fields. Barbarians are often superstitious, insular, and territorial. The closer to the northern pole they are, the less rational they tend to be. The further south the tribe resides, the more civilized it is.

BLACK MAGE – a mage who does not resort to blood and death as power sources but will use his magic for personal, and usually wrongful, gain. Black mages will sometimes also dabble in low-level necromancy practices.

BLOOD MAGE – a mage who uses the blood and death of anything living being in order to generate magical energy. Blood mages tend to also practice daemon summoning and necromancy. They are considered anathema and are usually executed after a swift trial, if any trial is given at all.

THE BLUE TOWER – the Trinity College of Artisanry and the natural stone column it perches on. It is part of the Trinity and the nick-name is derived from the blue tiled roofs featured on all school and town buildings.

BROTHER FILTAN – (pronounced *Bruh-thehr Fihl-tahn*) one of the monks at the shrine of Destiny's Way. He tends the stables.

BROWN – the horse of Absol Omine. A somewhat skittish horse of undetermined bloodlines, it was named by I'k'Nole soon after Absol found the child in the Spirlan Forest after the Great Earthquake.

CAMEN DESERT – (pronounced *Cay-mehn*) a desert found in the south-western portion of the Annian Continent. The region does not have very many cities but the few it does have are known for their princely architecture, the rare spices for sale, centers of philosophy, and myriad theologians.

CAPIL OCEAN – (pronounced *Cah-peel*) the largest ocean on Einlienn, it sits between the continents of Annia and Orthanor.

CAPTAIN TERIK WAYFORD – the captain of the small cargo vessel called *Fisher's Delight*.

CARTER FAIRWRIGHT – one of the foremost generals of his time, known for his many victories in the Daemon Wars preceding the Flood. Most of the details concerning his life and deeds have been lost to time. He is believed to have been killed at Carter's Rock during a pitched battle that was almost lost to the daemons. His death and his forces' victory are carved upon the rock that bears his name.

CARTER'S ROCK – a town east of Winede in northern Orthanor. The town was built on what is believe to be the site of a legendary battle between the human forces of Carter Fairwright and a small daemon army in the last years prior to the Flood. The rock, from which the town drew its name, is a boulder sitting atop a rocky outcropping jutting up from the crest of a hill. It is carved with a relief depicting the battle. The town surrounds the outcropping. It is considered to be a waypoint for Mancers in the north.

CEDANE HARVIER – (pronounced *Seh-dayn Har-vee-ehr*) the alias that Ba'tvian Delthanurk used at Winede Village. The persona is that of a journeyman trader from Menie Port who is on his first solo trading tour of the north.

CHALBROOKE – (pronounced *Chahl-bruhk*) the largest city on the eastern side of Orthanor. Chalbrooke has the unique distinction of hosting houses from every Guild in Orthanor, including the solitary Mancer Guild House. This has enabled the city to thrive and has given it the nickname the City of Guilds.

CHESRA – a board game featuring two opposing sides, each with twenty pieces, five of which are important to the game as they represent a royal family. Each side has a different set of moves. The object of the game is to capture all five members of the royal family. If any one of those pieces reaches the opposite side without capture, all captured royal pieces for that side is returned to the board.

CLERIC'S ROOM – a concealed room within the Trinity College of Magery that is used for judgments of student transgressions, questioning of students on serious matters, and other sensitive meetings involving school staff members.

CREATION MYTHS – myths that detail the creation of the universe and the world of Einlienn. The most common version includes the introduction of Death, and the beginnings of what may lead to the end of the universe. The story states that the One created the universe and began to fill it with worlds, dimensions, planes of existence, stars, etc. He did this by speaking. The universe heard the words spoken, then would help make it reality. Eventually, He became lonely in His task and created the Eldarae, a race of demi-deities, to keep Him company as He worked. His children took an interest in what He was doing so He granted them the power to create by speaking to the universe. There was only one rule to be obeyed: they could not destroy anything that had already been created. Each of them was an expert in one thing – one aspect of life – though they were able to create whole worlds, races, flora, fauna, and other cosmic things. The Eldarae known as Hell, one of the One's older children, fashioned a plane of existence known as Hell which spanned all dimensions. It was rigid and harsh in design, possessing mostly straight lines, jagged edges, and no beauty. He was praised for his work and basked in the accolades. Then Xera, one of the younger Eldarae, created the world of Einlienn, a place of serenity, beauty, and joy. The world quickly became beloved by all. Jealous, Hell coveted Einlienn and offered to trade Xera his plane for the world. Xera refused. Twice more the offer was made. Twice more it was turned down. At the third refusal, Hell bespoke Xera's destruction. Unwilling to break the one rule, yet bound to obey the words spoken, the universe tore a hole in its heart and cried out. Furious at the failure, Hell tore Xera to pieces. It was then that Death entered the universe for the first time. Xera's remains were merged with the world he loved so much and Hell was imprisoned with his plane as punishment. He is to remain imprisoned until he allows himself to be made into the bandage that will heal the universe's wound, or the universe dies. Until then, the Eldarae use Hope to close the wound and wait.

CROSSING – see Portal.

DAEMON – a race descended from the Eldarae known as Hell. They are from a plane of existence that parallels Einlienn's. That plane is also called Hell, or Hell's Plane, after the race's progenitor. It is the goal of daemon race to help Hell to break free of Hell's Plane in any way possible.

DAEMON LORD – a daemon of the purest blood, highest status, and most power. They are also the daemons whose loyalty to Hell goes unquestioned.

DAEMON WARS – (pronounced *Day-mon*) a war on a global scale in which the daemons fought against all other races of Einlienn in a bid for conquest. They were led by their sire and king, the Eldarae known as Hell. The Daemon Wars ended when the Flood came, cursing the surviving daemons and drowning most of the world's population. Also called Hell's War.

DESTINY'S WAY – a small village sitting on the boundary between the Plains of Gastaeia and the Wood of Destiny. It is a pilgrimage destination for believers in the One.

DERSTI – (pronounced *Dehrs-tee*) a member of the deer family that lives in northern climes. It is the size of a small horse (approximately 14 hands at the withers) and sports a set of antlers whose central tines often fuse together as they grow. Females shed their antlers winter. Males keep theirs year round.

DRAGON'S HEAD TAVERN – a tavern and inn at the Red Tower that is popular among the students of the College of the Magery.

EASTERN CLIFFS – the coastal cliffs ranging along the upper eastern coast of Exile's Peril.

EINLIENN – (pronounced *I-n-lee-ihn*) the world in which Descent Into Darkness is set.

ELDARAE – (pronounced *Ehl-dahr-ay*) the children on the One, demi-deities who took part in the creation of the universe.

ELVANARAE – (pronounced *Ehl-vahn-ayr*) a subspecies of elves that live underground and have close ties to the earth. The racial name is derived from the Old Tongue term Eldarae, in an effort to indicate their close spiritual association with Einlienn and the spirit of Xera. The Elvanarae have slate blue skin, white hair, and their eye color can vary from black, white, gray, and purple. They are a peaceful, and deeply religious race, if rather insular. Their society is simple, with no social ranking other than that of the priesthood, and they are governed by the High Priest. Most of the Elvanarae dwell in their subterranean city of Jevanel, having little contact with the outside world. Individuals do, however, venture out from their city for the purposes of tending to surface crops, trade, or education. A point of interest is the trademark characteristic of their naming system: male names incorporate "si le", meaning "son of", while females incorporate "se li", meaning "daughter of".

ELVANAERAN – (pronounced *Eh-vahn-ayr-ahn*) of or pertaining to the Elvanaer.

EMP – (pronounced *Ehmp*) a shortened or slang form of the word Empath.

EMPATH – (pronounced *Ehm-pahth*) an individual who possesses empathy – the ability to experience, sense, and/or manipulate the emotions/emotional psyche of other living things.

EXILE'S PERIL – a large, barren island or subcontinent that is home to only two settlements. On the eastern side, south of the Eastern Cliffs, is a fishing village founded by escaped and/or paroled prisoners from Exile's Port, which lies on the northern coast. The Port is the largest prison facility in the world. It receives inmates from major cities in Orthanor and Genoria. The island is called 'Peril' due to its lack of anything edible or drinkable throughout most of its terrain.

EXILE'S PORT – The largest prison facility in the world, it is its own city-state. Built with the labor of prisoners, it was constructed with the intention of retaining criminals whose crimes were bad enough to warrant incarceration without execution from other city-states. Over time, the city-states began to deport a certain number of convicts awaiting execution due to crowding in their own prisons. Generally, prisoners are either put to work in stone quarries used to build more prisons or repair existing ones, or hung in due time. In return for taking their convicts, a tithe of supplies is sent by all city-states who choose to deport their criminals. The Port is ruled by the Warden, who is assisted by a company of guards. The guards are enlisted from the various city-states and are placed on an annual rotation schedule. The schedule allows guards to leave their families at home while they work as it considered potentially dangerous to allow them to stay at the Port due to the prison population.

FISHER'S DELIGHT – the ship Absol took from Menie to the Trinity while pursuing Ba'tvian Delthurnak.

FISHERMAN'S POINT – a small, autonomous fishing village on the eastern of Exile's Peril, just north of the Eastern Cliffs. The fishing folk there are descended from freed criminals who had served their time at Exile's Port and did not want to return to the mainland. It is an insular, self-sustaining community, reliant on the sea for all its needs.

FLOOD – a global event that wiped out most of the races and populace of Einlienn. Only isolated groups of elves, humans, and the shape-shifting Were-Clan survived. They employed methods of survival that varied from climbing mountains to avoid the flood waters, retreating to the Northern Ice Fields where the waters were frozen, sealing themselves inside subterranean caverns, and, in one instance, petitioning the One to be transformed into beings that would not drown. The Flood lasted for three years before it receded. To commemorate the year the Flood ended, the survivors restarted their historic calendar.

GATE – see Portal.

GENORIA – (pronounced *Jehn-orh-ee-ah*) the smallest of the three major continents of Einlienn.

GLASTEN PORT – (pronounced *Glah-stehn*) a once prosperous sea port south of Menie. Though lacking a natural harbor, its proximity to fishing villages made it the best choice for the exportation of seafood. It fell out of favor when the Port City of Menie lowered the fees for its natural harbor.

THE GOLD OR GOLDEN TOWER – the Trinity College of Knowledge and the natural stone column it perches on. It is part of the Trinity and the nick-name is derived from the yellow tiled roofs featured on all school and town buildings.

GOOSE-BREE – a small farming community, loosely called a village, east of Menie and northwest of Destiny's Way.

THE GREAT EARTHQUAKE – the greatest earthquake on record. Originating off the eastern coast of Genoria, it affected the geography of the whole southern hemisphere. This event occurred in the first chapter of Descent Into Darkness: His Own.

HEALING HOUSE – a small hospital facility where healers, herbalist, and/or doctors tend to the sick or injured.

HELL – an Eldarae who turned against his brethren out of jealousy. As punishment, Hell was confined to his stark domain, Hell's Plane. There, he sired a race and strives to plot his way to freedom once again.

HELL'S WAR – see Daemon Wars.

HIGH JUDGE HAMAL – a human male serving as the senior court official of the Trinity's Red Tower. He weighs in on the most grievous cases. Just now approaching his sixth decade, he is a close friend of Master Oknare.

IBESTOR – (pronounced *I-behs-tohr*) a barbarian mage from the Northern Ice Fields. His arcane skills lie mostly in the making of living amalgams of various creatures. Cast out of his own tribe as a child, he has managed to survive in the icy wastes by means of his magic, but has become feral in nature. He was driven south of the Northern Ring by the other barbarian tribes. At the time of Descent Into Darkness: His Beast, Ibestor is twenty-three years of age.

I'K'NOLE – (pronounced *I'kay'Nohl*) an orphaned boy found by Mancer Absol Omine in the Spirlan Forest after the Great Earthquake. When not with Absol, he is being cared for by Master Abbott Dannon in Destiny's Way. A gifted child, he wants to be a Mancer like Absol. At the time of Descent Into Darkness: His Beast,

I'k'Nole is eleven years old.

IVERNESS – (pronounced *I-vehr-nehss*) a town north-west of the Wood and the Relds.

JEVANEL – (pronounced *Jehv-ahn-ehl*) The subterranean city-enclave of the Elvanarae, located on the northwestern coast of Orthanor. It is where most of the race is concentrated, is their religious center, and where they are ruled by the High Priest. It is sometimes referred to as "the earth's womb". Jevanel is the birth place of Nerisse se li Astorae.

KING'S FOLLY – the small cargo ship that took Ba'tvian into exile. It was later found adrift at sea, with all hands dead on board.

KING OF HELL – the Eldarae known as Hell.

LABIYAL BIYALBAN – (pronounced *Lah-bee-yahl Bee-yahl-bahn*) the half-daemon/half-human son of Daemon Lord Biyal.

LORD BIYAL – (pronounced *B-i-yahl*) a Daemon Lord of high favor. He is the sire of the half-daemon Labiyal Biyalban, and is one of the very few first generation Daemons left in service to Hell.

MAGE – someone who uses magic. There are four main ranks among mages: apprentice or student, journeyman, master, and adept. Each mage starts out as an apprentice and must pass a series of tests called Mastery Trials in order to ascend to the next rank. This is down under the tutelage and supervision of a mage who is a Master or Adept.

MAGERY – the practice of manipulating natural forces commonly referred to as magic. The term is also used to refer to the magic itself, or one's ability to use it.

MALTEK BAY – (pronounced *Mahltek*) a great northern bay that separates the Maltek Mountains in the west from the Trelum Mountains in the east. The entrance of the bay is frozen over and is part of the Northern Ice Fields.

MALTEK MOUNTAINS – (pronounced *Mahl-tehk*) the mountain range that spans across northwestern Orthanor, from the Capil Ocean to Maltek Bay, and makes up part of the Northern Ring. It home to several barbarian tribes.

MANCER – a warrior who is often also a minor mage whose sole occupation is to defend the living against daemon kind and mages who have gone turned to the bad. Mancers exist outside most societies, do not claim citizenship, and give no loyalty to any ruler. They adhere to a code that incorporates most of the existing laws. They are few in number and seldom stay in one place for long. Frequently, authorities faced with a black or blood mage or other preternatural activity will send for a Mancer to aid them.

MASTER ABBOTT DANNON – the Master Abbott at the shrine in Destiny's Way. He is a long-time friend of the Mancer Absol Omine and sometime caretaker of the orphan, I'k'Nole. As a member of the Order of On'Desae, he has strong faith in, and a close spiritual relationship with, the One.

MASTER OKNARE – (pronounced *Ahk-nayr*) a human male serving as a teacher of advanced or prodigious students of magic at the Trinity College of Magery. Though he is commonly called 'master', he is in fact an adept level mage. He was mentor to Ba'tvian Delthanurk until the student's exile. At the time of Descent Into Darkness: His Own, he is in his late sixties.

MASTERY TRIAL – a test, or series of tests, whereby a student of magic proves his or her magical prowess. By passing this trial or trials, they are able to ascend to the next mage rank, whichever rank that may be. A mage's ability to pass the Mastery Trials is dependent on his/her skill, knowledge, and the amount of magic he/she can utilize at any one point.

MENIE – (pronounced *Meh-nay*) a minor port city on the western coast of Orthanor, to the east and slightly north of the Trinity. Though it has no king, it is a fully independent city-state ruled by a lord who holds the majority of the lands surrounding the city.

MERCHANTS GUILD – the regulatory body of which mainland and maritime traders are members. Guild members trade primarily in high-end goods or wares garnered from other continents. They ply their trade for money, as opposed to bartering or services, and their guild fees are higher than those of the related Traders Guild. Their seal consists of an ewer, a small bundled sack, and closed wooden chest super-imposed over a coin. The guild's motto, "For Fair Value, In Goods, In Profits", is not featured in the seal. As proof of membership, every guildsman carries a medallion made from a real coin with the seal stamped on one side, and the motto engraved on the other. By tradition, the coin used to make the medallion is the first coin earned by the individual that carries it.

THE MONSTER OF MENIE – (pronounced *Meh-nay*) the label given to Ba'tvian Delthanurk after the events of Descent Into Darkness: His Own. The name did not become well-known until after the events of Descent Into Darkness: Her Lord.

NERISSE SE LI ASTORAE – (pronounced *Nehr-ees say lih Ahs-torh-ay*) a young elven mage and Empath originally intended for the earth priesthood of her people, the Elvanaer. She is apprenticed to Master Oknare in the aftermath of Ba'tvian's exile. At the time of Descent Into Darkness: His Own, she is sixteen years old.

NORTHERN ICE FIELDS – a vast frozen sea in the northern polar region of Einlienn. It is hemmed in by the Northern Ring and is largely featureless. At the very center of the Northern Ice Fields is an endless blizzard. It is alternately called the Northern Snow Fields.

NORTHERN RING – a ring of mountain ranges that enclose the northern polar region of Einlienn.

NORTHERN SNOW FIELDS – another name for the Northern Ice Fields.

NORTHERN WILDERNESS – the region of Orthanor north of the Wood of Destiny and south of the Northern Ring. It is a largely wooded area with the Sradieen Trade Route as the only maintained road. Villages, lone trappers' cabins, and small towns are scattered far apart. Most villages and towns are stockade as a defense against bandits and the occasional barbarian raid from the mountains. There is no central governing body in this area. Most of the economy is based on fur-trapping, logging, some mining, and alcohol distilled from root vegetables and herbs.

THE ONE – the supreme being who created the universe with the aid of His children, the Eldarae.

ORDER OF ON'DESAE – (pronounced *Ohn'Deh-sa*y) a monastic order devoted to worship of the One. The order is known for its generosity, open-minded acceptance of others, and efforts to preserve sites or monuments associated with the One or the Creation Myths. Their most renowned shrine is located at Destiny's Way, just outside the south-eastern edge of the Wood of Destiny. The order is less known for its other purpose: supporting the Mancer Guild as it fights against Daemons, blood magery, and black magic. They open their monasteries to traveling Mancers, supply them on their journeys, and offer sanctuary for Mancers who need healing, or survive their profession long enough to retire. The order also passes along news and maintains libraries of Mancer lore.

ORTHANOR – (pronounced *Ohr-thahn-oh*r) the largest of three major continents of Einlienn.

PIETE TOWN – (pronounced *Pi-eht*) a barricaded town situated north of the Wood of the Destiny. It is one of the largest settlements in the northern wilderness. By tradition, the town's foremost healer, who is usually an Empath, lives just outside the town. An unspoken pact with local bandits grants the healer and his/her family immunity provided that they tend to anyone injured who arrives at their door.

PLAINS OF GASTAEIA – (pronounced *Gahs-tay-ya*) a stretch of open grasslands dominating the the lower central region of Orthanor. To its east lies the Spirlan Forest, to the north stands the Wood of Destiny. The Plains were gently rolling open spaces before the Great Earthquake. The Great Earthquake caused the eastern portion of the Plains to become rough, uneven. Gorges, sheer drop-offs, and even small canyons can be found in the east while the western side remains flat or gently rolling.

PORTAL – a rift in the time-space continuum that allows near-instantaneous travel between one point and another. The mage skill and power required to create a portal is such that only adept-caliber mages or higher are able to create and sustain them. Portals are also called gates or crossings.

RED – the name used by Ba'tvian Delthanurk to refer to the blood mage with whom he has a contract. In exchange for information, Ba'tvian must pay him with a victim to use in blood rites every full moon. This agreement was made at the end of Descent Into Darkness: His Own.

THE RED TOWER – the Trinity College of Magery and the natural stone column on which it perches. It is part of the Trinity and the nick-name is derived from the red tiled roofs featured on all school and town buildings.

THE RELDS – (pronounced *Rehlds*) a swamp in the northern wilderness of Orthanor, to the north and east of Menie, it is located along the southern half of the Telmar River. In winter, the swamp is semi-frozen. As the ice tends to be thin and fragile in winter, and the area much too boggy for travel in summer, it is generally avoided. It is sometimes used as a haven by criminals or refugees as their pursuers are reluctant to follow them into it. However, the terrain is so hazardous that only one out of four men that venture into it survive.

SAGE – the fourth and highest class of magery. Sages are extremely rare. They can be so powerful that a more primitive culture could mistake them for gods. They are masters at manipulating magic, dimensional space, and even time.

SAERLAN SI LE THEIAN – (pronounced *Say-her-lahn sih leh Thehr-yee-ahn*) the High Priest of the Elvanarae residing in Jevanel. A gentle, compassionate man in his late fifties, he bears the slate blue skin and white hair of his race. As High Priest, he is also the theocratic ruler of his people. It was Saerlan who had noticed Nerisse se li Astorae's potential and claimed her for the priesthood, and it had been him who had made the decision to send Nerisse to the Trinity to complete her mage-training before her induction.

SEA'S BURDEN - the ship Ba'tvian Delthanurk used to return to the Trinity in Descent Into Darkness: Her Lord.

SHADOWED ONES – the cursed, first generation of daemons sired by Hell. They are condemned to be the lowliest of the low, and their once mighty origins have been forgotten by all but a select few. They exist as ethereal creatures that feed upon death. The more life force they consume, the stronger they become. Eventually, they are able take on a physical form for a time. Once they are corporeal, they are able to hunt and feed upon anything, living or dead. Because of the danger they pose, they are routinely hunted by the Mancers.

SILMON OF WINEDE – (pronounced *Sihl-mohn of Wihn-eed*) the proprietor and bartender of the only tavern in Winede.

SKELETON COAST – See Spirlan Coast.

SOUTHERN ICE FIELDS – an area consisting of the outlying parts of the southern polar region of Einlienn that is dominated by frozen, rocky tundra and snow. Ice storms are frequent.

SPIRLAN COAST – (pronounced *Spihr-lahn*) the portion of the south-western coast of Orthanor that makes up the seaside boundary of the Spirlan Forest. It becomes known as the Skeleton Coast once the Spirlan Forest begins to die off in the aftermath of the Great Earthquake.

SPIRLAN FOREST – a large forest, consisting mostly of the gigantic spire trees, that spans a few hundred miles up and down the south-western coast of Orthanor and a little over twenty miles inland. The forest was largely destroyed by the Great Earthquake.

SPIRE TREE – a gigantic tree whose branches grow in a spiral pattern up its thick trunk. They can grow up to a half mile high on average. Because of the sturdiness of the tree, and the close proximity of the branches to one another, it is not uncommon for villages to be built in them, with the spiraling branches acting as the only road.

SRADIEEN TRADING ROUTE – (pronounced *Srah-dih-een*) the main route for the northern fur trade. It winds through the northern wilderness of Orthanor and traditionally ends at Glasten Port. Since the rise of Menie as a major shipping port, however, most of the traders stop there instead of heading on to Glasten. The trade route is one of the few roads that is mostly paved. The paving stones are ancient, having been laid down by a culture that existed before The Flood. Though that civilization was lost to history, some of their stonework remains with the names of roads and places carved deeply into the rock. The name Sradieen can be found etched into the stone pavers that have survived the onslaught of water and time, thus the trade route is known by this name.

SUNDOWN – a small fishing village situated on a desolate stretch of coastline between Menie and the Spirlan Forest.

TELMAR BRIDGE – (pronounced *Tehl-mahr*) the bridge over which the Chal-Edon Trade Route crosses the Telmar River. The bridge was built by the Traders and Merchants Guilds and is maintained by them. It left unmanned in the winter, when traders are less apt to travel but is manned by guildsmen in the spring and summer when a toll is instituted to help fund the bridge's upkeep.

TELMAR RIVER – (pronounced *Tehl-mahr*) a river that runs from the Maltek Bay, through the Northern wilderness of Orthanor, through the Relds, and by the town of Goose-Bree. It is crossed by the Chal-Edon Trade Route. See also Telmar Bridge.

THALENE – (pronounced *Thah-leen*) a pre-Flood human civilization known for its advanced technology and sciences. When they became caught up in Hell's War, they began genetically engineering warriors to defend them, thus creating the shape-shifting race now called the Were-Clan. Unfortunately, their child race could not prevent their decline or protect them from the effects of prolonged global war. By the time of the Flood, there were no human Thalene left, only the Were-Clan they had created.

TIMBREL JODREK – (pronounced *Tihm-brehl Johd-rehk*) a Mancer in his late twenties who patrols the northern wilderness of Orthanor. During the events of Descent Into Darkness: His Beast, he is tracking Ba'tvian Delthanurk.

TRADERS GUILD – the regulatory body of which traveling mainland traders are members. Guild members trade primarily in low-end or raw goods. They are allowed to barter their wares for other goods or services. Their seal is a quartered circle ringed by the Guild's motto, "Provision of Goods to All, For Fair Trades or Barter". Each quadrant of the circle holds one of four symbols: scales for fairness, a book for accounting, a wool bundle for raw goods, and a candle for general goods. Every traders carries a chitty with their guild's seal on it as proof of their membership.

THE TRINITY – three columns of natural stone rising out of the eastern Capil Ocean near the coast of Orthanor. They are about 10-12 days sailing time out from the mainland. Atop each of the stone columns is a college of advanced learning and a small town. They, and the columns, are collectively referred to as the Trinity Schools, the Trinity Colleges, the Trinity, or the Trinity Towers.

VELTAN – (pronounced *Vehl-tahn*) a small town west of Destiny's Way.

WERE-CLAN – a shape-shifting race descended from the human civilization called Thalene. Before the Flood that ended Hell's War, during a time when advanced technology had a place in the world, the Were-Clan had been genetically engineered as warriors to face the onslaught of Hell's daemonic forces. By the time of the Flood, the Thalene technology and civilization had been abandoned, or killed off. The Were-Clan went on to survive the Flood, eventually establishing themselves as clans of nomadic mercenaries on the continents of Genoria and Annia. Though individual Were-Clan have been known to venture into Orthanor, the Were-Clan have never established themselves there.

WINEDE – (pronounced *Wihn-eed*) a village to the far northwest of the Wood of Destiny. It lies the east of the Sradieen Trade Route and is surrounded by a stockade. Most of its people are trappers, hunters, or loggers.

THE WOOD OF DESTINY – the world's most ancient wood, created by Xera before his death. The Wood has a collective consciousness that is aware of the myriad paths of the past, present, and future. The Wood sings, reaching out to touch its visitors through the endless song. Its mind has child-like, ageless qualities, and possesses a limited means of communication. Its main method of communication is through visions that it weaves around its visitors through song, drawing on the visitors' past, present, and possible futures to do so. This has often spooked people, and in some cases, has driven them mad.

XERA – (pronounced *Zehr-ah*) one of the Eldarae and the creator of Einlienn. It is believed that, when Xera was torn to pieces by his brother, Hell, his remains were merged with Einlienn. It is for this reason that most of the races of the world are referred to as Xera's Children.

ABOUT THE AUTHOR

DORIS Ross lives in Jacksonville, FL, where she slaves away at her day job (aka the Evil Necessity) and sneaks in writing whenever she can. If she finds that she can't write at home, she takes off for Coffee Roasters of Florida, a local roaster and coffee shop, where the coffee is excellent, the people are awesome, and she never fails to get her chapters done. When she's not writing, or working at the Evil Necessity, she is usually hard at work for Trinity Gateways LLC, the independent publishing house she founded with fellow authors Tricia Sparks and LJ Gastineau. In the little spare time she had, she's hanging with friends, playing video games, playing with graphic art, or consuming books in print, e-book, and audio formats.

DESCENT INTO DARKNESS
PART 4

HIS COMMAND

BY DORIS ROSS

THE Mancers are falling, hunted and slain by the blood mage they call the Monster of Menie: Ba'tvian Delthanurk.

With the aid of his companions, the elven lady Nerisse se li Astorae and the barbarian Ibestor, he has begun a quiet war, leaving nothing but death in his wake. As he blazes a bloody trail across the breadth of Orthanor, he will make new allies, meet his enemies head-on, and carve his name deep into the history of Einlienn.

Yet the decision to fight comes with heavy consequences. The Mancers will not die easily under his blade, nor will they standby to watch their brethren perish. With a single message, they have set in motion events that will force the Monster's most devoted follower, a once-intended priestess, to make a terrible choice in order to survive – and when Ba'tvian gives his command, that choice will be no choice at all…

TURN THE PAGE FOR A PEEK AT
HIS COMMAND.

LATE WINTER, *1306 AF*
THE NORTHERN WILDERNESS OF ORTHANOR,
EAST OF THE TELMAR RIVER

THEY hunted.

Shadowed Ones flowed over the ground, through the trees. Following close behind were three riders, mounted on things that had been deer and horses in a previous life. Now they were both, yet neither, keeping the best traits of both while possessing an endurance that the natural animals lacked.

Ba'tvian Delthanurk rode ahead of his companions. Clad in the dark clothing of trapper, cloaked and hooded, most of his mind concentrated on the hunt. One portion kept track of the time of month; the full moon was in a few days. He had a contract to uphold, a fee to pay. It meant that after this hunt, there had to be another. There would be little time between the two.

He was beginning to resent the obligation, yet wasn't brash enough to renege on it. He'd signed the contract in blood. That was more binding than anything signed in ink.

He had to admit, however, that the information Red provided him in exchange for victims was worth the aggravation. It had kept him ahead of the pursuit. Now it allowed him to hunt his hunters.

There was a Mancer in the area. Ba'tvian was determined to find him.

So winter-bound forest provided them with a boon: tracks in the snow. His prey wasn't following a road; those were few and far between in the northern half of the continent. It meant no witnesses.

Another asset was the snow itself. Freshly fallen from the night before, it was deep enough to muffle sound, yet shallow enough that their beasts could gallop when needed.

The Shadows surged forward, putting on more speed. Their mounts matched the pace. Ba'tvian narrowed his eyes. He arrowed a thought at the leader of the pack.

What have you found?

The responding mental voice slithered into his mind with a hiss.

The Mancer you seek, lord. He is not far.

Good.

Keeping a corner of his mind tuned to his minion, he glanced over his shoulder at his companions. Nerisse se li Astorae, the Elvanarae girl he'd taken from his former master, rode close behind him. Ibestor the barbarian-mage they had made their own, kept in line with Nerisse, his gaze absently taking in the scenery. Feeling Ba'tvian's eyes on him, he turned his attention to his lord.

"He's been sighted." Ba'tvian pitched his voice low. He didn't need to raise it much in the quiet of the forest. "You know what to do."

Ibestor nodded once before veering off to the right. Part of the Shadow pack went with him. Nerisse hesitated for the barest instant.

"Be careful, lord. This one is supposed to be more experienced than the last." She flushed, then angled her mount to the left. She was out of sight within seconds, an escort of his creatures trailing after her.

Keep them both in line, he ordered. He felt the assent from the myriad minds of his loyal followers.

He dropped all mental links, redoubled his personal shielding. A whisper of power deadened any sounds his steed made as it cantered through the snow. Then he reached for the small, loaded crossbow hanging by its strap from the saddle horn. It was the almost impossible to re-load while mounted, and took time to do so on foot. He would have only one shot with it. The others had similar weapons, each with bolts dipped in a special concoction that Nerisse had come up with.

Surprise was their primary weapon.

Tapping into the nearest Shadow he used as living reservoir, he drew the power needed to form and sustain an arcane 'net' – a kind of shield that would capture mage messages and dampen a mage's ability to fight back. It had taken weeks of work to devise the thing. It wasn't perfect, working best when anchored to something physical such as a cross bolt. Still, it sufficed. It only had to last long enough for Nerisse's drug to take effect.

Within minutes, he spotted his prey. The Shadowed Ones had faded into the merest hints of outlines, just flickers of darkness at the edge of vision. Picking up the psychic threads that linked him with the minds of his comrades, he synced with them on the mental plane. They had reached their positions.

He made his move.

Urging his mount into a full gallop, he raised the crossbow, aimed, fired. The bolt hit the cloaked man in the shoulder. A second bolt hit his thigh as he stumbled. The leg collapsed under him. The Mancer fell to the ground.

With two good hits, the third – Nerisse's – wasn't fired. Ba'tvian allowed his beast to carry him past the Mancer into the trees beyond, then wheeled the steed around. He kept out of sight of his prey, checking the net he'd created. He could see it in his mind's eye, a dome of woven power lines the color of blood.

Around the wounded man, the Shadows swirled. The Mancer held a hand in front of him, palm out. It glowed, flaring bright yellow as a burst of magic shot out to disperse the half-seen creatures surrounding him. It passed through the net, losing momentum and power as the net flickered around it. For a bare instant, it visible to the naked eye. So, too, was the emblem that Ba'tvian had devised, a set of arcane runes that identified him as the maker.

He wanted his enemy to know who was killing him.

He tightened the net around the man as he struggled to his feet. The dark things crept in closer. His prey let another volley loose with less effect than the first. He yanked the bolt from his thigh, went for the bow and arrows at his back. Ba'tvian ordered his Shadowed Ones to disperse as the arrows began to fly. The blood mage engaged his mind with Nerisse's.

How long do we have?

There was a pause. He could sense her checking the integrity of the Mancer's shielding.

A minute, perhaps less. His personal shields are beginning to fail. Once they do, the only defense he will have will be his physical weaponry.

He re-focused his attention, probing the crumbling shielding. They were fading, one after another, as the drug shut down the arcane centers of the man's mind. He could his panic now, the confusion, as he tried another power blast to no avail.

Ibestor. Ba'tvian felt the dog-like acknowledgement of the barbarian's mind. *Disarm him.*

He sat back to watch as Ibestor galloped into view, throwing himself from his saddle to tackle the Mancer from behind. What the barbarian lacked in intellect, he made up for in brute strength.

Ba'tvian sat back on his mount to watch the show.

www.ingramcontent.com/pod-product-compliance
Lightning Source LLC
Chambersburg PA
CBHW021949170626
46808CB00001B/76